LIGHT OF INFIXUS

DYLAN CARRIGAN

TABLE OF CONTENTS

CHAPTER ONE

Alarms wailed over the speakers on the bridge. "Calling every crew member to operative stations, please be on standby," the loudspeaker blared. Thatcher turned from the intercom, peering back onto the deck. Her pale-toned face was flush pink and panicked, and her slick-back blonde bun was hanging slightly looser than she liked. She ran across the black floor of the deck, pushing through crew members who were running all about. Thatcher stopped before the main window, peering out into the pitch-black space. Stars could be seen all around. She looked out to try to calm herself, but it didn't work. Her mind was buzzing. Her reflection showed her blue eyes, and it brought her back. She turned back towards the chaos that was ensuing.

"How could you lose a half-billion-dollar space probe just out of nowhere?" screamed Commander Thatcher. Everyone on the bridge was frantically running around, checking panels and monitors, trying to grasp exactly what was happening. The ship's bridge hadn't been in this state since it launched from Earth four years ago. As Thatcher watched, she could feel a knot in her stomach forming. "Drake is not gonna like this," she thought. She moved around the bridge to see if anyone had seen anything.

"Ma'am, we might have found something," said a soft-toned Private sitting at the security array. Thatcher walked swiftly over to the Private sitting at the desk full of screens. She reached him and leaned in to look at whatever mess was shown on the screen.

"Private Manson, what did you see?" Thatcher asked expectantly.

"I believe one of the probes onboard cameras caught something right before the signal and transponder went dark," the Private said

"Were the systems on board able to relay the recording before it went dark?" asked Thatcher.

"No, ma'am. The weird thing is I have no file backups from the last 30 minutes, which has never happened before," the Private said, still sounding scared.

"But did you see the video feed?" asked Thatcher.

The Private mumbled under his breath, "Yes. But I don't remember what I saw."

"What do you mean you don't know what you saw?" Thatcher said, raising her voice but still trying to maintain her composure. She knew she couldn't lose it in front of the whole crew. The entire bridge was watching the situation unfold. All at once, the crew members around Thatcher moved to attention as there was a shout, "ATTENTION ON DECK."

The gray doors of the bridge slid open as an olive-skinned six-foot man walked onto the deck. His magnetic features drew people in, and his presence commanded respect. "Commander Thatcher, do we have an update on the situation?" Drake asked as he walked over to where she was standing towards the side of the room.

"No Admiral. Private Manson saw the footage but cannot remember what he saw before the relay blackout." Drake looked down at the floor with his dark brown, almost black eyes. He thought for a moment.

"Take him to 15." Drake said. Everyone was shocked and started whispering to themselves. Level 15 was top secret. Only a select few actually knew what was on that level. Everyone was told it was memory banking. Something very experimental. But in the short time it was used, it was 100 percent effective. It sends radiation particles through the brain. It would rebuild neural pathways, allowing valuable information to be recovered. Rarely used, if ever. It was only installed on the ship for situations just like this one. But that probe was vital to the mission. Drake knew this. But he also knew the Private would have a 25 percent chance to live afterward. The machine had no way to dictate which pathways to restore, so it would more than likely leave the patient without any motor functions, and it would shut down the heart. But the mission... Manson knew this as well.

"No, please just give me a moment." Manson pleaded, knowing what fate would await him. Commander Thatcher stepped over and placed her hand on his shoulder.

"That's an order, soldier," she said firmly. Manson bowed his head.

"For the greater good," Manson said proudly as he saluted Admiral Marcus Drake. "For the greater good" was their motto. A code they all lived by. Drake saluted him back. Any crewmate would do the same, and Drake knew that.

Drake would do the same. He would lay his life down for this crew and ship if called. Manson turned, saluted his other crewmates, and walked to his almost inevitable demise. The whole bridge returned the gesture. Drake looked around at his crew.

"Let's get this figured out," he said commandingly. The bridge returned to its previous frenzy. Drake turned to leave, and as he did, he gave Thatcher a concerned look, leaving the bridge to go to his quarters.

Drake walked through the gray halls, reaching quarters. Being the top dog on the ship had its perks from time to time. He walked into his living room. The quarters were significant compared to the other crewmates. Enough to fit the admiral and his whole family. Except he didn't have any family. He had lost all of his family, every single one of them. His three beautiful daughters to some thieves two years before they launched. A few thugs deemed their lives invaluable compared to the extra food rations in their house. The global food shortages were terrible, but taking away his daughters for a little extra food? Drake would never understand why. His wife passed away a few years prior due to post-labor complications. But the ship was already almost complete. The family's cabin was already built. He had offered it to his second in command, Thatcher. But she insisted that she didn't want all that space to be kept clean. The cabin was a constant reminder of what he had lost. But he chose not to dwell on that most days; this crew was his family now.

Drake walked over to his bed and sat down, putting his head in his hands. He knew that Private Manson was gonna die. A 25 percent survival rating. It was actually lower. More like 22. But they said 25 because it sounded better. But if he didn't find out what happened, pandemonium would be aboard the ship. "Why now?" Drake thought. "Why when we are a year away from completing our mission?" Drake walked through his living room. It was cozy, for sure. The same gray walls as everywhere else, but pictures of his family all over the walls. Back home, this would be a small studio. But on the ship, this was the penthouse. He sat at the desk on the far side of his quarters and opened the tablet he brought everywhere. Drake opened his messages as he did most of the time he got on his tablet. He constantly had messages from all over the ship. There was a message pinned at the top. He had almost forgotten. He looked at the message he had received 2 weeks before the day. He couldn't read it when he had first received it, which was extraordinary, but there was a small countdown on the message. It had 2 weeks on it. The message was unlocked today. The title Read "URGENT FOR ADMIRAL- Alpha clearance required- Complete Bethany."

Drake was confused when he received this message. He had heard about Bethany before, but nothing else had ever been explained to him besides a vague explanation. It was a backup plan that had never been explained to him. Also, that class system had never been used by the Interplanetary Expedition Corp or IEC for short. Drake had top-level clearance but couldn't access this message no matter what he tried. Just as Drake was about to open the message again, someone knocked on his door. "Can I come in?" asked Thatcher. "Sure," Drake answered. He recognized the voice. He had known her for a long time. He was one of the first people he had met when he was recruited to the IEC. The door opened, and Drake looked up, seeing Thatcher. She was pretty but also adamant. She wasn't tall but not short either. She stated she was 5.9, but Drake knew it was more like 5.7 or 8. Fair-skinned, she was very fit. One of her true passions. She always seemed to wear a shell around people. Never truly let anyone in unless she really trusted you. And that trust took a long time to build. Her straight blonde hair, always up in a tight bun, hung a little lower. Drake could see the stress in her light blue eyes. She walked past Drake into the kitchen, grabbing a glass. "Mind if I grab some water?" she asked.

"Sure thing," he responded. "It looks like you are going to, no matter what I say," Drake said, laughing. Thatcher walked back into the living room.

"The private is currently being run through the mind banks to see if we can recover some of the recordings," said Thatcher. Drake just stared at the polished steel floor of his quarters.

"Well, is there anything else you need before the debriefing?" Thatcher said.

"No," said Drake, "but tell me, Thatch." Drake had called her that for the last year and a half, and Thatcher hated it.

"You know I hate that nickname," Thatcher said with an annoyed face.

"But you know I'm a nickname kinda guy, Thatch," he said through a half attempt at a smile. He was still obviously distressed but was trying to cover it up. "What do you think caused this?" Drake asked.

There was a lengthy pause. "I have no clue," Thatcher responded to him, "but honestly, after a year of silence, I don't know what to expect," Thatcher said. "I don't feel great about what we will see when we recover the footage." Drake stared at her.

"How long have we not had contact with Earth again?" Drake asked.

"One year and three months," Thatcher responded. Drake stood up from his bed. He started pacing his quarters.

"Look, Thatcher, we are alone out here in every way. Whether we like it or not, we knew this was gonna happen." Drake paused to look back at her.

"That's correct, but we thought the communication dead point wouldn't be till six months from now," Thatcher said in a concerned tone.

"We have to be prepared for whatever it is," Drake said as he stopped before a porthole, staring out into the vast nothingness. Drake said to Thatcher softly, "I need you here with us." Drake turned around, a tear rolling down his cheek. "Fiona, I sent that kid to be killed. He's our family, and I sent him to be killed in the mind banks. And why? Because he saw a video that didn't get saved to our faulty recording systems." Thatcher was taken aback by this reaction; she had never seen him cry. She rarely, if ever, heard her first name spoken. Especially since they left Earth. The last time she heard that name was from her father. He was the one who raised her, the one who made her into who she is today. This took her by surprise. Her usual upright, perfect posture slouched. She walked over to Drake and handed him a tissue. She never showed emotions. But she still felt them. She knew Drake took the only course of action available to him.

"Drake, you did what you had to do. No one else could have made that call. No one has the guts to." Thatcher leaned in, getting closer to him. "That's why you're the leader. No one's gonna hate you for this." Drake wiped the tears and sat on his brown leather sofa. One of the only things he brought from home.

"Drake, I need you here with us," Thatcher said one more time.

"I'm here, Thatch," Drake responded to her. "Just give me a few." Thatcher nodded at him, and she headed for the door.

"See you at the debrief," Thatcher said. After Thatcher left, Drake pulled up his tablet and returned to that email. The time lock was off. Drake hesitantly opened the email. In it was one video file addressed MARCUS. He clicked the video. His best friend popped on the screen. His best friend was the head of the IEC and was a huge reason he had gotten this position. Not that Drake wasn't qualified. Some called Drake overqualified. But still, Corbin had been the one to solidify this spot for him. Drake immediately knew something was off. Corbin Huxley, known for his bright and funny personality, was a solemn man in this video. When the video played, it showed just his face. Corbin was sitting in his office back at the IEC headquarters. The video had horrible quality, and the audio cut in and out, but Drake knew his best friend's voice. The short thirty-second video held twenty-nine words that Drake couldn't forget.

"MARCUS... EARTH... DONE... FINDING SECONDARY... IF THIS IS... BRACE... US."

But the last few words came in as clear as day. "MARCUS BUDDY, I'M SORRY. IEC IS DONE, EARTH IS DONE. I LOVE YOU BUDDY. FINISH THE MISSION. COMPLETE BETHANY."

2

CHAPTER TWO

Drake felt like he couldn't breathe. Could he really believe what he had just heard? Drake played the message over and over again to see if he could get the entire message to play. But it was the exact words every time. Earth compromised, finding secondary brace. The last part is what chilled him. What Corbin meant by IEC is done; the Earth is done. And there it was again, Complete Bethany. Just like it had said in the email header. It just didn't make sense. There had to be a mistake, an answer to all of this. Drake immediately began pulling up every file the world had on anything he had just heard. But just his luck, any information update was exactly one year and three months ago when they received their last transmission from Earth. So there was no new information or update or anything going on there. Drake was unsettled. They had expected a communication dead point, so it wasn't a shock. It's just that it happened so soon. Drake had to steel himself. He couldn't freak out. If he did, everyone else would as well.

"Come on, Marcus. Take a deep breath. Breathe," Drake thought to himself. "Feel it; now face it," he said out loud. After an hour of reviewing files, he got a message from the mind banks. Private Manson hadn't survived the mind-banking process. Drake threw his tablet across the room, throwing it hard into the ceramic walls of the kitchen. He saw this coming; it was his decision to send Manson to be slaughtered. "Drake pull it, together," he said to himself. Drake sat there for a moment. His mind raced, but he tried to settle it and prepare for whatever came next. "I won't let this happen again," Drake said to himself. He got ready to head out to the debriefing. He did his best to cover the emotions in his heart.

Drake walked through the halls of the X-Caliber, a name he had actually gotten to pick out himself. He had an affinity for medieval times, his favorite being King Arthur. It also helped that the gigantic ship was almost sword-shaped if looked at from the right angle. Drake considered what he might say in the debriefing. It's not like he didn't have enough trouble keeping 500 people alive aboard the ship, but now he had to deal with this. As Drake walked into the debriefing room, everyone snapped to attention. He took his seat at the head of the table.

"All right, everyone, I know we aren't sure what's going on, but we need to try and work through this a piece at a time," Drake said. "Commander Thatcher, could you please state what you got out of Private Manson before he perished," asked General Helks.

"As far as we got in the mind, banking before he perished was shocking," Thatcher said, straightening up in her seat. "He saw the whole thing but only remembered its last five to ten seconds."

"Did he have any kind of mental illness that causes short-term memory?" Helks asked.

"No, absolutely none; that's what makes no sense," Thatcher responded.

"Out of all this, what doesn't make sense?" Helks said. Drake sat motionless at the head of the table. The room wasn't huge, but big enough to fit the ten highest-ranking officials aboard the ship. Drake played with the flash drive in his hand. He had stored the message from Corbin on it. Drake wondered if he should share the message with his fellow officers or keep it to himself. What would the consequences of either choice be, Drake wondered.

"Drake," Thatcher said.

"Oh yes, sorry." Drake had been lost in his thoughts. "So, what did the recording hold?" Drake asked.

"Let me just show you," Thatcher said. She turned on the screen, which dimmed all the lights in the room, and closed the curtains on the glass windows looking out into the hallway. The clip was only about 5 seconds long. It was a recording of probe 5's onboard camera. Probe 5 was the last probe to be launched precisely two weeks ago from that day. The probes' mission was to go ahead of the ship to spot potential threats and find viable landing zones for X-Caliber on Pluto. Probe 5, in particular, was a threat analysis probe. Meaning it looked specifically for things that would harm the ship or crew. The video showed nothing but a faint dot in the distance; Drake assumed it was Pluto. You could see 4 shiny metal reflections ahead of probe 5, the other 4 probes. The video showed the probe moving slowly through space while light reflected off the different probes in front of it. Then, at the end of the recording, they all saw something they could never unsee. There was what looked to be a ship on the far left-hand side of the screen. It was super blurry, and the details were super visible. But the sun hit it just right. You could see the outline of a spacecraft. The room was vacant of air. No one said a word except for Helks. A man Drake had known for a long time. Always known to be the obnoxious and loud one.

"Play it again," Helks yelled. "Is that a ship in the corner?" They all saw it. Drake didn't need to see it again, but they played it repeatedly.

Drake finally broke the silence. "So we aren't alone," he said.

"We always suspected this," Thatcher said quietly. "In the whole universe, there had to be some life, but who are they, and what do they want?" she asked.

Helks stood from his chair, racing to the direct communication phone in the debrief room. The phone that hadn't worked in one year and three months. It was a direct line contract to the IEC. The last time it had worked was when Drake contacted Corbin to give the weekly all-clear. Corbin had been more quiet on that phone call. But Drake didn't pay it much attention. He didn't know it would be the last time he would hear his friend's voice.

"We have to contact Earth," Helks said, panicking. "We have to let them know we are under attack." Helks picked up the phone and dialed the emergency number. The phone rang as every desperate attempt had been made before that one, and no call was connected.

"Drake, what's the move here? What do we do?" Thatcher asked. Drake looked down again. Staring at the old polished oak table.

"I may know something else," Drake said hesitantly. Drake sighed, "Corbin sent a message." Right at that moment, all the lights aboard the X-Caliber shut off.

"There's no way this could get any worse," Drake said with a chuckle.

CHAPTER THREE

2 WEEKS EARLIER

Drake woke up to an alarm clock blaring in his ear. As always, he was ready for the day. Simply continue on a five-year trip aboard one of the best ships in the entire IEC. Heading deeper and deeper into space than any human before. The goal of the mission was even easier. Set up a base on Pluto. Or so that's what the general population was told. It didn't hurt that he would be the first to set foot on Pluto. Today's goal was to send out 5 deep space probes toward Pluto, and that's what he intended to do. Drake got up and looked in the mirror; his grayish-black hair stuck up all over. In his 43 years, he had never had much luck controlling his rebellious hair. Most days, he kept it in his old, worn-out Yankees cap. His olive skin always seemed red in the mornings. He splashed cold water onto his face to help wake himself up. He had excellent features. Nothing too crazy. Drake turned from his mirror and looked around at his cabin. As expected, a single man with his own place looked tidy but not neat by any standards. But it did just fine for him. Drake made breakfast and coffee. Drake sat on his old leather sofa and read his Bible as he did most mornings. He got dressed in his usual joggers and a shirt. As usual, he stopped by his door and put on his old Yankees cap on the way out. He picked up a framed photo he kept right by his door. He said each of his three daughters' names. He said his wife's name and told them he loved them. Setting it down softly, he made his way out the door.

He walked to his office, just a short five-minute walk from his cabin. Once he got there, he stepped into his sanctuary. His home, he called it. The place where he would make history, as Corbin had said when he gave the ship's first tour. Drake smiled at the thought of his old friend. Today was the first real progress they had seen since they had taken the year to get around Jupiter's moons. They were finally in range to send out the probes. They were at step 8 of a 10-step plan to establish a base on Pluto. That's what everyone was told. Drake knew the real intent, and so did most of the crew. The Earth was dying; it had been for two hundred years. So, in its place, Project Genesis was born.

Named after Noah for saving the human race from extinction. Holding a small part of humanity to live onward. Everyone knew Earth was in bad shape, but no one knew how bad. So the plan was laid out. Live on Pluto. Becoming living legends on Earth in the process is what they were all told. Be humanity's first line of defense against asteroids, extraterrestrials, etc. Everyone laughed at that part. Alien life had never been proven.

However, the crew members were commissioned, the IEC was formed, and the Genesis missions were created. The X-Caliber and Admiral Drake being one of the three missions. The Moon, Mars, and Pluto. It was considered the hardest of the 3 by far. But most aboard welcomed the challenge. The public was told that three manned vessels were to be sent to each location, set up bases, and wait till they were needed. The Moon and Mars were a cakewalk. Resupplies happened monthly to the Moon and yearly to Mars and Pluto in a few years. On the bright side, the X-Caliber was self-sustaining and would remain their home even when they landed on Pluto. They were in the home stretch now. One year left. But at the end of the day, it wasn't really the whole truth. They were, in reality, a backup plan. Drake knew they were the human race's contingency plan. If Earth was toast, at least humanity would live on thanks to the nearly 200,000 human embryos aboard level 15. Hence the name Project Genesis. If needed, they would all begin again. But none of them thought it would come to fruition, at least not in their lifetime. It was hard to fathom that the Earth, Humanity's home, would be gone someday. The hardest part of the mission was that there would be no return voyage for the 500 crew members aboard the X-Caliber. More personnel would eventually be sent, but that was fifteen years from now. But it didn't matter. If you went to Pluto, you would die on Pluto, and most, if not all, of the crew welcomed that fact. Drake pulled up the day's to-do list. And, like most days, it was completely full. But the launch of the probes was something special. Everyone's duties would be suspended before they launched. It was something to celebrate, one more step down in the mission. Drake had always been the glass-half-empty kinda guy but never showed it. He kept his skepticism to himself most days. Drake knew the importance of this mission. He had even helped make the plans. But there had always been this ping of guilt for the people they had abandoned on Earth. Drake brushed off this feeling and got to work going through his emails. The usual data reports from life systems, food supply analysis, and maintenance updates. Drake skimmed over these. Something caught his eye as he was about to move on to another task. An unread email was received at 3:25 am the night before. The title caught Drake off guard. The title read "URGENT FOR ADMIRAL- Alpha clearance required- Complete Bethany."

Drake immediately tried to open it, but he couldn't. The email had a time lock. It would open precisely two weeks from today. Drake stared at his screen, trying to see a sender's address. There wasn't one. Drake was at a loss. The only person he knew who could know what was going on wasn't going to like helping him; in fact, he didn't like helping anybody. Jason Ross is a man who could break into any firewall, crack any encryption, find any backdoor to a code or algorithm. Jason was one of the few who did not want to go on the missions; he said something about dying with dignity on Earth. He was a criminal, not violent, but a cyber-criminal. He went by many different names back on Earth. He was, in all regards, the best hacker to have ever lived. But as punishment, he was sent here with the rest of the crew. Everyone loved Jason, and that was the funny part about it all. Anytime he made jokes, they were almost always a shot at someone. But he had a personality where people just loved it. Drake picked up his tablet and called Jason.

"Jason, could you come to my office, please?" Drake asked. "I need you to look at something." The line was silent, and Jason didn't say a word, but Drake knew he was on his way. Drake leaned back in his chair and looked around his office. He had a mini X-Caliber on his desk. His shelves had pictures of his family. He smiled softly at the thought of them. It was a big ship, so it would take Jason about 10 minutes to get there. Drake finished going over the day's procedures. Drake was definitely more excited today; Launch Day was here. Something he had been looking forward to ever since he got on the tin can, as he liked to call it from time to time. Most of the day consisted of meetings till 4 pm. That's when they would launch. Drake finalized the plans and opened a folder he kept on his computer. Drake stared at the file titled FAMILY. He clicked on it, and more than 1000 photos and videos popped up. He scrolled through them all, grinning as he passed photos of his beautiful girls. Some photos of birthday parties, school plays, and just everyday life. His oldest daughter, Taylor, named after his wife's Grandmother, had graduated from high school the year before they all passed. It was one of the biggest accomplishments, considering there was no college anymore, nothing like that. If you made it through high school, you had done something exceptional. Drake stared at the photo of his daughter grabbing her diploma, her smile crossing her face. He looked at photos from the graduation party. Drake stopped over a picture of his wife at the party. Her straight, dirty blonde hair fell below her shoulders, and her deep blueish-green eyes pierced through the picture. She was beautiful. Anyone with eyes could see that. But she was also strong. Her smile could light up a room, and she held Drake up most days. She was Drake's soulmate. Carmen Barret, a woman he had met when he just turned 18, she was a year older than him. They met the day after Drake had finished high school, and from that day, they were inseparable. They did everything together. She supported Drake's ambitions. She was considered a genius herself in a lot of areas. But that's where the similarities stop: they were polar opposites personality-wise. Drake was reserved and sometimes cynical, while Carmen was the optimist. She always found a way to be happy and joyful. And it rubbed off on Drake throughout their time together. When she was around, he always lit up. He had never been happier than when she was with him. So they built a life together, and they were pretty successful for the day and age they were in. Drake worked for the IEC, and Carmen was an engineer for systems and infrastructure for the IEC. Carmen always laughed and said their differences were what made them stronger. They truly loved each other and loved life. Drake clicked play on his favorite video.

"Honey, look over here," Drake said in a soft, happy voice. In a hospital bed, Carmen was lying down, holding Taylor. She looked over and smiled. Drake felt a tear forming. Carmen looked at the camera. "Look what we made," she said excitedly. "How did this come out of me," said she in a funny voice. Drake moved the camera closer. "You are gonna be the best mother ever," Drake said to her. She looked at him and smiled. "We are gonna be the best parents," she replied softly. "I love you, Marcus," she said with a smile. The clip ended. He had seen that video over 1000 times, but he loved it. Drake looked up and noticed Jason standing in his doorway.

"Bad time?" Jason asked with a blank expression.

"Jason!" Drake exclaimed; "No, not at all," Drake said as he frantically closed the video on his computer. "I have something for you to look at." Drake quickly cleared his files, and Jason sat down behind the desk. Jason had a pretty decent build. He had been much more fit back on Earth. But the sedentary space lifestyle made him give up his fit physique. His glasses and red beard matched his red hair. He usually kept it pretty short. Drake really did like Jason. He even considered him to be one of his closest friends at times.

"What are we looking at?" Jason asked. Drake pulled up the email. Jason looked at it intently.

"Have you ever seen anything like this?" Drake asked. Jason's eyes got wide, and he sat back in his seat.

"I haven't seen it in a long time," Jason said, pulling up things on the computer that made no sense to Drake. "This jargon was rarely, if ever, used in the early days of the IEC," Jason said. "And the fact that there is a timer on the email makes no sense."

"Can you break into it?" Drake asked him.

"No," Jason said bluntly. "If I hack in or bypass the time lock, all files associated with this message will be erased." Drake shook his head at that.

"I definitely don't want that to happen," Drake said.

"These were used to send presidents crucial info about the impending doom of the Earth," Jason said with a smug, amused look. "I've never actually seen one in real life. Why you have one sitting in your inbox is beyond me," Jason responded, closing the email. "I would wait out the two weeks to see what's inside." Jason stood up, "I'll look into it," Jason said. "If I had to guess, either this was the only way someone could contact you, or some loser intern sent an email from a secure computer and had no idea what they were doing."

"What do you mean the only way someone could contact me," Drake asked.

"Well, considering we haven't gotten an external message in over a year and the first one is from a server that shouldn't exist anymore, whoever sent you this needed to do it quietly, or this was the only server left in their possession to send a message," Jason said tapping on his tablet. "That's just a theory, though," Jason said blankly. "Like I said, I'll look into it, but your best bet is for you to just wait out the timer." Jason said, heading towards the door.

"Some world's best hacker you are," Drake said, in a joking tone. Jason just looked at Drake.

"You couldn't breathe without me," Jason said in a monotone voice, "I'll shut off the ship's life support if you want."

"Get to work, Jason," Drake said laughingly.

"See you at the launch," Jason said as he walked out of the room. Drake sat back in his chair and slouched, staring at his computer screen. He didn't completely understand all that Jason had said. But he decided to put it in the back of his mind for the moment; he had a lot of bigger things to deal with today.

After a few more hours of work, Drake decided to walk through the ship. The crew seemed to be in higher spirits than usual. Everyone was excited for the change of pace. The crew's usually busy schedule would get a break with the launch of the probes. Drake passed by the offices of his fellow commanding officers. Drake popped his head into Thatcher's office.

"Hey Thatch," Drake said. "Is everything going well?" Thatcher grimaced at Drake, calling her Thatch.

"Yep, almost everything is ready to go," Thatcher said. "Also, if you keep calling me that, I will tell Jason you love him."

"But I do," Drake said, "and he knows it. Do you need anything from me before we start getting ready for the launch procedures?" Drake asked, leaning on the frame of the door.

"Nope, I'll send a notice if I need anything," Thatcher said, still looking at her monitors. Thatcher was head of operations. She was number 2, right underneath Drake. She ran most of the ship by herself thanks to her very administrative mind; she knew how to run things orderly. That's why they worked well together. Drake was a genius who could solve any problem but couldn't explain what went on in his head most of the time. That's where Thatcher came in. She knew Drake and could understand him. She didn't have the highest scores during training and testing in the IEC, but Corbin had assigned Thatcher to the X-Caliber because of the potential he saw in her. Drake walked around the offices, heading down towards the lower crew levels. He loved his crew. Drake made it his mission to always be there for them, no matter what. He walked into the cafeteria.

"Hey Louris," Drake said to the main cafeteria lady. "How's the week been treating you?"

"Not too bad, Admiral," she responded to him. "It's been good to see so many smiling faces this week."

"That's all because of your cooking, Louris," Drake said with a wink.

"Oh, hush it, Drake," she said, blushing. "Here's your food," Louris said, handing Drake his food. He grabbed his tray and sat with some crewmates at a random table.

"Liam, Amelia, how are you guys doing today?" Drake asked as he sat down.

"Doing good, Admiral," Amelia said.

"We were just talking about some fusion experiments that we want to try when we get to Pluto," Liam said. "If we could get the right kind of gravity pocket, it could vastly open up how we move in space," Amelia said.

"We have infinite possibilities on Pluto," Drake said.

Liam nodded; "We already have the rudimentary system aboard the ship. But we are thinking of one infinitely more powerful." They ate their meal together and talked for a while. At 3:30, Drake made his way to the bridge for the launch. Walking past the sliding door, the bridge hadn't looked like anything Drake had imagined when he first saw it. He always imagined it looking sleek and pristine, like the ones from the space movies he had seen as a kid. But in all reality, it was a workspace. It was two levels, with a command deck that held three seats, one for Drake, one for Thatcher, and one for Ackin, better known as RJ. It was short for Thomas. It made no sense, but that's what he told everyone. He rarely, if ever, came out of his quarters. But that was his job; he was a reserve. If Thatcher or Drake were gone, that's when RJ jumped in. It's not like he was anti-social; he just preferred to keep to himself. Not surprisingly, Jason and RJ spent most of their off time together. The walls of the bridge were black, clean, and tidy. Monitors hung everywhere. It was a large room with over 70 crew members going about their daily tasks. It wasn't like the movies, where there was a huge open view of the vastness of space. There were a lot of cameras with feeds on monitors. But there was one giant window in the front, so you could see out into the vast space. The room was made in a sort of half-octagon shape with two levels. Drake entered and walked up the stairs to the command deck. Thatcher was already in her seat, looking over the diagnostics of the rockets that would be used for the launch. Drake sat in his seat in the middle and pulled up his monitor to look at the timeline and ensure they were on schedule. The bridge was bustling with movement, and everyone was scrambling to make sure everything was good to go.

"RJ walked in at the last minute, "Sorry I'm late, guys," RJ said, slouching into his seat. "I woke up late today," he said with a half laugh. RJ was still very obviously tired and out of it.

"Are you gonna be okay?" Drake asked RJ in a stern voice.

"Yeah, sorry, Marcus, I'm good," RJ said as he tried to straighten his shirt. Drake logged into the bridge's intercom.

"All systems check-in," Drake said. "Propulsion check, probe technician check, launch bay check, external systems check." The entire thing was being broadcast to the whole ship. All of the X-Caliber stood in silence.

"All systems go for launch?" Drake asked the bridge. He stood by for any objections. They all gave a thumbs-up for the launch. This was it; they had been waiting for it for a year. One step closer, Drake thought. Drake stood from his chair, walking to the edge of the command deck. The whole bridge looked up at him, holding their breath.

"X-Caliber... Launch at will."

CHAPTER FOUR

BOOM... the sound shook the ship as the first probe ejected from the ship. Everyone held their breath. The next few seconds dragged forever; there was another loud boom, then another. Then there was one last boom, the sound rattling the entire ship. "Probe 5 launch confirmed," the tech said. They weren't in the clear just yet. Drake stood at the railing, watching as the probes went in front of the window. Then a roar they hadn't heard since the day they launched from Earth echoed through the ship; all at once, the probes' engines fired on, shaking the whole ship. The probe tech looked up at Drake as he spoke through the intercom.

"Sir, the parameters are set, and the path flight is engaged. Probes are set for a course to Pluto." The entire ship erupted into cheering; Thatcher jumped up and hugged Drake. Everyone was yelling and celebrating. It had gone off without a hitch. Probe 5 passed in front of the window on its way to Pluto. The bridge looked on with excitement. Drake got onto the intercom.

"Crew, we did it," Drake said, full of pride. "One step closer to home." The crew on the bridge were jumping, high-fiving, and hugging each other. The cheers from the rest of the ship were audible even from the bridge. The celebration went on into the night. People just sat around, talked, and had a great time. Drake walked through the halls and different areas of the ship. He talked to everyone he came across and thanked them. It wasn't just his accomplishment; it was everyone's.

Drake continued to walk around the crowded hallways. He passed by a group of crew members all talking to themselves. He knew them well enough. They were the workers from level 15. They rarely, if ever, branched out and talked to others. Especially about their work. Most knew them as the mind bankers, which was their primary job. Only a few on the ship actually knew they were the caretakers. The ones who looked after the embryos. These men and women were selected by Drake himself by hand. Most of them resented the job because it was all a lie. And even though no one from Earth would ever find out, they had to keep the entire operation a secret. Drake walked by, just giving a small nod, not wanting to talk business at that moment. The caretakers seemed to only ever talk to Drake about their work. He was usually okay with this, but tonight wasn't for work. It was for a celebration. Drake felt a hand touch his shoulder.

"Drake, we need to talk," a man said from behind him. Drake looked behind him and saw Rowan Hayes, the lead caretaker. Rowan had gone to the same high school as Carmen, so that's how he had his in at the IEC.

"Rowan, can this wait?" Drake asked him. "People are having a good time." Time had not been kind to Rowan. His hair was almost gray despite only being 3 years older than Drake. Rowan wasn't fit by any standard, but definitely not fat either. But still big enough to see a slight belly through the standard uniform that all crew members wore. His eyes looked tired as if he hadn't been getting enough sleep.

"Drake, this can't wait," Rowan said, still holding onto Drake's shoulder. "You need to see this now." Drake continued to walk away.

"Rowan, I promise you it can wait till morning. Let us have the night." Rowan moved in front of Drake to stop him.

"Marcus, you have to trust me. You need to see this." Rowan pleaded to him. Rowan had always been serious, but Drake knew when he meant what he was saying.

Drake sighed, "Okay, let's make this fast."

"I don't think that's gonna be your concern after you see what I'm talking about," Rowan said, looking at the ground as they walked. Drake, Rowan, and two other caretakers went through the ship to the elevator. Once inside, Drake turned to Rowan.

"Is it the embryos?" asked Drake in a concerned voice. Rowan stayed silent for a moment.

"You just need to see for yourself," Rowan said quietly. They arrived at floor 15. The nicest and cleanest floor on the whole ship, mostly because only 10 regular crew members were stationed on this level. Everyone else just stayed away. As they walked through the dim halls, the automatic lights shot on. Offices sat on either side of the halls. There was a door at the end of the long hallway; the sign overhead said "Mind Banking." They turned and walked into Rowan's office on the left. Once inside, Rowan pushed a button under his desk, and a door on the opposite side of the wall slid open. Drake knew about this room from planning and construction but had never been into it with the embryos. They walked through the decontamination room and into the main vault. Their breath was visible in the freezing room. A large table with four chairs was in the middle of the space. It wasn't huge, but there were rows and cryo shelves. The table in the middle had one computer.

"Drake, please sit down," Rowan said softly. Drake sat, as did the other three men.

"Drake, you know the purpose of this mission, correct?" Rowan asked him.

"Yes, of course, I do," Drake said confidently.

"Let me explain again," Rowan leaned forward. "We are the human race's last contingency plan. The Moon is a research facility, and Mars is where they wanna move people." Rowan paused for a moment. "We are nothing but a backup plan."

"I've known this, Rowan," Drake replied.

"Then what is our mission before we are needed?" Rowan asked him.

"To set up a base and testing facility," Drake said, seeming confused at the question.

"Correct," Rowan said, messing with the monitor in front of him. "Then why did this happen two hours before the probes launched?" Rowan moved the monitor around so Drake could see it. He pulled up a list of cryo shelves. All of the names were highlighted in red next to the number. The screen showed them all in sleep mode except one. Drake looked at the screen.

Shelf 01 Name: BETHANY

Drake's heart dropped.

"Sir, what's going on?" one of the other men asked. Everyone's eyes were on Drake. Drake thought back to his friend. Corbin had kept one secret. The day the ship left Earth, Corbin brought Drake to his office and told Drake the last piece of the puzzle.

"You know your mission," Corbin said, "but there's one more thing. The embryos on your ship. They mean a lot more than you know." Corbin paused. "You can't activate them. Not until you arrive, at least." Corbin paused for a moment. "The only one who can activate them before you arrive is me. The only way I will ever activate them is if I need to." Drake made a confused look at him. "I can't tell you why yet, but it has a purpose. If shelf Bethany activates, you and your crew must be prepared for anything."

"What does that even mean?" Drake asked. "You sound crazy right now." Corbin just sat there motionless, not answering him.

"Why Bethany? Why's that necessary?" Drake asked him.

"Because Marcus, that's where the tomb of Lazarus was," Corbin said, tapping his hands on his desk, still visibly nervous. Lazarus was the one whom Jesus raised from the dead. Shelf Bethany has a higher purpose. One beyond just saving the human race. Bethany is how we come back more robust than the flawed ways of our ancestors." Corbin paused for a moment. Drake felt lost at this moment. He didn't truly understand the gibberish from his friend's mouth. "Those aren't just any embryos on that shelf," Corbin said leaning back.

"Who are they then?" Drake asked.

"That's for another day, Marcus," Corbin said, looking right into Drake's eyes. "But listen to me. If shelf Bethany is activated, you have to protect it at all costs," Corbin replied.

"Corbin, how am I supposed to protect something If I don't even know what I'm protecting?" Drake asked, trying to get through to Corbin.

"I know you don't, buddy," Corbin said. Obviously trying to finish the conversation. "You just need to trust me, can you do that?" Corbin asked. Drake nodded in agreement.

Looking down at the monitor in the cryo room, Drake tried his best to not show how distressed he was. He had yet to move in a solid 20 seconds.

"What's going on?" Rowan asked. Drake looked over at Rowan.

"Where is Bethany?"

CHAPTER FIVE

Rowan walked Drake all the way through the shelves towards the back. They stopped at shelf Number 1. There was a glowing green cabinet sitting in front of them.

"Usually, there are 250 embryos per shelf," Rowan said. But Drake had never looked into any of the specifics of the cryo room; he had never had to. Corbin had told him to not worry about it. But here in front of him sat an empty shelf. Illuminated green. Except for one. Just one embryo sat on the entire shelf designed to hold much more.

"Rowan, what do you know about this?" Drake asked Rowan, still staring at the shelf.

"Nothing," Rowan said quietly. "It's all completely classified. I have no access to anything on this shelf." Drake knew this embryo was unique because Corbin had said so. But he didn't know in what way. Rowan looked puzzled.

"That's weird," Rowan said. "Usually, this process is all automated."

"What do you mean?" Drake asked.

"It should unthaw from cryo, and then the development process begins...I don't know what's going on here. It's not unthawing from cryo. It's really not doing anything at all, actually," Rowan said, looking confused.

"What does that mean?" Drake asked, perplexed.

"I'm not sure," Rowan responded. "There must be different coding on this shelf in particular."

"Is there a way to deactivate it?" Drake asked.

"No," Rowan said abruptly. "We are caretakers. It's our job to look after the embryos. If I shut it down, the embryo dies." Drake looked away from the shelf and the embryo. He knew that Bethany was important. But he never truly understood to what extent. Drake had to let his fellow officers know. They deserved to know what was going on. But how would he tell them? Drake stared back at the individual capsule.

"Rowan, keep me updated," Drake said. "I need to think." Drake walked out of the vault, Rowan right behind him. Rowan had always been the persistent type.

"Marcus, what are we gonna do about this?" Rowan asked, sounding desperate. "This wasn't supposed to happen for 4 more years; we don't have anything set to raise any of these embryos if more are activated." Rowan was almost pleading at this moment. He knew Rowan was right. The correct procedure didn't have these pods activating for years after they had landed on Pluto. Drake stopped and leaned against the metallic wall.

"Look, Rowan, I don't know, to be very honest with you," Drake said. "I need to look and see if there is anything else Corbin might have said or left on the mission logs that I haven't seen yet. I need this to stay under wraps for now," Drake said, leaning closer to Rowan. "Things can't fall apart when we are this close to completing this mission." Drake turned back towards the door. "I'm gonna go back out there. I encourage you to do the same. We might not have very many average days left on this ship."

Drake walked into the elevator. How am I gonna explain this to everyone? he thought. Drake knew all along there were other motives behind sending them to Pluto. But he didn't really care. With his family gone and the Earth dying, Drake was okay with taking whatever responsibility came with his role. Drake remembered his friend's words. "Those aren't just any embryos." Corbin had never elaborated on it. Even in the three years they had open communication from Wart to the ship, there had never been another mention of Bethany or the embryos. It was always the same thing between them. Earth still sucks; the Yankees lost again this season; how's the crew doing? People are losing faith in the IEC. Same old stuff.

Drake was a genius. He knew it; everyone knew it. But Corbin was a genius in his own respect. You had to be a genius to convince every government on the globe to give up on Earth and give everything they have to make space their new home. The IEC was formed when Drake was only 18 years old. It took a long time to gain traction, but Corbin was at the helm the entire time. Drake had gone with Corbin simultaneously but mostly worked behind the scenes. They still paid him well, but he made it a condition to accept the position. He didn't want to be publicly known. The last thing he wanted was to work constantly and in the limelight. He had his small, blooming family and didn't want to focus on much else. Life on Earth didn't last as long as it once had; most life ended by your 40s or 50s, so Drake didn't wanna make his whole life his work. Family meant too much to him.

On the other hand, Corbin didn't have a family except for his dad. The IEC was his life. Since the IEC was a global partnership, Corbin met with the world's most elite. Anywhere from billionaires to presidents to religious leaders. Everyone wanted a stake and a part of the IEC, so naturally, there would be some shady dealings, things Corbin couldn't talk about. Drake knew this. But it didn't matter to him in the end. Drake wasn't there anymore. But it still concerned him. He knew some sketchy dealings went down, and people wanted their own version of the missions. Drake was in charge of the plans, but Corbin would always go in to add to or take away. Corbin always finalized everything. So Drake knew there were things he didn't know about.

But Bethany. It was something that Corbin had let Drake in on. But why he told Drake and didn't give any details still confused him. The ding of the elevator brought Drake back to reality. The door opened, and Drake stepped out into the hall. The celebrations were still going as strong as before. Drake let himself smile at their happiness. Drake looked at his watch. It was 12:34 am. Drake knew they would be up well into the morning, so he decided to talk to a few more people and then turn in for the night. Drake passed the infirmary on his way back to his quarters. He decided to pop in. The infirmary always seemed to be quiet. There wasn't a lot of sickness aboard the ship. Rarely, if ever, someone would come down with a cold or mild flu and check themselves in. Everyone usually just enjoyed the week off of work that came with it. But it still wasn't the funniest thing. Drake walked over to the nurse on duty.

"Oh, Drake," the woman sitting behind the nurse's desk exclaimed. "It's so good to see you! Congratulations on the successful launch today, dear."

"Thank you, Nan," Drake said kindly. Short for Nancy. Or Nana, everyone looked up to her as their grandmother aboard the ship. That's even what she called herself. "I'm everyone's grandma," she liked to exclaim. She had never met a stranger and was the sweetest soul. She had been head of emergency medical services back on Earth for some of the biggest disaster response services ever. And Earth sure did need a lot of disaster relief these days. It wasn't just famine that ravaged Earth; tornadoes the size of skyscrapers. Volcanoes, earthquakes. And to top it all off, the Earth had massive food shortages. It truly felt like the end of the world was there. Instead of going into complete anarchy, people decided to fight for the greater good. To try and give humanity a fighting chance.

"How's everything been running down here?" Drake asked.

"It's been swell dear," Nan responded. "More and more get out every day, and there are fewer coming in, but we know flu season is around the corner, so it'll be a nice little break for a few weeks," Nan said with a compassionate grin. "Oh, here, look at these," Nan said as she walked over with her medical tablet. She pulled up a picture of her dogs; it was her favorite thing to do. She loved talking about her "little rascals," as she called them back home. She swiped through a few pictures. The cute dogs reminded Drake of the one he left back home. Drake had always been a dog man and always had one growing up. But no animals were allowed on the ship except for control test animals. So Cody had to be left behind. Drake didn't name his dog. It was his 2nd daughter, Savannah, who named him. The first trip Cody went on was through Cody, Wyoming, so from that day forward, Savannah called him Cody. Drake loved it. He honestly just loved anything that reminded him of his girls.

Nan continued swiping for a while, and Drake sat there with her. He knew it was late, but being with his crew filled his heart. At 1:30, Drake decided to call it a night. People still sat in the halls and talked as he made his way through the halls. Drake eventually made the walk back to his quarters. Drake input his code for his door. The door slid open. Drake fell back when he saw someone standing in his living room.

CHAPTER SIX

"**D**rake, it's just me," Thatcher shouted right as he hit the floor, scared half to death.

"What the heck, Thatch," Drake growled; it was almost two in the morning. "What are you doing here?" Drake asked as he got up from the floor with an annoyed look.

"I'm sorry," Thatcher responded. "I just wanted to make sure everything was okay."

"Yeah, why wouldn't it be?" Drake answered as he made his way into the living quarters. Drake stopped to put his old Yankees cap on the coat hanger in his living room.

"No reason," Thatcher responded. "I just saw Rowan giving you a hard time earlier, that's all."

"Rowan?" Drake asked, "nah, he's harmless."

"Are you sure?" Thatcher said, shooting Drake a severe look. "He looked pretty serious when he was talking to you."

"First off, you gotta quit stalking me," Drake said with a smile, grabbing some water from the kitchen.

"In your dreams," Thatcher responded quickly. Something that Thatcher was very good at was telling when someone was lying, and Drake was the worst liar ever.

"You know when you lie, you shift your weight forward, and your left eye slightly twitches," Thatcher said with a stone-cold expression.

"What the heck, Fiona? How could you possibly know that?" Drake said in a surprised voice.

"Marcus, you know I hate my first name. No one calls me that, but you," Thatcher said, sounding displeased.

"I know that's why I call you that. Not because you hate it but because I'm the only one who calls you that. I doubt more than 5 people know your first name on this ship," Drake stated.

"Very accurate," Thatcher said as she shot him a look. "Let's try to keep it that way," she said with a serious face. Thatcher was leaning against the kitchen counter, and Drake was sitting on the back edge of his couch, looking at Thatcher. Thatcher stood up.

"Look, Drake, you don't have to tell me, but I know something happened tonight with you and Rowan."

"Thatch, I don't know where to begin," Drake said, pausing; he still had a hard time comprehending it himself. "It's a lot."

"Good thing we live on the same ship," Thatcher said as she walked over to the recliner in the corner by the artificial fireplace. Drake sighed. He rolled over onto his couch, sitting in the middle of it.

"Where do I begin?" Drake said as his face stared at the floor. Over the next hour, Drake explained the best he could about Project Bethany. If Drake could trust anyone, it would be Thatcher. But in a way, it still felt like a betrayal of Corbin. After all, Corbin had trusted Drake with the secret. But Drake told her everything.

From the contingency plan to the embryos, which she already knew about. To everything Drake knew about Project Bethany, which was not a lot. What Drake suspected of Corbin's dirty dealings within the IEC. Drake explained the shelf activating that day. Thatcher looked unfazed at the end of it. Her face showed a mixture of it almost being 3 in the morning, shock, and a slight bit of betrayal. Thatcher looked up at Drake.

"Marcus, do we even know the real reason we are here?" She asked with a concerned look.

"You know I can't answer that," Drake said, pausing. "I thought I knew, but it feels like everything is changing under our feet," he said, meeting her eyes. They just looked at each other.

"Look, Drake, I know you were not keeping anything from me. But I hope you understand if I'm cautious," Thatcher said.

"No, I understand, trust me, I don't know how I'm gonna sleep tonight," Drake said, messing with his hands.

"Well, we're gonna have to try," Thatcher said, standing up. "Get some rest, okay?" she said as she left the room. Right before she left, she turned back to look at Drake. "Hey, just so you know. I got your back."

"I got yours, Thatch," Drake said. Thatcher walked out of the room, the door sliding closed behind her.

Drake couldn't believe that day he had just had. Trying to process all of it felt like a never-ending flowing lava pit. His mind didn't end in a comfortable place in every direction he took. Thatcher didn't even know about the email. It still gnawed at him. Why would someone send an email in the fashion that he had received it? It didn't make sense. Then, the launch went so smoothly. This was supposed to be a happy day for the crew and Drake. But it ended with more questions than answers. Drake decided to sleep in for the first time in a while; he felt like he deserved it.

Drake woke up, His head felt dizzy, and everything seemed to move around him, but he wasn't awake. He looked down at his hands, which appeared to be blurry, like his feet. Drake stood from his bed but immediately knew it was a dream. What he saw couldn't be real. Drake walked forward into the room in front of him. His three girls, Taylor, Savanna, and his youngest, his princess, Sadie, all sat in front of him. Sadie was named after Carmen's middle name. Carmen had died 5 months after giving birth to her. Drake and Carmen kept the pregnancy a secret from everyone except Corbin and Carmen's mother. When there's barely enough food to feed yourself, having more than one child is looked down upon, let alone three. But they wanted to keep her. But the moment Sadie was born, they knew something was wrong with Carmen. She never got her color back. It was all of a sudden, and her body just decided to give out. The first few months were okay. But the last two are where Carmen really went downhill. Drake stood by her side, caring for Sadie and giving his wife the best last few months he could. She passed, and Drake said it was from the famine. He wouldn't let anybody know it was because of Sadie. There was a special bond between Sadie and Drake. It was the last gift Carmen could give him, and in a particular sort of way, the two girls before had Drake's eyes, deep dark brown. But Sadie had the fierce blue-green eyes of her mother. Drake lost his breath when he saw her. Sitting there on the carpet playing like she did all those years ago. The ground below her was fuzzy like it could give at any minute. Drake ran over to her and scooped her up in his arms. He knew this wasn't real, but he would enjoy every second with her. His other two girls scooted in beside him. They sat on the ground, looked at each other, and smiled. Drake was overcome with emotions. He looked up, and his wife was standing in the doorway. She walked in and sat down with all of them. Drake had not been this happy in a long time. Everything he cared about was right here.

"Marcus," his wife said, staring into his eyes. "Complete Bethany," she said in a very soft voice, Drake's heart dropped.

"Carmen, what did you say?" he asked.

"Complete Bethany, Marcus." Carmen said again. This time, a little louder, Taylor looked up at him.

"Complete Bethany, Dad," Savannah said, joining in.

"Complete Bethany, Daddy," Sadie said. They were all saying it in a frantic voice. Drake was getting overwhelmed.

"Complete Bethany, complete Bethany, complete Bethany." They were all standing in a circle around Drake, screaming the exact words at him, "COMPLETE BETHANY." Then, all of a sudden, it stopped. Taylor and Savannah had disappeared. Carmen looked up at Drake. She kissed his head and then placed her hand on Sadie's chest.

"Complete Bethany, my love," Carmen said in a sweet-sounding voice. Then, like that, Carmen was gone. All that was left was Drake and his baby girl. She looked up at him, and Drake held onto her tightly, trying to enjoy it the best he could.

CHAPTER SEVEN

A week had passed. Drake did what he did best, and he pushed forward. He continued to meet with Rowan daily for updates about the cryo shelf. But he kept on with duties as usual. Except there was even more work now, which was good in the grand scheme of things. It kept his mind busy and off of that night. He couldn't unsee his daughter's eyes staring into him. He couldn't forget his daughter's voice. He couldn't forget seeing his wife again. It had all just felt so real. But Drake brushed it off. He had work to do. New data poured in from the probes hourly. They were rocketing towards Pluto and were expected to arrive in 4 months, just 6 months ahead of the crew. Drake was in charge of Probe 1, which would be the one that would find a landing spot for their home. So it had to get there sooner than the others. And it would be a month ahead.

Drake poured over topography maps already collected by the probe in his office. There was a knock. Drake looked up to see RJ.

"Hey, bossman, sorry to interrupt, but I just thought you should know Helks is calling for a council meeting," RJ said, standing slouched in the doorway. Drake sighed. These meetings were always dull and took way too long, but Drake had to go.

"Thanks for letting me know," Drake said with a half smile, "see you there, RJ."

"Oh, I'm not going," RJ said, laughing. "I got a ton of paperwork to go through."

"Like what?" Drake asked.

"Oh, you know. The critical kind," RJ said as he slouched off towards his cabin. Drake sighed, standing up from his desk and leaving his office.

Drake walked to the meeting room, wondering what it could be about. These meetings didn't happen often, but there was usually a point behind them, which was good. A council meeting was held with all the heads of departments and then the 4 lead council members: Drake, Thatcher, Helks, and RJ. Drake had always wondered how he got this job. He was good for anything but leadership, but somehow, he had gotten this job. It was basically a vacation for him. Drake didn't mind too much, though. RJ mainly stayed out of everyone's way. The only person he honestly annoyed was Jason. But it was more of a friendship kind of annoyance.

As he arrived, he saw that everyone was already present. Drake took his seat by Thatcher and leaned over to her.

"Do you have any idea what the meeting is about?" Drake asked.

"I have no clue," Thatcher said. "I ran some supply sims, and then RJ busted into the lab, saying they needed me quickly."

"Why wouldn't they just message us to have us all meet?" Drake asked, confused. "And why would they make RJ come round all of us up?" Drake asked.

"No clue," Thatcher said, looking unamused, "but I hope this goes by fast." A few more stragglers made their way into the meeting room. The last one was Rowan. His head was down, and he was obviously distressed. Drake stared at him, but he wouldn't meet his eyes.

"So what's this all about?" Drake said, raising his voice. Helks stood up and walked over to Drake.

"This man is a great leader, and we couldn't have done this without him," Helks said, patting Drake on his back. At that moment, RJ busted into the room with a cake in his hand and music playing.

"Happy birthday, nerd," RJ screamed. Everyone joined in; "HAPPY BIRTHDAY, DRAKE!" Everyone exclaimed. Drake had forgotten entirely. It was hard enough remembering what month it was. But how could he forget his own birthday? Drake looked at the cake and saw the number 43. Everyone sang the same old birthday song and cheered at the end.

"Make a wish," Thatcher said with a smile. Drake smiled. He closed his eyes to make a wish, but all he saw were his three girls and his wife right before him. Drake blew out the candles and smiled. He didn't have his family, but this one was still here for him. It made his heart happy. Drake spent the afternoon talking to friends and the crew. Some would drop by at random times to wish Drake a happy birthday. Some would stop to tell stories about Drake. Thatcher had some pretty bad ones on Drake. Everyone seemed to love them.

The party ended, and everyone returned to their rooms for the night. Drake walked Thatcher back to her room.

"Thank you for everything, Thatch. All this means so much." Thatcher stopped at her door. She stared at Drake.

"Always," she said with a smile. "You're my best friend. I would do anything for you." She opened her mouth to say something else but stopped herself. "I'll see you tomorrow," she said. Drake felt something. Like what she was gonna say was important. But he didn't want to harp on her.

"Alright, Thatch, I'll see you tomorrow," Drake said with a kind look in his eyes. Thatcher lingered in the doorway for a moment, and then she turned and went into her cabin. Drake turned and walked away. That was odd, he thought to himself. Drake hadn't dealt with knowing what a woman felt in a long time. And up until that point, he didn't really care to. Ever since his wife, it didn't matter. But Drake pondered on that thought as he walked back to his cabin. He put up his old Yankees hat and turned in for the night. 43, Drake thought to himself. For the day and age, he had beaten life expectancy. They said 50s, but most didn't make it past 40. But that's just who Drake was, a man who defied the odds.

CHAPTER EIGHT

25 YEARS AGO

For a man who grew up in the worst times the world had ever seen, Marcus Drake was able to pull himself out of the waste. Call it fate or luck, but Drake had found a way to make it. He grew up in a small town named Rustin. Formally known as Central Kansas. His family was from Oklahoma, where he was born in Coffker. They migrated when all the super-tornados started forming in upper Texas and Oklahoma. Plus, living in Tornado Alley wasn't precisely a good decision when the tornados were as giant as 3 miles wide and as tall as the most prominent buildings still standing in the world. The town was named Rustin. There were about 10,000 people there. Everyone just wanted to get out and head north. But that took a lot of work to do. The roads were shot, and owning a vehicle was next to impossible, considering the price of owning and operating it. The town was old and run down. And had a significant drug problem. Most would travel to Rustin to get their drugs. Drake and his family had seen a person traveling through. They knew they weren't from around there because no one in Rustin drove that nice of a car. But the man had on a shirt, and the words on his shirt said: "I got my drugs from Rustin." Poor taste, for sure. But that was just the atmosphere. But no one really did anything about it anyway. Everyone just looked out for themselves.

Drake's sophomore year would change everything for him. Drake was in his 1st-hour human history class when the door opened, and the Principal walked in with a kid no one had ever seen before. It was a smaller school with about 100 people in the grade, so everyone knew everyone.

"Hey class, I just wanna introduce our new student Corbin Huxley," the Principal said. Everyone just stared at the new kid. "Well, okay, Corbin, let me know if you need anything," the Principal said awkwardly. "Class, please make him feel welcome." The Principal walked out, and Corbin just kinda stood there. The teacher smiled.

"Hello Mr. Huxley, go ahead and find a seat," the teacher said with a half smile. The room was already packed as is. She wasn't happy about cramming another student in the overflowing space. And as fate would have it, Corbin Huxley sat right beside Drake. They didn't really talk much the first couple of weeks. Drake never really spoke to anyone. But the class had a mid-term project, and you had to have a partner. The teacher paired students with whoever they were sitting by, so Drake and Corbin worked together on the project. Corbin went to Drake's house one night to wrap up the project. At this point, Drake still hadn't opened up to Corbin. They had mainly worked on the project at the local library or the only pizza shop. He was still a stranger to him. Drake did not trust easily. He never had. He didn't like sharing what he felt. But Corbin being around was like a thorn in his side. His personality rubbed Drake the wrong way. Corbin always joked around. Very rarely did Drake crack jokes. He was reserved for the most part. He was not isolated, but he just preferred to keep to himself. But Drake had no choice; they had to do this project. Drake went along with Corbin. Half laughing at the jokes. But there was one thing they had in common. It was the one thing Drake truly loved. Baseball. Corbin had noticed all the Yankees memorabilia around Drake's room. And that's what sparked the friendship. That was the crack in Drake's armor. Since Drake was little, his grandpa had taken him to one Yankees game yearly. His grandpa would save up all year so he could go with his grandson. Drake's favorite gift was a Yankees cap that his grandpa had gotten him on one of their last trips to see the team play. Drake and Corbin started talking about their favorite teams. Drake loved the Yankees, and Corbin loved the Astros. Some call it simple. But it's what Drake needed. That's all it took. The next day after school, Corbin invited Drake over to throw around a baseball and talk about their favorite sport. And from that day forward, they were inseparable. They weren't just friends in baseball, though. Their love for space was also mutual. They both knew so much was possible in the realm of space travel. Drake liked to point out the discoveries they could make if they hadn't been born into the worst period in human history. Even though college was never an option, they excelled in their classes. Both are at the top. Most people didn't really care. The school didn't really do anything for anyone anymore. But it was something that both Drake and Corbin pushed each other in. Their academic prowess didn't go unnoticed. Years passed, and neither boy had a plan for what they wanted to do after school. But they knew they wanted to work together. They weren't just friends anymore. They were brothers.

It was graduation day. Something that didn't matter much anymore, but they still did it out of tradition. Drake wanted to skip, but Corbin wouldn't let him. They both walked, and the ceremony was held. Afterward, there were pictures and smiles. Just as both the boys' families were about to leave, Corbin and Drake were approached by some men at their graduation. It was an odd thing to see. Only family ever showed up to these events anymore. So the men in all-black suits really stood out, especially next to the drab, worn-out clothing worn by most people in Rustin.

When the men approached, Corbin and Drake's families walked towards the door. "Corbin Huxley, Marcus Drake?" one of the men asked.

"Yes, Sir, that's us," Corbin said with a puzzled look. The men peered at the boys' families.

"If you could excuse us for a moment. We just need a word with your sons," the taller one said. Drake and Corbin followed the men over to the deserted side of the gym. Most people were already leaving, so they were able to talk privately.

"Hello, my name is Agent Helks." The man was short and not in shape but had thick blonde hair. He looked like he was in his late 30s, but that was getting up there for the day and age. He wore thick glasses, but they suited his face.

"We work for the United States government." The two boys just stood in confusion.

"A paper that you wrote, Corbin, ended up on my desk," the taller agent said.

Corbin smirked, "I wrote a lot of essays; you're gonna have to be specific," Corbin said, his ego popping through. The men didn't look amused.

"Look, I said we don't have much time here," Agent Helks said. "But what we are about to tell you is very, very important. Remember that paper you wrote about gravity distortions and human life in space?"

"Vaguely," Corbin mumbled. Corbin was infatuated with gravity and what it meant for the greater universe. He didn't talk about it much to anyone but Drake; he liked to keep his cool guy persona. But, as an 18-year-old, he knew everything there was to know about physics and gravity.

"What does that have to do with anything?" Corbin asked in a curious voice.

"We have a new agency in the government being talked about, and we think you would be a great addition to its beginning stages," the taller agent said. Corbin looked shocked.

"You mean to tell me that the US government wants to hire me to help develop a new agency?" Corbin asked, laughing. "I'm 18, dude."

Helks looked sternly at Corbin. "Not only are you one of the brightest minds we've seen in a generation, but that should also show how desperate we are. We are at an 18-year-old's graduation," Helks said in a snarky yet semi-serious tone. Corbin leaned against the wall.

"Well, how could I say no," he said in a joking tone. Drake looked up at them; he'd been staring at the laminated wood floors of the gym that were about 20 years past and needing to be redone.

"Then why am I in this conversation?" Drake said, confused.

"Did you not read your friend's work, Marcus?" the taller agent asked. "You are stated over 300 times in this article as an assistant and a close advisor in this theory." Drake loved space but didn't have all the knowledge as Corbin did. Where Drake excelled was the unexpected. Thinking outside the box. Seeing things Corbin didn't. "That's why we want you and Mr. Huxley to come together." Drake looked at Corbin, who just shrugged back at him.

Drake's mind raced for a moment. A kid who shouldn't have a shot at anything being offered a job in the US government. Something unheard of. Especially in this part of the country. One of Drake's first times defying the odds.

"When would we start?" Drake asked in a serious voice.

"Four months," Agent Helks responded. "Take this time to get your lives straight here back home. You won't be back to Rustin much after you leave," the taller agent said.

"Where are we going?" Corbin asked.

"That's classified," Agent Helks said. "We will be in touch," the other agent said as they walked away past their families. "Congratulations, boys," they said as they walked out the door.

The two boys walked back to their families. "What was that about, boys?" Corbin's father asked.

"I think our lives are about to change," Corbin said with a laugh, putting his arm around Drake.

Drake didn't show it, but he was excited about this opportunity. He stared at his bedroom ceiling for a while that night, just thinking about things. There was a light knock at his door. His Grandpa walked in.

"Hey, Pops," Drake said.

"Hey, kiddo," His Pops said in a kind voice. "Wanna fill me in on what all that was about earlier in the gym?"

"They were from the US government," Drake said, messing with one of his car models. "They are forming some new agency. And they want Corbin and me to be a part of it. But they want me to work alongside Corbin," Drake said, still looking at the model car.

"Doing what?" His Pops asked him.

"They actually didn't tell us," Drake said, looking up at his Grandpa.

"Well, what is your heart telling you?" His Pops asked, pressing further.

"I'm not sure, Pops," Drake said, lying down and looking at the ceiling.

"What is God telling you?" His Pops said in a genuine voice. That's something Drake was eternally grateful for. His Pops was a firm believer. He had instilled that belief into Drake.

"Do you believe in destiny?" Drake asked his grandfather.

"Son, I believe in the will and plan of God," he responded to Drake. Drake smiled. "I guess you could call that destiny," Pops said with a genuine expression.

"I feel like there's something more to this than what I can see right now," Drake said.

"Then follow it till the road runs out," his Pops said as he stood from the side of the bed. "I'll see you tomorrow, son." Drake smiled. It was his favorite thing that his Grandpa had told him. It gave him permission to follow what he felt was right. He would always say that if it was God, the road wouldn't run out, and if it did, you would know it wasn't Him. Drake rolled over and got some sleep.

Drake and Corbin's family took them to a graduation dinner the next day. They had to take the bus for two hours because Rustin had no excellent restaurants. So they had to take a bus to one of the only places in the entire state that didn't serve fake lab-grown meat. They walked in, and all sat down around a big circle table. The place was a decent size and not super busy. But the place had a very old diner feel to it. They got their drinks and menus. They all browsed over the different steak options the place had. Drake had begged his Grandpa for a steak for graduation. It was a stretch for him to afford it, but he wanted to make it happen for Drake.

Just then, a voice came from behind Drake. "Hey guys, I'll be your waitress today. Are we celebrating anything today?"

Drake's Grandpa looked up. "We sure are, our boys just graduated yesterday," his Pops said with some pride in his voice. Drake still hadn't turned to look at the voice behind him. He had been fixated on the menu in front of him. It wasn't every day he got authentic steak.

"Congrats, you two," the kind voice said behind him. Drake decided to turn around to say thank you. When he did, his life changed forever. The woman smiled at him, "My name is Carmen; what can I get for you guys today?"

CHAPTER NINE

ehind him stood the most beautiful girl he had ever seen. She stood with grace, but right away, Drake could see the strength in her. Their eyes locked, and Carmen let out a little laugh. Drake, being a complete idiot and not knowing how to handle his feelings, reached out his hand.

"Hi, I'm Marcus." Corbin, who had been wide-eyed at the interaction, face-palmed himself.

"Hi Marcus, it's great to meet you," Carmen said in an obviously nervous voice. Carmen snapped herself out of it, remembering she was at work. She cleared her throat. "So what can I get you, lovely folks?" She said, writing down the orders. When she walked away, Drake looked down at the table with a slight grin. He looked up and saw everyone looking at him.

"Corbin laughed, a real smooth idiot." Drake threw his napkin at him.

"Shut up, man."

After their meal, they paid and walked outside to wait for the bus home. But Drake just couldn't shake a feeling he had. Drake leaned over to his Grandpa.

"Pops, I just gotta go talk to her again." His Pops smiled and looked at him.

"Till the road runs out, son," his Pops said, putting a hand on his shoulder. Drake hugged him and told him he would be home later. As he ran back towards the restaurant, Corbin shouted at him.

"Dude, what are you doing?"

"Something stupid," Drake shouted back. He walked inside and up to the host.

"Excuse me, can I speak to Carmen?"

"She gets off in 30 minutes, but I'll let her know," the host said, not looking very amused.

"Great," Drake said.

"You don't mind waiting?" the host asked.

"Not at all," Drake said as he sat in the front waiting area. A few times, Carmen walked by, and she glanced at Drake and smiled shyly. When she got off, she met Drake at the front and walked out to wait for the bus with him. Drake, a nervous mess, walked out with her.

"So I just thought you were really cool, and I was wondering if I could have your number?" Carmen, smiling the whole time, looked at him.

"Of course," she said with a smile. Drake had had a few flings and girlfriends, but nothing made him feel like this girl did in the two hours he knew she existed. They stood by the bus pickup, waiting for ten minutes.

"So where are you going back to?" Carmen asked.

"Rustin," Drake said. "What about you?"

"Woodmarls," Carmen said. Definitely a more sociable city than Rustin, but luckily for Drake, it happened to be on the same route towards Rustin for an hour.

"Well, look at that," she said, "headed the same way. Wanna sit by me?" Carmen asked in a shy voice.

"Sure," Drake said in a voice he noticed sounded too excited. They talked nonstop for the entire time until they reached Woodmarls.

"Call me?" Carmen asked as she got up to leave.

"Of course," Drake said as he watched her get up and go. She took one last look before she walked off the bus. Drake slouched in the seat and just smiled. He looked up; "What just happened?" he said with a smile.

The next few months were a dream. Drake and Carmen spent every moment they could together. Corbin would hang out with them from time to time as well. Drake eventually asked Carmen to be his girlfriend, and she accepted. Time was growing closer for both the boys to leave, but they still hadn't heard from the agents and had no idea where they were going. Drake explained the best he could to Carmen what would happen, but he honestly had no idea himself. As time passed, Drake knew he had a decision to make; he didn't know if they would let Carmen come with them. But he knew he couldn't live without her.

The three of them had all decided to walk to their favorite spot in town. A blacked-out vehicle way too high-class to be from Rustin pulled up. Agent

Helks stepped out.

"Boys, nice to see you again. And who is this?" Helks said casually.

"This is Carmen, my girlfriend," Drake said nervously. It had been a few months, but it still excited him to talk about it.

"Good for you," Helks said. "Two weeks, meet me at the Hillbaton airport. There, we will head to your new home."

Corbin jumped up in excitement. "Finally!" Corbin said. "I thought you guys had been messing with us." Drake was torn. That meant he would be leaving Rustin and Carmen.

"See you guys then," Helks said, stepping back towards the car. "Carmen, it was a pleasure." Drake jumped up and ran over to Helks.

"Sir, can I talk to you for a second?" Drake asked him.

"Sure, what's up?" Agent Helks asked Drake.

"Listen, I know that this is for me and Corbin, but Carmen, she's the brightest person I know," Drake said, trying to not sound desperate. "She's more of a genius than Corbin and I combined." Which was true. Carmen could do practically anything. She had graduated top of her class and had an offer from one of the only remaining universities in the country. Helks looked at him intently.

"I'm not authorized to give that invitation out of the blue," Helks said.

"What if she was my wife?" Drake said in a last-ditch effort.

"I suppose I couldn't separate you two at that point," Helks said hesitantly. Drake smiled at that response.

"Expect one more person on that plane," Drake said with a smile. Helks nodded, then stepped back into his car and drove away.

Drake knew from the bus ride that first day he wanted this girl to be in his life forever. He didn't know how much time he had to make it happen. That night, Drake rode the bus with Carmen back to Woodmarls. He asked her mother for her hand in marriage. At first, she was hesitant. But she saw that any life outside that place was better than she could offer. The two got married three days later. It was a smaller ceremony with the local judge. Drake's Grandpa and Carmen's mom were there supporting him. When it was time to leave, the three of them, plus their families, took the three-hour trip to the airport. Drake's Grandpa rode with them, along with Corbin's dad and Carmen's mom. They were all there to see them off. No one left their hometowns anymore, so this was a big deal. The three had never even stepped inside an airport in their lives. They eventually arrived at the terminal. They stood outside the loading area. Drake's Grandpa hugged him tightly. He looked him in the eye.

"Son, there is so much in you, so much potential; there is destiny in you, I see it, something extraordinary." His Grandpa stepped back for a moment. "Follow God's plan and his will. Follow that road until it runs out. You always have a home here," his Grandpa said as a tear flowed down his face. Drake let a tear fall as well. He had never seen his grandpa cry, but the tough, caring man let tears stream down his face. They boarded the plane. He saw his Grandpa looking at the aircraft through the plane's window. Drake was okay with never seeing Rustin or the wastes again, but his Grandpa was the one who had always been there for him. When his parents left. He didn't know he would never see him again. Drake peered back at him through the glass of the plane, watching the man who gave him a shot at life fade away as the aircraft rolled onto the tarmac.

CHAPTER TEN

DAY OF THE PROBE DISAPPEARANCE; PRESENT DAY

The emergency lights came on with all the systems that powered life support, but the rest of the ship remained dark.

"What's going on?" Helks yelled.

Drake stood up. "Everyone remain calm," Drake said, trying to maintain control. A power outage was typical back on Earth, but it was next to impossible aboard a ship like the X-Caliber. Really, the only way for power to actually go out could have two different reasons: someone had deactivated the main reactor, or, the worst option, it had been turned off on purpose by someone. Everyone knew the likelihood of this happening was very low, making the situation that much more uncomfortable.

"Drake, what's going on?" Thatcher asked.

"I don't know, guys. I don't have an answer yet," Drake said, trying to remain calm. Drake looked down at his fist with the flash drive. He debated internally. The video screen returned online, replaying the same clip they had been watching a minute prior. Once again, it stopped just as a ship appeared on the left side. Drake decided it was now or never. He plugged the flash drive into the port located by his seat.

Why not add to the fire, he thought. The video of Corbin popped up. Drake stood up before he played the footage.

"Listen, everyone. I don't know what's happening right now," Drake said, trying not to show his nerves. "A lot of strange things have been happening. I wish there was a procedure or protocol for all of this. But I've been doing my best to handle it as it comes." There had never been any procedures for what was happening to them. He had to play this all off the hip. Drake explained the message he had received from Corbin two weeks prior and that he had just seen it earlier that day. He played the video for them. As expected, no one said a word. Blank expressions all around the room.

"So the Earth is gone, then?" Tomlin asked. Tomlin was the head of life support operations.

Helks butted in. "Well, we are all dead, so what does it matter?" Helks said, getting slightly unhinged. "What are we doing here, Marcus?" Helks yelled. Funny for the man who had brought Drake into all of this to ask him. Drake looked straight at Helks.

"We are surviving," he said with a straight expression.

Jason, who stood motionless until now, was standing in the corner. "What is Bethany?" Jason asked. He always seemed to ask the questions no one else would. Feeling overwhelmed at this moment's pressure, Drake leaned against the old oak table.

"I wish I knew, Jason," he said.

"Lock the ship down until we know what caused the loss of power," Thatcher said, hoping to help Drake in the moment. Drake walked to his seat, grabbing the phone beside the flash drive, which was still plugged in. Drake connected to the ship's main intercom.

"Attention, crew of the X-Caliber. This is Admiral Drake," Drake said into the phone. "Please remain calm; we are in a very unusual situation. We are already working to resolve the power issues." Even Drake himself could hear how unconfident he sounded. He cleared his throat. "Please lock down wherever you are until this issue is resolved. Thank you." Drake hung up the speaker almost a little too frantically. He turned to Jason standing in the corner.

"Do we have a remote connection to anything on the ship?"

"Not at the moment," Jason said, tapping on the tablet he had always had with him.

"Not even to the backup systems?" Drake asked.

"No, nothing. Something is keeping me out," Jason said calmly while he tapped away. "Never seen this before," Jason said as he slouched back into the corner. Jason never showed emotion. So, seeing him distressed just added to the tense situation. Drake knew he had to do something. He was the leader. He breathed in, then breathed out.

"We are going to figure this out. You have my word. Everyone stay in here," Drake said. "Thatcher, come with me."

"Where are we going?" Thatcher asked.

"To try and get the power on," he said. "Everyone else, stay in here. Contact the head of your respective departments. Make sure everyone is okay. We will talk more about our other issues when this is resolved," Drake said as calmly as he could, trying to be reassuring. Everyone just nodded in response. Even Helks just sat there in what looked like disbelief.

Drake walked up to the automatic door and almost ran into it when it didn't automatically open. "Crap," he exclaimed as he felt around for the manual release. Finding the release, the door made a hiss, and it opened slowly as Drake turned the crank mechanism. Thatcher closed the door behind them as they left the debriefing room. Both of them had emerged into a very dimly lit hallway. The only thing lighting the hallways was the red backup lights built into the ceiling. It would be a long walk to the bridge in this condition. Drake walked forward a few steps when he felt a hand behind him touch his shoulder.

"Drake, wait," Thatcher said in a concerned voice. Drake paused and turned around, barely able to make out her standing before him, but he knew it was her. Drake didn't say a word. "Look, Drake, maybe I'm losing my mind, but none of this makes sense. First, Rowan with the embryos, the email. Then, the probe. Now, the video and the power. We obviously aren't alone out here, and now we have confirmed sightings of an alien ship," Thatcher said, breathing heavily. Drake's eyes widened. He had never seen her in this state. He felt it, too. He knew what she was feeling. He was there himself. But it was usually him showing emotion and Thatcher being there for him. Drake stepped forward and placed his hand on her shoulder.

"You have to breathe, Thatch," Drake said, compassion behind his voice. "If we fall apart, so does everyone else on this ship. We have a different weight to carry." She closed her eyes and placed her hand on his hand.

"I know, Marcus, but this is all we have. This tin can and a few hundred souls. And it's our job to keep them alive," she said, meeting Drake's eyes in the dark. Drake nodded.

"I know, Fiona, and that's exactly what we will do." She didn't even flinch at her name. In some weird way, hearing Drake say her real name comforted her. At that moment, Drake realized his hand was still on her shoulder, and her hand was still placed on top of his. They both stepped back as if they realized at the same time how close they had been. There it was again. That feeling. The one Drake had felt the night after his birthday. Even in the dark, Drake could see Thatcher's eyes locked onto his. He knew what she was thinking. She had a face when she was thinking. Thatcher broke the awkward silence.

"Thank you for being there for me," she said as she brushed past him while walking down the long, dark hallway. Drake smirked and shook his head.

"This is crazy," he mumbled. He followed close behind as they navigated the different walkways and hatches of the ship.

"You never really know how big this ship is until you have to open every door by hand," Thatcher said in a half-laughing, annoyed tone. "Where are we headed?" Thatcher asked after they had been walking for a while.

"To the bridge," Drake said as they walked. "We need to check life support and see if they have seen a cause for this outage." Along the walk back, they ran into some crew mates sheltering in one of the emergency stairwells. Drake didn't see them at first until one of them called out to them.

"Admiral, what's going on?" one of them said in a scared voice. Drake stopped and crouched down next to them.

"Some power issues, friends, no need to worry," Drake said with a smile and a compassionate voice. "Are you guys doing okay?" Drake asked. Anyone could see how much Drake cared for these people. Drake recognized these crew members; they were all sanitation workers. He reached out his hand and reassured them.

"Ethan, right?" he asked.

"Yessir," the man responded.

"Thank you for everything you do, friend," Drake said. "You guys stay here. The power will be back on soon, and we will be back to normal in no time," Drake said as he stood up. In his mind, he knew he shouldn't promise that. He had absolutely no idea what was going on. But that was his job. To stay strong and keep these people safe.

"We need to keep moving," Thatcher said in a quiet voice. Drake nodded to her.

"Do you guys need anything else?" Drake asked.

"No sir," Ethan said, "If you ever need anything, I'm at your service, Admiral."

"I'll remember that," Drake said with a genuine smile. They both continued up the stairs. As they walked, Drake thought about everything going on. There was never any sort of training for this. He was taught how to effectively run this ship. Part of that training was keeping all of it from falling apart. But most circumstances accounted for were never remotely close to this. He learned how to counteract mutinies and fix breaches in the plan. But they never trained for random spaceships flying through and taking the probes. He kept walking, pushing that out of his mind. He had to be strong. Not for himself but for the 498 other souls still alive on this ship. Drake grimaced at the thought. He had almost forgotten. How could he? The first crew member to die on his watch. It was his fault as well. But he went willingly. He knew anyone else would have as well. It didn't stop the stinging feeling in his heart. No one else on the ship knew about that either. Drake knew there was about to be a lot of explaining to do. Thatcher snapped in front of Drake as they walked.

"Are you still with me?" she asked. Drake snapped out of it, "Yeah, sorry about that." A lot to take in, Drake said, blinking.

"I know, Marcus, but you are here for me, and I'm here for you. Whatever's going on, we can face it," Thatcher said, trying to comfort Drake. He nodded at her. They had arrived at the main hall where the bridge was located. Outside, people sat along the walls. Drake half jogged over to where the crew mates sat.

"What's going on, guys? Is everyone okay?" Drake asked.

"Yes, we are all okay," one of the crew members responded. "As for what's going on, we have no clue. We were coming back from lunch when the power cut. The bridge's emergency doors had shut when there was power loss, and none of us had clearance," the crewmate responded. These were all deckhands, and there were no official officers with emergency door authorization on deck. Drake walked to the door. The electric keypad was off, but there was a manual keypad on the other side of the door for this issue. Drake input his code, and a mechanical click could be heard. Drake and a few crewmates grabbed the now unlocked emergency door and slid it out of the way. A navigation specialist named Conwell grabbed the manual release for the door. The two heavy metal doors slowly moved open as they all pulled the doors to the side. Drake stepped into the bridge.

CHAPTER ELEVEN

TTENTION ON DECK. All the crew on the bridge snapped to attention as they had earlier that day. Drake looked around the dimly lit bridge. His eyes landed on the empty seat at the security array where Manson worked. He gritted his teeth. In his mind, he was losing control, but on the outside, he had to keep a calm composure. Behind the now-standing crew members, Drake could see the giant window at the front peering out into the vast nothingness. There wasn't anything but stars. No probes, no strange alien ships.

"Lucian," Drake called out.

"I'm here, Sir," a man said as he stepped from behind a workstation. Lucian was the ship's main head of bridge operations. The man walked over. His fit physique was noticeable to almost anyone. He had jet black hair that was always neat, and it complimented his dark skin complexion.

"What's going on here?" Drake asked.

Lucian tapped on his pad. He mumbled something in Spanish under his breath.

"What was that?" Drake asked as he stepped closer to him. They were on the bottom level of the bridge. Most of the bridge crew was down on this level.

"Nothing good," Lucian responded. "We are still moving but have no movement control, front sensor array, or way of avoiding anything." Thatcher walked over to the window, peering out into nothingness.

"Do we know what caused it from here?" she asked.

"Not yet, but we know that the only things working on this ship are life support and backup lights," Lucian said, scratching his head. Thatcher nodded. She started walking around to the different crewmates and talking to them.

Drake stepped into the middle of the floor. Everyone had resumed trying to fix what was going on. He cleared his throat.

"Excuse me," Drake shouted, and everyone turned to look at him. "I don't know what's happening, but we have the best crew in this galaxy. We are gonna fix whatever's happening. Commander Thatcher and I will head to the main reactors to see if we can find a solution." Everyone applauded them. Once again, Drake felt guilty. He didn't deserve applause, but he knew his crew was thankful.

"Lucian, can we talk?" Drake asked.

"Of course, boss." They stepped to the far side of the bridge, vacant since none of the monitors would even power on at the moment.

"Listen, there's more going on than I'm telling," Drake said, whispering to him. "Just me and the other officers know. But things are about to get a lot more complicated here." Lucian looked confused.

"What do you mean? Complicated how?" he asked.

"We are figuring out the extent right now," Drake replied to him. "We really don't know," which was true. Drake didn't know if it was just one crazy alien or thirty crazy aliens close by. "We will have a briefing when we get the power back on. We will go over everything," Drake said, trying to reassure him. Lucian gave a half smile and nodded. They both turned and walked away from one another. "And hey, Lucian," Drake said as he was walking away. "Keep things under control here; if you need me, the intercom is still functioning."

Lucian walked back to him and patted him on his shoulder. "I will do all I can," Lucian said with a genuine tone. Drake found Thatcher, and they exited the bridge. Taking a right towards the back of the ship, Thatcher and Drake walked for about thirty minutes. It was a huge ship, not small by any standard. In comparison, it made the ISS look like a toy; it had taken 10 years to complete. Looking back, it was no easy feat, especially where the world was at at that point. Drake ran his hand along the walls of the ship as they walked. The metal sides were black, and the floor was made of the same material everywhere, a light steel color. It made for an interesting contrast, but it worked. Drake had been in charge of most design choices on the ship, and Corbin had also been in charge of certain things. They collaborated on most of it. Corbin insisted on an aggressive design choice that leaned more toward sleek and maneuverability. Drake didn't see the point in that. Longevity and durability were where he wanted them to focus their efforts. So they compromised, and X-Caliber was born. The ship had 17 levels. All with a different purpose. Some had a few other uses.

Level 0 wasn't a level; it was its own thing. It was in the front of the ship and was slightly elevated. It was the bridge and primary controls. It housed around 70 crew members and served as the forward operating base for the entire ship.

Level 1 was a vast area that could hold much more, including launch bays where other ships would dock when they came to Pluto in the distant future.

Level 2 was where the offices and administrative offices were held. It was where Drake and Thatcher's offices, along with those of the other top officials, were held. This is also where the briefing room was held.

Levels 3-4 were cafes, the hospital, and rec spaces. On the lower levels, there was a full-sized gym. This is where most of the crew hung out when they were off. There was also a bowling alley, movie theater, and swimming pool.

Levels 5-7 were crew quarters. Drake's quarters were also on this level. He had a special elevator that took him to his office so he could get there quicker. Most officers were on the upper levels if they needed to get to the bridge faster.

Levels 8-10 were all science labs. Drake didn't go through these levels much.

Levels 11-14 held maintenance, engine rooms, and things of that sort. The main reactor was on level 12.

Everyone knew what level 15 held, or at least they thought they knew.

Level 16 was restricted and never accessed. It housed an armory and access to the ship's limited defense systems. Only Drake, Thatcher, and the head of security, Langston, had access to that level, and they never planned on needing to use anything on that level.

Level 17 was the most extensive level by a long shot. It was storage. It held decades' worth of supplies and provisions. It also housed the generators and the main fusion reactor that powered the ship. They had unlimited power at their disposal, which is why the ship's power being off brought so much stress.

Two other ships were made alongside the X-Caliber. One for Mars and one for the Moon. The one for the Moon was tiny in comparison. The Valiant was the name of the ship. It held a crew of roughly 50, sleek and slender. It was still more significant than anything humanity had ever created. It was commanded by Admiral Bartus. The Mars ship named the Andromeda, is named after our closest sister galaxy. The ship was about 20 times larger than the X-Caliber but was designed more as a humanitarian vessel. It launched a few years after the other two ships, taking a portion of the Earth's population to live on Mars. It was deemed possible, so people were drawn out of a lottery. Drake knew there was another purpose for Mars, just like with Pluto. But he was never filled in on that. He knew the Andromeda was gigantic and the most enormous thing humanity had ever built. It also housed smaller spacecraft. The Andromeda was run by Admiral Clovis. Drake knew her well. More of a mother figure to him than anything else. Older than Drake but still as sharp and spry as ever.

You didn't get this job by chance; you were hand-selected. She had long, dark, curly hair and a dark complexion. She had a charming Southern accent. In the old world, that accent was from Georgia or Louisiana. But she called Texas her home. It's one of the only places to not get a new name. In their time training at the IEC, Drake could see two sides of her. In a way, it reminded him of Thatcher. She was sweet and caring to those who needed it. But in an instant, she could flip her switch to get what needed to be done.

CHAPTER TWELVE

Walking through the halls, they kept passing crewmates and conversing briefly with them. The walk took forever since it took a lot of work to see in the hallways. Drake sent a message to Lucian on his tablet, and he responded quickly.

"Lucian, any update on the bridge?" Drake's message read.

"No, Sir, nothing has changed. We aren't slowing down, which is suitable for time, but we are still just kinda floating," Lucian responded.

"Okay, thank you," Drake replied back. "Thatcher and I are almost to the reactor room. I'll let you know when we make it," Drake said, typing as fast as he could.

"That sounds great. I'll keep it afloat up here," Lucian responded.

Level 17 was much darker than the previous levels. There were no emergency lights there because it was just storage. No crew was stationed on this level except for the inventory managers and the reactor workers. There was one head over the main fusion drive.

"Tony, you in here?" Thatcher yelled. It was Saturday, Earth time. They still had off days on the ship, so no one was scheduled to be on this level today except for the food people grabbing next week's meals. But they had done that earlier in the morning. So it was empty. There wasn't a response. Drake called out again. They waited a second, and still no response.

"Do you think Tony tried to make it back into the reactor room?" Thatcher asked.

"I would assume so. This is his life. He would be down here if I told him a piece of trash was on the floor," Drake said, trying to make light out of their situation.

Tony really did run a tight ship in his department. And Drake appreciated that about him and his work ethic. They were walking through rows and rows of shelving. All are organized into sections and years on when use would be appropriate. Most of it was food. Some water was stored here, but most of the water on the ship was recycled. But they would need some when more people arrive years from now. They made their way through the maze of crates and boxes piled high. Drake tried one more time to call out to Tony. There was still no response.

They got close to the reactor section. It was at the very back and was very clearly sectioned off. No one was allowed in this part of the ship except those authorized. Thatcher and Drake walked into the room and saw Tony pacing frantically.

"Tony, what's going on, man?" Drake shouted over the noise of the reactor. Tony screamed when he heard them walk in. He stopped for a moment and caught his breath.

"A little jumpy?" Drake asked as he looked around the room. Tony didn't answer his question. Instead, he just pointed at the reactor, which made sense. Why was he freaking out? The reactor was still on and running normally. This means there should still have been power going to the entire ship.

"What does this mean?" Thatcher asked. Tony still had yet to answer.

"I've done everything: reset the system and overridden the reboot protocols, but nothing works. That's our fail-safe, Drake," Tony said frantically. "If I can't manually override the system, that means something is intentionally keeping our reactor from powering the ship."

Drake understood why Tony was freaking out. They truly had no control over the situation.

"Say that again," Thatcher said in a scared voice.

"I mean, something or someone has hacked into our ship's systems," Tony responded.

"That's impossible," Drake said in disbelief. "In all regards, we should be entirely impenetrable." Thatcher paced back and forth, talking to Tony and throwing out ideas or things they had yet to try. Drake sat in a chair in the room. He put his hands on his head. Drake prayed under his breath.

"God, I need your help. I know you didn't bring us out here to be stranded. Show me what to do. We're really in the wrong spot," Drake prayed, his head still in his hands.

Just then, a man came running into the room. It was Jason. He was out of breath from running. He was hunched over for a second but forced himself up.

"Drake, you gotta see this," Jason said through his heavy breath. Drake stood up. His face was now stone cold. He already had the weight of the world on his shoulders. He could take whatever came next.

As Drake, Thatcher, and Jason left the reactor room, all the lights suddenly came on. They all stopped.

"What in the world?" Thatcher exclaimed.

Drake sighed a sigh of relief.

"We aren't out of the woods yet," Jason said as he urged them to keep walking.

"Where are we going?" Drake asked several times as they walked. Jason didn't answer right away.

"I don't know how to explain it," Jason said, looking ahead.

"Then take a second to think and explain it to me, Jason," Drake said, trying his best to not sound annoyed. "There's enough I already don't know. There needs to be some clarity, and it needs to happen very soon," Drake said, sounding commanding.

Jason turned to him from the tablet he was typing on as he walked. He paused for a moment before he spoke.

"They are trying to talk to us." Drake and Thatcher both stopped in their tracks.

"Who is they?" Drake asked.

"If I had to assume the ship that stole our probe," Jason said calmly.

"What did they say? How are they even contacting us?" Drake asked him.

"They have been trying for about 15 minutes to connect to our communications array." Jason held up his tablet, showing a bunch of lines of code; in the center, there looked like a bunch of red lines that Jason was keeping out somehow. "I've been able to keep them out. But I also had to come to find you."

"Why didn't you just call us or message me?" Drake asked him.

"I don't know if we are being monitored. We just can't play this too safe," Jason said as they walked. Drake knew Jason was right, but he had a pit in his stomach and was scared. He wouldn't tell anyone and did his best not to let it show on his face. But Thatcher could see it. She saw how frightened he was.

With the power now back on, that meant the elevators worked.

"Where to?" Jason asked.

"Take us to the debriefing room; we need to let everyone else know what's going on," Drake said. "It needs to be in a controlled environment if we talk to them."

"If we are even able to speak to them," Jason muttered.

"True, we might not even be capable of communicating," Thatcher said. She seemed scared but also slightly excited at the prospect of talking to aliens.

"We have to speak to the crew first," Thatcher reminded Drake.

"Right," he thought to himself. He was getting caught up in the moment. He had to refocus himself. Carmen would have to help him with this sort of thing back then. She was always there to help his mind stay on track. It tended to run in every direction if not put in check. Thatcher reminded him of her sometimes. Just the small things she did.

They returned to the debriefing room, taking less time with the elevators working. As Drake walked in, they all saluted him. Drake found that even in this crazy situation, their respect for him was something he thought was undeserved, but he cherished their loyalty. Drake walked to the front of the room.

"Jason, have you filled everyone in?"

"Yeah, I have," Jason responded as he connected to the monitor.

"Good," Drake replied. "So you all know what circumstance we are in. We believe whoever these people are have hacked the X-Caliber and stopped our reactor from sending power to the ship or engines. They have given it back, and Jason is working on setting up a workaround so it doesn't happen again." Drake paused for a moment, taking a breath. "They are trying to establish communication with us, but we haven't let them through yet."

Helks stood up.

"What do you mean? We aren't gonna talk with space pirates," Helks explained.

Drake was calm now. "Do you mean aliens who have the capability to shut down our ship from who knows how far away?" Drake asked in a quiet voice. This made Helks sit down. Another officer raised his hand.

"Sir, if I may ask, what do they want with us?" The officer asked.

"I have no clue," Drake responded, "but we are about to find out. Jason, please connect me to the bridge." Drake asked, turning towards the monitor.

"For sure," Jason said with a tap. The screen showed the bridge and people in a somewhat calmer state bustling around the bridge.

"Hello, Admiral," a crew member said.

"Looking for Lucian?" The crewmate asked.

"Yes, please," Drake said kindly.

"I'm here," Lucian screamed as he ran over to the console. "Boss, you got the power on," Lucian said excitedly.

"It wasn't me," Drake said.

"What do you mean?" Lucian asked.

"Keep the bridge calm, but I need you to stop the ship."

"What? What about the timeline, boss?" Lucian asked him, confused.

Drake interrupted. "It doesn't matter anymore. Stop the ship," Drake said in a cold voice.

"Right away," Lucian said as he turned and shouted to the bridge. "Stop the ship, Admiral's orders."

Like a well-oiled machine, everyone got where they needed to be to operate this beast of a ship. Everyone felt the ship decelerating as the engines powered down. After a minute of deceleration, the ship was still.

"Keep the bridge ready, Lucian; I'll keep you updated," Drake said. Before you go, Lucian said, getting Drake's attention.

"Can you let the 2nd crew swap with these men?" Lucian asked. Drake remembered. They were the same crew that had been there since morning. They hadn't been relieved for rest.

"Of course," Drake said. "Go get some rest, Lucian."

Lucian stepped forward. "I won't be leaving, boss. I'm here until this is resolved, whatever it is," Lucian said, saluting him.

"Thank you, my friend," Drake responded, saluting him back. He really was grateful. Loyalty was in everyone's hearts. They were all any of them had out there. Drake backed away. He didn't realize how worn out and tired he was; it had been almost 24 hours since the drone disappeared. Drake pushed sleep out of his mind.

At the same time, Thatcher was on the intercom addressing the ship. "Attention, everyone. Please listen closely," Thatcher said, trying to keep a steady voice. "We are figuring out a situation. Please remain calm and in place for the time being. If you have an essential job, please go to your post. For the greater good," Thatcher said as she signed off.

You couldn't hear it, but everyone aboard the ship said it back to themselves quietly. They were all in this together.

CHAPTER THIRTEEN

Drake positioned himself in front of the camera, Thatcher to his right and the other officers behind. "Let them through," Drake said with a cold expression. Drake was still determining what he would say or do or if he would have words at all. He was about to contact extraterrestrials. He had no idea what they would look or sound like. Or if they would even talk. The first man to speak to someone, not from Earth. In a different circumstance, this would be spectacular. Something to be written about for ages to come. But for all Drake knew, they were the last humans and everyone back on Earth was dead. So, it meant something more to him. It meant more to his family. This crew, this ship, this mission.

Jason tapped a few buttons. "They are coming through," Jason said. The black panel in front of them lit up. It was distorted at first, but it cleared up. The screen showed what looked like a big hangar. On the far side, probe 5 could be seen in pieces. Drake swallowed but determined to not show any emotion.

"Hello?" Drake asked in the most poised, courageous voice he could muster. "Is anyone there?" The whole room was silent. In the right-hand corner, a figure walked into the frame, and the figure bowed to the camera. They had on a full suit from head to toe. So it was impossible to see them. It was a black suit and what looked to be some sort of space helmet. It reminded Drake of some super futuristic space armor; the helmet was reflective, and there were no holes in the mask. It looked like one piece of glass wrapped around the entire figure's head with a screen displayed inside. When the figure was entirely in the frame, they stopped and stared at the camera.

Drake didn't know what he expected. But this thing looked normal. Extremely humanoid. The limbs were proportionate, and it walked strangely normal. Thatcher had grabbed his arm. She was breathing lightly and hadn't noticed she grabbed his arm. She let go when Drake stepped forward.

"I am Admiral Marcus Drake; this is the X-Caliber; we represent the IEC and Earth. Who are you?" Drake asked commandingly. The figure didn't say anything. It walked closer to the camera and picked up what looked to be a piece of paper and a writing utensil. It wrote something on the paper and then held it up.

WHO I AM IS NOT IMPORTANT…

Thatcher whispered in Drake's ear. "It knows how to write in English," she said, trying her best to whisper. It wasn't pretty, but it was still English. Drake didn't let his demeanor change.

"Then what do you want with us or our probe?" Drake said calmly. The figure flipped the paper over and began writing again, and after a moment, it held the paper up again.

YOU WILL KNOW SOON ENOUGH. IT'S NICE TO MEET YOU, MARCUS DRAKE…

Drake didn't know what to say after that. Helks stood up and walked over. "You better start explaining yourself, or you'll have the wrath of the IEC coming after you," Helks said, trying to be intimidating. Drake knew this was an invalid threat. There was no one close to them, and Helks also knew this. The figure grabbed a different piece of paper and scribbled something out faster this time.

CONTROL YOUR OFFICER ADMIRAL…

Drake shot a look at Helks, and he backed away. Drake noticed something as the figure went back to writing. Why was this thing writing on paper when it had the capability to remotely hack their ship. And how did they know how to write in English? This created more questions. Thatcher stepped forward.

"I'd like to introduce myself," Thatcher said, trying to sound kind. The figure stood still for a moment, then bowed. Thatcher let out a little grin. No matter how tense or crazy this was, they were still communicating with a being from outer space. "I am Commander Fiona Thatcher, 2nd in command on the X-Caliber." The figure wrote again.

HELLO FIONA THATCHER…

"Why'd you tear apart our probe?" Thatcher asked. The figure turned to look across the hangar it was standing in. It took another piece of paper and wrote for a while longer than it had previously.

WE NEEDED IT. THE ONLY WAY WE COULD COMMUNICATE WAS YOUR PROBE'S RELAY DEVICE. OUR SYSTEMS TOO ADVANCED…

Everyone stood quiet. Too advanced, Drake thought. Who were they dealing with, and what did they want with his ship and crew? They had very standard relays, and almost any frequency could be reached with their systems. It didn't make sense. Drake decided he had to be bold. He stepped forward again.

"No disrespect, but you stole something from us and hacked into our ship…not very peaceful if you ask me," Drake said to the figure. The figure stood motionless like a statue. It weirded them out. Drake asked one more time. "What do you want with my ship and my crew?" Drake could be intimidating when he needed to. And it showed through in this moment. The figure again stood motionless. A white-gloved appendage came into the frame, handing the mute friend another piece of paper. The figure read it and then turned it around.

YOU WILL KNOW WHO WE ARE SOON ENOUGH… WE ARE COMING…

The figure walked out of frame, and the screen went black. Drake stared at the black screen in disbelief. They were coming. He didn't know who they were or what they wanted. Drake turned around to his fellow officers. "We are in danger, and it's time to defend our ship…Activate protocol 16."

CHAPTER FOURTEEN

Langston, the head of security and defense on the ship, usually had a cushy job. He had never really had to work to secure or defend the vessel. His job was one of redundancy, a just-in-case job. It was now time for that. Langston walked over to the intercom.

"Attention, Langston here. This is not a drill… activate protocol 16."

This put the ship into complete fight or flight mode. Drake inputted a code into his pad. Alarms once again blared on the ship. Portholes were covered. The X-Caliber wasn't equipped with many offensive measures except for a few 50-caliber turrets on either side of the ship, ten in total. They also had a few missile bays with some warheads on them. They had one nuclear warhead to use in massive emergencies, typically meant for gigantic asteroids that threatened the X-Caliber. But with protocol 16, everything was activated. There were no defensive measures, just extra metal plating that slid in front of windows and vulnerable parts of the ship's exterior. But it wasn't a war vessel; it was never its intention. But Corbin had insisted on being ready for whatever might play out. Drake fought him on this, seeing it as a waste of space. He was grateful his old friend had overruled him.

"Keep comms open," Drake yelled. "You see anything, you talk directly to me. Thatcher, Jason, with me." Drake said, running out of the debriefing room.

They didn't hesitate to listen. They practically ran to the bridge, passing crew on the way. They all looked frantic but determined. They made it to the bridge rather quickly. They walked in. Thatcher and Jason broke off, going their respective ways on the bridge. Drake walked up to Lucian, standing at the front of the bridge, peering out. He called out his name as he approached. Lucian turned around; Drake could see how tired he was.

"Lucian, get some rest, friend. This isn't going to be over soon, and I need you at your best."

"What's going on, Drake?" Lucian asked in a voice that almost sounded hurt. "You aren't telling the crew anything, and these people are going mad. No one knows what's going on, boss."

Drake patted him on his shoulder. "Go to Thatcher, and she will explain it all. I'm taking control of the bridge for the time being."

Lucian nodded and walked away. He was right, though; his crew had the right to know. Drake didn't know how long he would have before they would arrive or if they even would. He had no way to know. Nothing had been picked up on the radar yet. Langston arrived on the bridge.

"Everything is ready, Admiral," Langston said.

"Thank you, stay here, would you? I need to talk to my crew." Drake responded.

Drake felt like he had done this a thousand times today. He was exhausted. He could feel it in his eyes. But they needed him right now. That's something Drake had plenty of. He had grit. He wouldn't give up on his people.

"Hello, crew of the X-Caliber. This is Marcus Drake." Drake said into the intercom. Thatcher looked over at Drake, unsure what he was about to say. "As all of you know, we have had a very stressful and crazy day, but you all deserve to know what's happening." Drake breathed in deeply. "We retrieved the footage from Manson. We saw an unidentified foreign ship take probe 5. We were then hacked by said ship, and our power was cut off. They then returned power to our ship and attempted to make contact with us. We established contact and had a brief conversation."

Drake stopped. You could hear a pin drop on the ship, and everyone was silent. "They didn't say who they were or what they wanted. But they are headed to us. Drake paused again. Be prepared for anything, family. We aren't alone. We are gonna get through this. For the greater good, my friends."

Drake hung up the intercom and turned his head towards the windows leading out into space. In the distance, he could see the dot that was Pluto.

"We made it so close," he thought to himself. "I'm sorry, Corbin," he mumbled, "I'm sorry, Carmen."

He walked to the second story of the bridge and sat in his command chair, putting his head in his hands. Thatcher was beside him.

"Go get some rest, Marcus." she urged.

"There's no way I can leave right now," he responded.

"Like you told Lucian, we need you at your best," Thatcher insisted. Drake agreed. He couldn't fight her on this; he was exhausted.

"Are you gonna be okay, Fiona?" Drake asked.

"Yes, I am, I promise." She responded kindly to him, reassuring him. Drake put his hand on her shoulder as he walked toward the door. She placed hers on top of his again and squeezed his hand. He looked back one last time and saw her looking right at him. He flashed back to the day he had first looked at Carmen. Drake didn't want to feel this, especially not right now. But he was too tired to fight it. She gave him one last reassuring smile.

"I'll be back in a few hours," he said.

"Trust in me, Marcus. I can run this while you rest." Thatcher said.

He nodded and smiled slightly as he walked out and headed to his quarters. The ships started moving again, trying to regain their original pace.

Drake walked back to his quarters with his mind completely blank. He needed to think and work through all this, but his mind wouldn't let him. Drake barely reached his couch before flopping down like a child and passed out. He had a dream, which wasn't usual for him. He never did. The only time he ever had dreams was when they meant something to him. His dream two weeks prior still perplexed him, and he thought about it often. He loved seeing them again, even if only in a dream.

He found himself in the seat of a plane. He looked around, trying to figure out where he was. Looking around, he saw a sign that said Hillbaton Airport out the window. He knew exactly where he was. He knew it was a dream, but he had no control over his actions. It was like he was watching a replay of the day he left for the IEC. His head turned from the window, and he saw a much younger Corbin on the car seat next to him and his Carmen in between them in the middle. They were both smiling so big. The excitement was tangible even in the dream. Drake couldn't hear them speaking at first. He couldn't remember what they had been talking about that day. It had been so long ago. Why this? Why was he dreaming this? Suddenly, Drake got control of his body during the dream. He could hear again and could feel. He reached over and grabbed Carmen's hand. It felt so real. Like he was really holding her hand again. Drake cried in his mind. His body in the dream didn't cry, though. She squeezed his hand back in nervous excitement. He decided to just let this happen. He didn't care what it meant. He just got to be next to his wife, and that's all he cared about. He watched the events play out as they had that day. They took off and flew for a few hours. He talked with Carmen and Corbin and just relished this break from reality.

A few hours into the flight, Drake felt off. He looked up, and there was a man at the front of the plane staring at him. It was off. Drake knew he had never seen that man on the plane. So why was he seeing him now? Drake looked back at the others to try and get his mind off it. The plane landed, and they still didn't know where they were. Helks hadn't told them. They grabbed their things and walked off the plane. Drake knew nothing had seemed off to him when this happened in real life. But this time, he couldn't help but look at the man he had seen earlier. The man wasn't even trying to hide it. He was staring directly at them as they walked off the plane. He should have been one of the first ones off, but he was staying behind. The entire time, just staring at him. Not the other two, just Drake. As they walked past, the man's eyes followed him, and he got in line to exit right behind them. Drake was freaked out. How were the other two not seeing this? He knew this was different. He would have remembered this. When they got into the terminal, Drake turned to say something, but it was like, at that point, he had lost all the control he had gained. He couldn't turn to talk to the man. They walked to the exit to wait for whoever would pick them up. They looked up and saw a sign that said welcome to North Reaches, formerly North Dakota. "North Reaches?" Corbin asked in a surprised voice. "Why are we in the North Reaches?" Corbin laughed.

Just then, Drake saw the man walk out the door in front of them, shooting the kids one last look before he disappeared into a crowd of people. He still didn't understand it, but this dream didn't feel like a dream anymore. It felt more real every moment he was here. He was living out his past in a dream for whatever reason. They had all noticed how much better everyone dressed here in the North. A lot more money and food here. Still, not enough, but more than back home, and the constant familiar smell of dirt was gone here. It was definitely cleaner. The kids were in awe. They weren't used to this nice of a place. Still, this was considered poor for the upper levels of wealth in the US. Only a few cities still held the standards of the old world. They stood out in the crowd. But not too bad. Just enough to be slightly noticeable.

They walked out the door, looking for where they were supposed to go. They saw a man dressed in the same attire that Helks usually did, but it wasn't him. Corbin started walking over to him. "I guess this is where we are supposed to go?" Corbin said, being upbeat. Drake looked around one last time for that crazy man. He didn't see him. Drake let it roll off his back. He got into the car, and they were off. Drake, in his mind, knew where they were going. But it all felt like he was living it for the first time again.

"Where are we going?" Corbin asked the agent. Corbin was always curious and asked questions; Drake and Carmen were the type to just go with it. The agent hadn't said a word yet. Which was weird. The agents usually at least said something. Corbin waved a hand in front of the man's face. "Hellooo," he said in a mocking tone. The man did a long blink. "Hello, friends, I'm agent Bartus." Bartus was cold. Not a happy man. Literally never. His buzz-cut hair didn't help his very round face. But he was definitely a man. Intimidating and strong-looking. It didn't bug Corbin, though. Nothing really scared him. "Where are they taking us?" Corbin asked Bartus again. "Washington," Bartus said monotone. "Like DC?" Carmen asked in an excited voice. "No, the state," Bartus said with a fake smile. Carmen's smile went away. "Don't look too excited now," Bartus said. That did make him laugh a little. They rode in a car until they arrived at a smaller airport with one of those smaller private planes. They boarded along with Bartus, and Helks joined them at this point. There were snacks and drinks and unlimited food. "A treat for you guys," Helks said with a smile. For how annoying he was, he wasn't so bad back in those days. He didn't do well in stressful situations. They feasted on foods they had never seen or heard of before. They were all laughing and telling stories, waiting for the plane to take off. As the plane turned to leave, Drake looked out the window. Something again he knew he didn't do at that moment. The man looked directly at Drake, pulling the fuel truck away from the plane. Drake reacted in his mind. He wanted to scream, but he couldn't. He had almost forgotten this was a dream by this point. That brought him back to reality. But he still couldn't wake up. He was walking this day out. No matter if he wanted to or not. They landed, exhausted from their day of travel. "Almost home," Helks said as he stood to exit the plane. "You mean we aren't there yet?" Corbin exclaimed in an annoyed voice. "Nope, but very close," Helks responded. "Welcome to Canada," he said with a chuckle. They stepped out into the freezing cold. "Canada?" Drake asked, confused. "Yes, but don't worry, you'll work in the US. You'll see it in about 15 minutes." Helks said reassuringly. They loaded up one last time into another blacked-out SUV and drove. Drake, in his mind, had completely forgotten this was a dream. He was in it all the way. As they drove, they reached their hands out the window, enjoying the pure air and scents of nature. Drake looked over and saw Carmen taking it all in. It made him smile seeing her happy. They were stopped by some guards at a border crossing. "What's going on?" Corbin asked. "Not sure," Drake responded as he looked out the window at the guards. He saw the name Point Roberts Border Patrol embroidered on his shirt. Bartus flashed his government ID, and the guards immediately let them pass. They pulled into a small street with a few homes on it. Helks got out and opened the doors for the kids.

   DYLAN CARRIGAN

"Welcome to Point Roberts," Helks said with a smile. "Are we even in America?" Corbin asked. "You sure are," Helks responded. "Welcome to Little America. Completely detached from the US and the perfect place to lay low as we lay the frameworks for what we are building." Helks said, stretching as he stepped away from the car. "There's nothing here," Corbin responded. "Not that you can see," Helks said with a wink. "Let me show you your homes. We start work tomorrow," Helks said. Carmen and Drake walked into their home. "Sorry, it's kinda small," Helks said as he dropped them off at the front door. "Here's your key. Some basic information on the counter about trash and the internet and stuff." Carmen and Drake's eyes were wide. They walked in together, and Drake could feel a tear rolling down his face. He looked over and saw Carmen with a tear rolling down her cheek. He reached over and whipped it for her. "We get to have a life, Marcus," Carmen said to him with a huge smile. She jumped on him in a hug. They walked around the house; it was fully furnished. It had everything they could ever want. Way more than they had ever had back home. It was surreal. They were winding down for the night when Drake got a weird feeling. He knew he had also remembered to check all the door locks and windows that day. He heard a knock at the door. His stomach dropped. Who would be here at 12 at night? But he got the courage to go check. It had to be Corbin, he told himself. He walked into the living room, and then there was another knock. Then it hit Drake. He wasn't really here. He snapped back into it. He remembered this was all a dream. Why was this happening? Why did he have to live this again? It didn't make sense at all. Another knock could be heard. He mustered up the courage, walked over, and flung open the door, expecting to see Corbin or Helks. Instead, his heart dropped. It was the man from the airport with the same angry look. Drake fell back. The man's expression changed from anger into sympathy. The man stepped in. Drake tried to scream and warn Carmen, but he couldn't. The man helped Drake to his feet. Drake felt instant peace. He had just had so much fear, but it was all gone. The man looked deep into Drake's eyes. "You are on the right path now." Drake cocked his head in confusion. The man's voice was familiar in a distant way. "Keep going, Marcus." He tried to respond but still couldn't. The man hugged him. He let go of him and started to walk out. The man looked back one last time. "Marcus…COMPLETE BETHANY," the man said in a compassionate voice. Drake's eyes widened, and he fell back. He felt himself lunge forward, hitting the cold floor of the X-Caliber.

CHAPTER FIFTEEN

Drake looked up at his ceiling, dazed for a moment. He had hit his head falling off his couch. His eyes came back into focus. He was back in his cabin. Everything felt dizzy. He had kicked his head really hard against the ground. He sat up and took a breath. There was a buzz coming from the couch. Drake crawled to the sofa and picked up his tablet. There was an incoming call from Thatcher. He answered it and heard panicked yelling and people running behind Thatcher.

"Drake, get to the bridge now," Thatcher said, sounding panicked.

He pulled himself together. "What's going on?" he asked. He could still hear the loud talking and commotion in the background. "Thatch, what's going on?" he said again.

"They're here," she said, trying not to fall apart. He'd never heard her sound so scared before. Before he knew it, she was shouting orders and running away from the comm. Drake felt another surge forward as the ship came to a complete stop.

That's what must've made me fall off the couch, he thought. His head was still throbbing, but his vision returned to focus. A mild concussion, he assumed. It would have to wait.

Drake sprinted out of his quarters towards the bridge. Along the way, he called up Lucian.

"Lucian, they're here. Get to the bridge now," he exclaimed as soon as Lucian answered his tablet, not giving him time to say anything before.

Lucian had felt the ship stop and was already on his way along with Drake; "already on my way, boss," Lucian shouted as he was running. Their quarters were on the same level, so they ran into each other in the elevator. They rode in silence for a moment. Lucian spoke up first.

"What do they want, boss?"

"They didn't say," Drake responded to him. "But one thing's for sure. They will have to kill me before they get my ship and my crew," Drake said, staring at the shining metal of the elevator's walls.

"I'm with you till the end," Lucian said as he stared ahead with Drake.

Drake felt compassion for this man. He knew he would do the same thing if he was in his position. Whether they had to defend or go down with the ship, every man and woman on the X-Caliber was willing to die for the ship and crew, their home. They arrived at the bridge and walked in. Everyone stopped and looked at Drake as he walked to the bridge's front glass window. Thatcher was already there staring out, looking at the now visible ship about 5 football fields away and slowly approaching. Drake put his hand on the glass, looking at the ship. He breathed in, feeling a knot in his throat.

"Father, help us," Drake said under his breath.

The ship was just as big or even bigger than the X-Caliber for the first analysis. It had a very aggressive design, and turrets of some sort could be seen all over the ship. Unlike the X-Caliber, the ship in front of them had obviously been designed as a war vessel. It was a dull gray color. A light yellow shimmer could be seen on the outside around the ship.

"What is that?" Thatcher asked as she noticed the shimmer.

Langston was standing there as well. "Some sort of shielding," he guessed.

"They are definitely way past us technologically," Lucian said to them. Drake looked over at Langston.

"What's the update on our weaponry?" Drake asked him.

"Sir, at your word, the turrets and missile bays will activate. All trained men are stationed at all access points," Langston said proudly.

"Good," Drake said softly. "If they try to board, we will have to defend the best we can," Drake said solemnly.

Langston saluted Drake and ran towards the door. "I'm going to join my men Admiral."

Thatcher had made her way up to the command deck. "Drake, are we actually gonna try to shoot at them?" Thatcher asked him as he made it up to the command deck.

Drake never thought he'd have to make this decision. Open fire on an unidentified vessel, he thought? He was an expeditionary, not a war general. But Drake wouldn't let his ship fall. He would do what had to be done. Drake sat down as he took his place at the head of the vessel. He looked down and scanned his finger on the touchpad to log into his command controls. The screen lit up green, and he punched in his code to unlock the weapons systems.

Drake thought for a moment as he struggled internally, he didn't want to be the one to make this decision, but he had to be.

"Set turrets and missile Bays to fire," Drake shouted.

Crewmates on the bottom of the ship ran around, and Thatcher grabbed Drake's hand. Drake turned to look at her.

"There's no coming back from this," she whispered in a pained voice.

"I know," Drake said, meeting her eyes.

"I won't let this ship or my men fall."

The ship shook as the large turrets emerged from the walls of the X-Caliber. Rising out from the dark gray, almost black metal of the ship. To anybody from Earth, the ship was the most intimidating thing around. Most people on Earth compared it to a sci-fi spaceship more than an exploration vessel. However, images of the ship in battle formation were never shared for obvious reasons. Why was it necessary? That would be the question people would have asked. Drake had wondered the same thing. Now, he was grateful. The ship shook one last time as the missile bays on the left and right sides of the ship opened up. It was dead silent for a few moments.

"OPEN FIRE," Drake yelled.

The ship shook violently as all ten of the war turrets erupted. The flashes could be seen outside the front window of the bridge. Within seconds, yellow sparks could be seen flying off of the other ship as the ship's shield took the impact. The shots continued for thirty seconds before Drake commanded a cease-fire. The last of the sparks shattered off of the shield. It almost looked like yellow glass flying off before it dissipated into nothingness.

"Sir, that had no effect," one of the crew members shouted.

"Fire missile bays," Drake commanded in a loud voice.

Two giant rockets shot out from the belly of the ship; the light was blinding from the engines firing off. Within 5 seconds, the missiles connected with the ship. A massive burst of light could be seen. Drake anticipated a shock wave.

"Everyone brace," he yelled as a shock way shot back through the X-Calibur. Drake grabbed Thatcher as it almost sent them onto the floor. A few of the crew members fell over as the ship was sent in an upward direction, blocking the view of the other ship. The crew reacted immediately by firing pressure cannons located all around the ship.

As the ship came back on course, everyone expected to see a hole in the front of the other ship. The crew was cheering as the ship came back into view. To everyone's horror, the ship was even closer now, roughly 3 football fields away and clear as day. Everyone saw the dull yellow shimmer perfectly intact around the vessel and no damage whatsoever.

"Sir, should we fire the Nuke?" a crewmate asked in a panicked voice.

Drake hadn't realized that Thatcher was still holding onto him. He patted her on the back, and she let go.

"No, we can't do that. The shock wave alone will tear this ship apart. It probably wouldn't even affect the other ship," Drake said in a severe voice.

Drake lowered his head. What have I done, he thought. He fired upon another ship. And not a thing they threw at them did a thing; Drake fully expected them to immediately open fire on them. But they didn't; they waited in silence for what felt like an eternity. Jason had walked up to the command deck. He tapped Drake on the shoulder.

"Drake, they are trying to make contact again."

"Let them through," he said quietly. Drake still had some fogginess in his head from the knot that had formed on the side of his head. All the explosions definitely didn't help; he walked down to the main deck;

"Communication incoming," Thatcher yelled.

Drake stood there poised and steeled. The screen faded in, and the familiar backdrop was once again present. The same figure strolled into view again. Bowing in front as it had done previously. Odd, Drake thought; why would they bow when we had just attempted to kill them?

Drake stood poised and motionless, his hands behind his back, waiting for the figure to speak. The figure held up a piece of paper.

PLEASE LOWER WEAPONS… WE AREN'T A THREAT

Drake had had enough; "Not a threat?" he exclaimed as he stepped forward. "Stealing parts of our ship, saying that you are coming to us. We don't know you, you've told us nothing about who you are and what you want. I don't know about you, but that is classified as hostile actions to us."

Drake realized he had been stepping closer to the giant monitor. His voice was raised but not yelling. Drake always had an assertive demeanor about him. Again, the figure stood motionless, almost as if the being was thinking. It grabbed a piece of paper from the white-gloved appendage again.

YOU ARE THE ONLY ONE BEING HOSTILE. YOU FIRED ON US. WE DID WHAT WE MUST TO COMMUNICATE…

The figure grabbed another piece of paper.

WE NEED YOU MARCUS… WE NEED BETHANY…

There it was again. Drake felt dizzy as if he could pass out from all of this. The weight of everything pressed down on his shoulders. How could these aliens possibly know what Project Bethany was? Drake tried to cover.

"Bethany? I have no idea what you are talking about," Drake said.

They again held up another piece of paper.

WE KNOW YOU ARE AN INTELLIGENT MAN. PLEASE DON'T LIE TO US…

Drake didn't have words anymore. His head throbbed, he was exhausted, and he was internally panicking. Drake couldn't hide the visible sign of shock on his face anymore. The figure bowed once more and held up the last piece of paper.

WE ARE COMING…

16

CHAPTER SIXTEEN

The screen went black, and the only noise on the bridge was the hum of computers and monitors. Even though the ship was right in front of them, the radar systems still couldn't pick up the ship. Drake looked out the window and saw the other ship move closer. It felt like minutes passed before anyone on the bridge said anything.

"Admiral, what's the plan?" a crew member asked from somewhere on the bridge.

Drake didn't know what to do. His head was fuzzy, and his vision went in and out. Drake knew he had a concussion from the fall, but he tried his very best not to show it. He turned to face everyone. His eyes met everyone else's as he looked at all of them. His eyes stopped on Thatcher. He saw a tear in the corner of her eye. It broke his heart; he had never seen her in such a state.

"I want a skeleton crew on the bridge," Drake said, trying to muster as much confidence as he possibly could. "Lucian is in command. I want everyone else to go into the safe rooms."

There were about six different safe rooms on the ship. Each one was equipped with a blast door and completely sealed rooms. An announcement came over the PA as most of the crew on the bridge scrambled out toward their assigned safe room.

Drake walked swiftly over to Jason, standing by some monitors and displays. He was just standing over them, not looking at anything, staring blankly at them.

"Are you okay?" Drake asked as he put his hand on Jason's shoulder.

Jason closed his eyes and sighed. "Yeah, um, I'm okay, Drake," Jason responded quietly.

"Look, we need to talk, but not here."

"About what?" Drake asked. "About all this? Look, I don't have any answers."

"No," Jason said with a blank expression. "We need to talk about something else," Jason said.

Just then, the proximity alarms went off. Drake looked forward and out the window. The ship had approached much faster than they had thought.

"Jason, get to your safe room. We will talk soon," Drake said as he ran past Jason towards Lucian.

"How did they get here so fast?" Drake asked him.

Lucian shrugged in a frustrated way. "I'm not sure, boss. All I can see is that they turned off whatever that yellow glow was around their ship. Must have uncloaked themselves somehow," Lucian said as the radars and alarms now blared at the incoming ship.

Drake looked down at the panel. The X-Caliber was slowly moving towards the other ship. "Lucian, how can we be moving if our engines are off?" Drake asked him. He knew what he thought it was, but he wanted to ask.

"I'm not sure," Lucian responded, messing with other controls. "They have control of everything. That's how they stopped our engines in the first place. But it still makes no sense how they've been able to override everything."

Drake patted Lucian on the shoulder. "You and the others should be safe here. The bridge is effectively the safest part of the ship," Drake said.

Drake walked back up the command deck and sat in his chair next to Thatcher. She was unspeaking. That was mostly the same with everyone on the ship. No one had words.

She spoke up. "I feel so helpless, Marcus," Thatcher said. "I wanna be strong, but I'm scared," she whispered as she sat beside Drake's seat. "I feel like we are lambs just waiting for the slaughter. We tried to defend ourselves, and it did nothing," she said.

They both sat silently for a moment. "Drake, how do they know about Bethany?" Thatcher asked.

"No clue, Thatch," Drake responded. "Nothing makes sense anymore. The last 24 hours have left me with more questions than I will ever be able to have answered," he responded.

Thatcher had been sitting cross-legged. She leaned her head up against Drake's knee. It surprised him. He knew trauma brought people closer, but this felt different. The same feeling from a few weeks back at Thatcher's door. The same feelings he hadn't felt since Carmen. But he was too tired to fight it. He let it happen.

Everyone was waiting in anticipation. The ship got closer and closer; it was evident that the alien ship was flying below the X-Caliber. Drake made a call to Langston.

"The alien ship is going to try to dock under us into 17," Drake said, monitoring the displays in front of him.

"Roger that Admiral, moving all men to intercept on that level," Langston responded to him.

"Copy Langston, keep an open comm channel, and update me if they breach."

Thatcher looked up and turned around. "What are the odds that they are actually able to dock with us?"

Drake hadn't even thought of that. There was next to no possibility that both ships had compatible docking bays. This made Drake feel slightly better for a few moments.

Right then, there was a giant crash into the ship. "Did they hit us?" Drake asked Lucian, hovering over monitors and talking to the few crew still running around the deck.

"Yeah Boss. Right on dock port 5," Lucian responded. It was on the very bottom of the ship.

"Langston, prepare for a breach in dock port 5," Drake said into the comms.

"Roger," Langston echoed through the comm. "Come on men, let's move," Langston yelled.

At that moment, Drake felt guilt. "I should be down there, Fiona," Drake said as he stood.

She grabbed him by the calf, still sitting beside his command chair. "Marcus, you are more valuable to this ship alive than dead," she said as she looked him in his eyes.

"These are my men, Fiona, I live and die by them," Drake said resolutely in his decision.

"Then I'm going too," Thatcher said as she sprung up, chasing Drake down the command deck stairs.

"Not a chance," Drake said as he stopped walking to turn and face her. "I need you here in case things go wrong."

"Things are already wrong, Marcus," she yelled, making the already quiet bridge even more silent. "I told you I have your back, and I mean what I say. If you are gonna risk your life, then I am too," she said, holding back a sob.

Drake grabbed her by her shoulders gently. "Fiona, this is no time to act on emotion," he said in a very calm, compassionate voice. She tried to respond, but Drake spoke again. "We can talk about that another time. But we both have jobs to do."

She didn't respond this time, but Drake could see he had gotten to her. She nodded slowly. Drake pulled her in and hugged her; he truly hugged her. He had in the past, but never like this. He felt his heart behind it and didn't know whether to be scared or embrace it. He thought that Thatcher did the same. She hugged him like she meant it. They let each other go.

"Be safe out there, Admiral," she said, trying to smile at him.

Drake grinned. "You do the same, Commander."

Drake turned and ran towards the danger. He only hoped he would get there in time.

Drake sprinted through the halls of his ship. He knew it by heart. This place was his home. He took every shortcut, and thankfully, the elevators were still operating.

"Langston, come in," Drake yelled as he talked into his comm.

"I'm here, Sir," Langston responded.

"I'm headed to you; give me a status update," Drake yelled back.

"You're what?" Langston exclaimed. "Sir, stay back on the bridge. I need you safe."

"This is my ship, and those are my men. I'll fight with them," Drake yelled.

There was a pause. "Yessir," Langston said in an exhausted voice. "They are right outside dock port 5. They haven't docked yet. I'm not sure why they are waiting," Langston said. There was obviously commotion behind him.

"Okay, I'm five minutes away," Drake exclaimed as he exited the elevator and sprinted toward level 17.

It was surprising even to Drake that he could sprint like he was at his age. He had always prided himself on being in shape but was never the fittest. He wasn't skinny, and he wasn't fat; he was healthy. He was just attributing it to the adrenaline and the mild concussion numbing most of the pain in his body and moving it to his head.

Drake reached level 17. When he stopped, he felt the pain in his head swell. The running and fatigue were getting to him. He leaned on the door frame and nearly collapsed. He doubled over and threw up. There wasn't much, given the lack of eating that had been done in the last twenty-four hours. Drake looked up to see Langston at the door with his hand out.

"Let me help you up, Sir," Langston said. There was respect in Langston's eyes. He knew Drake would do anything for this crew and truly honored that. He saw Drake as a real man.

"Thanks, man," Drake said as he grabbed his hand and got to his feet. They walked in silence. Langston reached to his side and grabbed the sidearm that was strapped to his leg.

"Here you go, Admiral. Need you armed if you are gonna be here with us," Langston said, looking ahead.

Drake had always loved guns back on Earth. He had only shot a few, but they always fascinated him. The weapon was warm from being strapped to Langston's leg, but it was silver and a hybrid between a 9 mm and a 40mm, a specially designed bullet for space. Designed to not penetrate the precious wall of the ship. But packed enough to take down what needed to be taken down.

As they walked, they felt another big bump. Drake raised his comm to talk to Lucian.

"What was that, Lucian?" Drake asked.

"Sir, I don't know how they did it, but they successfully docked onto us," Lucian said, sounding more panicked.

"Lucian, lock up the bridge. Thatcher, be prepared to blow level 17," Drake said calmly while still walking.

"What do you mean?" Thatcher exclaimed over the comm.

"Only as a last resort, Thatch. You have to trust me. I'll only make that call if there's no way we can hold them off. But if I tell you to blow it, you have to listen to me, Thatch," Drake said without a second thought.

There was dead silence. "Yessir," Thatcher said as the comm went dead.

Drake felt bad. He knew he couldn't do that if the roles were reversed, but he needed her to be strong. He knew she was mad at him. But she would have to forgive him. They walked close to the dock port, passing the armed men. They saluted as Drake and Langston passed by. Drake stopped in front of the blast door that sealed the port from the entry chamber. He turned around and spoke to the men.

"I need you all to be strong and of good courage. Pull on the strength within you. I don't know how this ends, but I will die for this ship. I will die for my men," Drake said as he stood unmoving in front of them.

All the men yelled at the same time.

Drake put his finger on the scanner, and the door opened. He walked forward and looked through the small viewing port that was supposed to view outer space. Instead, on the other side, Drake saw the same figure from the videos and a figure in an identical white suit. Drake assumed it was the figure actually writing the notes. Behind them stood about 40 men in suits that were similar but different. The other men wore gray suits and had what looked to be mostly metal helmets. There was a camera on the helmet, and Drake could see a HUD displayed inside. The helmets were see-through on the glass part, but the HUD skewed what the soldiers' faces looked like. Soldiers are what Drake assumed they were. They held large weapons. They all looked identical except for the two standing in front of them. Drake stared at them with a look of pure disgust. The two figures standing before Drake bowed.

Drake peered through the window into the other side. The walls were black, but it wasn't dark on the other side. It was well-lit with white floors. What an odd contrast, Drake thought to himself as the three men had a stare-down. Drake looked from left to right, looking back and forth between the two men. The one in white nodded at Drake. Drake didn't return the gesture.

"We are prepared to die with this ship," Drake said as he approached the door. Still, every man on the other side stood completely motionless. Drake turned back quickly, realizing how vastly outnumbered his men were. Drake had about half the men compared to the others.

"We won't let you in," Drake exclaimed.

Again, they stood motionless.

"We will blow this level if you don't leave, killing all of us," Drake said in a desperate attempt to get through to the motionless figures.

Drake saw the figure in black, the one he recognized from the videos. The figure pressed something on his wrist. It looked like the figure was bobbing his head, almost like it was talking through a communication device. Drake's comm started flashing along with Langston.

"Sir, they've tapped into our air supply," an engineer from the bridge shouted through the comms.

Drake looked back through the blast door window and saw the two figures turn to walk away. As they did, the soldiers split down the middle, allowing the two to walk away. In a moment of pure rage, Drake reached up and punched the glass. It did nothing to the glass, but the figure in white stopped and looked over their shoulder before turning down a corridor. Drake felt something in his hand pop. He knew he had broken a knuckle. Drake's arm shook with adrenaline and rage. He didn't feel it yet, but he knew it was only a matter of time.

Langston hadn't even noticed he was shouting at his men to get off the level. "What's going on?" Drake asked. Still dizzy and full of confusion.

"Sir, they are pumping gas onto the ship."

"How?" Drake asked, confused.

"We don't know."

Drake instinctively reached for his comm. "How are they getting gas onto the ship? Can we block them out?" Drake asked in a dizzy panic.

"Marcus, we can't; they completely overridden all our fail-safes," Thatcher responded to him. "We are dead in the water," Thatcher exclaimed.

"Where's Jason?" Drake asked, pacing by the blast door.

"He's running around trying to kick them out," Jason chimed in on the comm. "Drake, I don't get it. It's like they know all our passwords, overrides, and firewall breaks; they know this ship better than I do. It doesn't make sense," Jason yelled.

"Do we know what kind of gas?" Langston asked.

"No idea," Jason said. "We are effectively locked out of everything. Life support, all gas systems, literally everything," Jason said.

Drake looked down at his feet and mumbled under his breath. "I will die for these men."

Thatcher kicked Langston and Jason off the comm chat. "Marcus, I need to talk to you alone," Thatcher said.

"Thatch, is this really the time?" Drake asked.

"We may not have any other time, but you need to know this right now."

Drake was silent.

"I care about you, Marcus, and you asking me to blow up a level of the ship if needed is cruel, and I couldn't do it. I couldn't live with myself knowing I killed you."

Drake knew this was her way of trying to tell him how she felt. It shocked Drake. He didn't wanna accept the way he had been feeling. He had been married and didn't need to ever love again. Not that it was love. But Drake had not been willing to accept what he felt for Thatcher. But amid possible death, Drake let himself feel. And like a ton of bricks, the feelings laid on him. He felt feelings he had only felt for one other. Carmen flashed before his eyes. Drake felt a tear roll down his cheek; he didn't care. Then Fiona flashed in his mind, and he smiled. Drake snapped back to the moment. Drake smiled and sniffed.

"I care for you too, Fiona. And I couldn't have done that either. Thatch, don't let anyone onto the bridge," Drake said.

"Marcus, what are you doing?" she asked.

"You gotta trust me; I'll see you when it's over," Drake hung up the comm. He would see her one way or the other. Either in heaven or when they won this fight.

Drake walked over to Langston, who was speaking to 1st safety officer Mondin. "Alright, well, I say we wait 'em out," Langston said.

Just then, there was a hiss in the vents overhead, and a white cloud of gas flooded the room.

"Hold your breath, men," Langston shouted.

Drake looked up and saw the soldiers on the other side closing on the blast door. Drake drew his sidearm with his non broken hand and leveled it at the door. Langston stood next to him and leveled his rifle at the door. Drake's vision got blurry as his lungs burned for a breath. Drake's body forced him to inhale deeply. Drake felt the gas burn his lungs. As soon as he did, he felt his eyelids grow heavy, and he could barely stand. Drake looked over and saw Langston and Mondin on the ground. Drake fell to his knees. The blast doors hissed and began to open. Drake raised the pistol again to take a shot.

Drake yelled, as he felt a sharp pain in his rib cage, then a jolt of electricity. The gun fell, and so did he onto his back. The world was almost black as he saw gray figures walk past him. The last thing he saw was that white helmet standing over him before the world went black.

 DYLAN CARRIGAN

CHAPTER SEVENTEEN

Wake up, wake up, Drake heard it in a muffled voice. Drake painfully pried open his eyes as though they had been shut for years. The first thing Drake noticed was how absolutely pitch black it was where he was. Drake thought back to the last thing he was doing. The soldiers, the gas, his broken hand, his concussion, his ship, his crew, Thatcher… his mind lingered on Thatcher. Drake could move his hand completely fine. Almost as though it hadn't happened. That's impossible. That happened less than a day ago at most, Drake thought to himself. And his concussion was gone entirely. His head didn't hurt at all. To think of it, the last 24 hours had made very little sense to him. Who was telling him to wake up? He felt himself drifting back to sleep. He had to be on some sort of drug, he thought. This was too powerful to be his own body. Or maybe he was just that tired. It was already pitch black, so Drake saw no change when his eyes finally slid shut again.

Wake up… Wake up, Marcus. Drake bolted up from sleep. Feeling much less groggy than before. All the lights were on in his room this time. The walls were the same black he had seen on the other side of the blast door. He stood from the bed he'd been lying on and started pacing around the room. Drake immediately knew he wasn't on the X-Caliber. This wasn't his ship. Why'd they take him on board? Why didn't they kill him? Where were his men? His thoughts raced. He saw a door on the other side of the room and rushed over to it as best he could in his delirious state. He pounded his hands against the door. It felt solid. No give to it in the slightest. Drake didn't want to hurt his hand again. There was a small porthole in the door. Drake peered out of it. The outside of his door was pitch black. Drake stepped back, looking for anything that might help him. The room was pretty bare, only a bed and an end table with a glass of what Drake assumed to be water. Up until that point, he had forgotten how thirsty and dehydrated he felt. He didn't care if it was water or not. He rushed over and downed the entire glass. It felt like the first time he had water in years. The water tasted so pure and natural. He put the glass down and sat back on the edge of the bed. The lights in the room suddenly went out. Drake lay back on the bed, determined to not fall asleep again. But as what seemed like hours passed, he drifted once again. This time, it was different. It didn't fade to black as it once did. Drake opened his eyes in a bed he used to call his own. He turned over and saw his old room. This was his and Carmen's house. Drake looked over and saw Carmen sleeping next to him. He didn't know what to do. Why did he keep coming back here? To this place in time. He reached over and put his hand on his late wife's shoulder. It was warm, and Carmen rolled over to him. She smiled; good morning, love, she said to him. It broke his heart as tears fell from his face. This was like torture. Why'd he have to be back here again? He loved seeing his wife. But this felt too real. Like she was here with him. But she wasn't. She died from post-labor trauma. Drake watched as she got up and went into the bathroom.

"Can't believe we've been here for 6 months already," she said as she walked back out.

Drake knew this feeling. It was identical to when he dreamed about Corbin, Carmen, and him when they had moved to Point Roberts to work at the IEC. He was there again. He knew all he could do was live this out until he woke up. Drake followed his wife into the living room. He immediately knew something was off. The walls were completely bare. This puzzled Drake because Carmen was crazy about pictures. Especially family photos. Old ones of her family and recent ones covered the walls at their house, but not here.

"Carmen," Drake said in a concerned voice. "What did you do with all the photos?"

"What photos?" she asked.

"The ones we've always had up," Drake shot back.

"Oh, those? Yeah, I took those down," she responded.

"Why would you do that," he asked.

"Because it's time to start again, Marcus, I'm giving you a blank canvas," Carmen said compassionately.

Drake felt the breath leave his lungs. "Are you saying you want to leave me?" Drake asked, sounding heartbroken.

"No, my dear," she said, looking at Drake. "But you must let go of the past. Your destiny is in front of you."

Drake knew this never happened. She would have never really said anything like this. Drake walked towards her as she poured a cup of coffee for herself, then for Drake. She motioned for him to sit down. Drake sat on the stool while she stood across from him.

"I love you, Marcus, and I always will. But your destiny doesn't end with me," Carmen said as she looked intently at her husband.

"What do you mean?" Drake asked. "I love you. You are my wife. The mother of my daughters."

She hushed him. "I can feel your hurt, my dear. I know, but I was only your beginning. You have a purpose far higher than you can imagine," Carmen said, stepping closer.

"I don't want a purpose if you aren't in it," Drake said, feeling a knot form in his throat as he tried not to sob, his heart tearing in two.

She reached out and placed her hand on top of his. It soothed his heart.

"Marcus, she's a part of it," Carmen said in an understanding voice.

Drake raised an eyebrow at her. "Who?" Drake asked as his mind snapped back to Thatcher. But he was right in front of his wife. The love of his life. How could he be thinking about her when Carmen was right before him. He looked up. She was looking at him with compassion in her eyes.

"She is your future, Marcus; it's okay."

Drake closed his eyes. He felt ashamed. He felt like he was betraying her. But he knew she was right. He had to let go. He had to let go if he was to ever live the way he was supposed to. Drake looked up and saw his daughters standing beside Carmen. Drake stood up, rushed over to them, and hugged them all. They were all smiling. Drake felt a hand touch his shoulder. Drake looked over and saw his pops standing there smiling at him; Drake let all the pent-up emotions pour out. He wept in the arms of his grandfather. The man who had given him a start. His role model and his hero. They all hugged. Drake didn't want it to end. They spent the whole day together. Making food. Playing in the backyard. And playing old board games. This was happiness in Drake's eyes. Then he remembered. This wasn't real. What was it then if it wasn't real? It all felt like real life. It was surreal. Drake knew his time was short. He cherished every moment with his family again. As the night ended, Drake hugged his girls and his pops as his grandfather led his daughters out the door. They all looked back as they walked out. They waved as they faded out the front door. Drake turned to see Carmen standing up to leave as well. He reached out his hand for hers; she grabbed it and held it. She frowned at him.

"My dear, I'm afraid the road ahead is dim and full of trials."

Drake's face became long at hearing these words.

"Trust in yourself and in the gifts God has given you." Carmen paused for a moment as she smiled. "Don't push her away; lean on her, Marcus."

"Lean on who?" Drake asked.

She smiled and tilted her head. "Fiona, my dear," she said softly.

Drake responded abruptly. "How can you know any of this, Carmen?"

She leaned down and kissed his hand. "Because I do, my dear." She walked toward the door and opened it. "Trust God, Marcus."

Just as she walked out the door, she stopped and turned back one last time. "And Marcus, one last thing…"

"I AM BETHANY…"

CHAPTER EIGHTEEN

In an instant, Drake felt like he was sucked back into reality. His eyes shot open. He was breathing heavily and gripping the sides of the bed. His eyes immediately went to the figure sitting on a chair at the edge of the room. It was a figure in a white uniform. The one who had been handing all the notes to the figure Drake had talked to. Here he was, in the same room as him. Drake shot upright to get his breath under control. He didn't want to show fear. But he did at least a little bit.

"Hello Marcus," the figure said. It spoke English. The voice was heavily distorted but could still be made out clearly enough. Drake tried to talk, but no words came out. It was like his tongue was tied.

"Your voice will come back in a minute or two," the figure said. "You've been out for a while."

Drake forced his voice to work. "Where am I? Where's my crew and my ship?"

"They are safe; you are safe, Marcus," the figure said softly. "We told you we didn't want to hurt you. But we knew you wouldn't go quickly. That's something we admire about you, Marcus."

"Who are you?" Drake asked. The figure stood up and walked forward. The door to the room opened, and the figure in black stepped in as well.

Drake felt trapped. He looked around again at the same room he was in before he passed out. Nothing he could use. Drake decided to wait it out. To see the outcome. If they had wanted to kill me, they would have done it by now, Drake thought to himself. As the figure in black approached, it reached up and pushed a button on the side of its helmet. A metallic click and buzz could be heard as the helmet unsealed itself. Drake didn't have any idea of what to expect. What did an alien look like? The helmet was unclasped, and the figure took it off. Underneath the mask was a pale-skinned individual. But besides being pale, the figure was very much human. The eyes, the hair, the limb proportions. It made sense now why they looked so human-like; they seemed to be humans. The man bowed as he always did before, then spoke in what appeared to be English, just slightly off.

"Hello Admiral, I am Aziel," the figure in black said as he bowed. He had shortish-white hair that hung slightly messy around his face. His piercing gray eyes stood out the most on his very cut face. Drake was baffled and speechless. Aziel continued. "We apologize for how all of this has transpired." The man spoke English, but it was either an accent or a different dialect. It made Drake have to really think about what he was hearing.

"You must have a million questions," Aziel said as he motioned towards the white figure, and they stepped forward. With the same click and buzz, the figure reached up, and they took off the helmet. Drake did not register the face at first. But he knew the voice by heart…

"Corbin?" Drake said in a baffled tone. The helmet slid off, revealing the face of Drake's best friend. His beard was grown out, and his hair was shorter, but it was undoubtedly Corbin Huxley.

"Hey buddy," Corbin responded to him.

Was this really him? There's no way, Drake thought as he tried to put the dots together, but there was no hope. He was at the mercy of the situation. Corbin stood there, a dark-complexioned man with the knowing smile Drake had known his entire life. Drake didn't care what he looked like at this moment; he leaped up and embraced his friend.

"It's good to see you, Marcus," Corbin said. Drake had never been this emotional before. The stress of the last few weeks was coming out, and he broke down. He never did this. Only to Carmen a few times. Drake cried on Corbin's shoulder. Corbin motioned over to Aziel.

"Give us a few minutes, would you?" Corbin asked him. Aziel bowed and exited the room.

Corbin pulled up the chair from the corner of the room to the edge of the bed as Drake sat back down. "I have a lot of explaining to do," Corbin said with a chuckle. That was him. Always able to make light out of any situation. "But I can only say so much right now; there will be a debrief soon."

Drake butted in. "First off, are my men and my ship okay?" Drake asked him.

Corbin leaned over and patted Drake on the knee. "They are my friend. Commander Thatcher, Jason Ross, and Helks will be at the debriefing." Drake was happy to hear this. Especially knowing that Thatcher was okay.

Corbin smiled. "How's Helks been treating you?"

Drake smiled slightly. "As unstable as usual. Didn't take the last 24 hours very well," Drake responded, almost laughing.

Corbin's smile faded. "Buddy, it's been a week since we took you on board."

"A week?" Drake exclaimed.

"You had a bad concussion and a messed up hand; our doctor found it best to leave you out for a week to let you heal properly."

"I didn't wake up at all during this week?" Drake asked.

"Not one time," Corbin responded. "You've been under local anesthetic and under 24/7 watch."

Drake could have sworn he had woken up at least twice. He sat silent for a moment. "How is my hand not broken after a week?" Drake asked.

"They have technology way beyond our time," Corbin responded.

Drake leaned back on the bed. "Who are they?" Drake asked in a quiet voice.

"All will be explained, brother, I promise," Corbin said with a reassuring look. They both sat in silence for a few moments. Drake looked back up.

"So I'm on your ship?" Drake asked.

"Yes," Corbin responded. "But don't worry, we are still docked to The X-Caliber. We've already started overhauling the ship," Corbin paused, cutting himself off. "I'm getting ahead of myself. Like I said, there's a debrief in 15. Follow the blue arrows overhead when the doors open, a guard will escort you. I'll see you there," Corbin said as he rose and walked toward the door. Corbin patted the door edge as he walked out, leaving Drake once again alone in this room. He closed his eyes. Not knowing what to believe. Was this another dream? It had to be. None of this could be true. Aliens who are humans, Corbin being with them. Drake only hoped this meeting would help him find any sort of answers.

Drake was startled when the door opened with a hiss. A guard in the gray uniform he had seen at his blast doors stepped into view.

"Admiral, with me, please," the female figure spoke. She had the same accent that Aziel had. Drake followed the guard out the door. As they walked through the black corridors, they passed doors and more of the strange men.

Some had helmets on, some had them off, and they all looked so strangely human. Most had deep black; Drake was silent the whole walk. After 5 minutes and an elevator ride, they were in the debriefing room. The doors opened, and they stepped into a massive room. There were roughly 40 people by Drake's quick scan of the room. All of Drake's counsel was there. His eyes locked with Thatcher's. She smiled a grin more enormous than any Drake had seen from her before. All of Drake's men snapped to attention as he walked in. Drake scanned the room as he walked to the empty seat next to Thatcher. He sat down, and when he did, Thatcher looked at him and smiled.

"I'm glad you're okay, but we still have no idea what's happening," she whispered. "Engineers have been going on and off our ship, and they won't tell us what's going on. But it's Corbin, so we are all overruled here, I guess," Thatcher said, still whispering.

Drake looked at his men; he saw Thatcher, Helks, Jason, Lucian, and Langston. RJ wasn't there. Figures, he thought to himself. The room was well-lit, with a giant square table spanning the whole room. Corbin and Aziel stood in the middle with another man Drake didn't recognize. All of Drake's men sat on one side of the table. The rest of the table was occupied by whoever these other men were. The man Drake didn't recognize stepped forward. The man had solid white hair, but there was no way he was over 30 years old, and from a brief glance, Drake could tell that he and Aziel were brothers. Their medium-sized noses and pointed chins with an almost overbearing brow gave it away. He was wearing the same thing as Aziel but all gold. Their clothing definitely made them look more intimidating.

"Crew of the X-Caliber, welcome aboard the Seraph, I am Atlas," the man in gold said. He spoke better English than Aziel. He didn't seem to have as deep of an accent as the rest. "You all must wonder what transpired this last week and what the purpose behind it is. First off, on behalf of all Drezmians and the Solraes Imperium, we say welcome."

Drezmians? Solraes Imperium? Drake thought.

"I will let your leader explain everything," Atlas said, stepping back.

Corbin stepped forward. "Thank you, Atlas. Atlas is the head of the entire Drezmian military," Corbin explained. "I am sorry this all had to happen this way. But it's the only way things could be put in motion." Corbin walked more into the middle. "These plans have been in the works long before our time.

This plan and its groundwork were laid at the beginning of the human race's start on our planet, Earth," Corbin said, pausing.

A screen popped up on the wall behind Corbin. "But we aren't from Earth." A video of the planet played, and the shot panned out as another planet ten times the size of Earth came into view. Corbin pointed at the beautiful planet; it had gigantic oceans of blue and large expanses of green with moon-sized cities on it. It reminded Drake of how the Earth looked long ago before the planet was polluted. There was much more land mass on this planet, though.

"That's Tyradis, the home planet of the Drezmians, Home of the Solraes Imperium," Corbin paused for a moment. "The original Home of the Human race."

CHAPTER NINETEEN

ou could hear a pin drop in the room. Almost as though no one wanted to take a breath for fear it would be too loud.

Helks spoke up. "Excuse me? How was the IEC never informed of this? How was the higher command never told any of this," Helks yelled.

Corbin shot Helks a look. "Only a select few knew; none on the mission Admirals knew anything," Corbin responded, "Please let me finish, Helks."

Helks, who had stood up, sat back down. The video on the screen panned out to show the entire solar system Tyradis was located in.

"This is the Eclion System," Atlas said. "In this system resides the civilization of the Drezmians, and the empire that reigns over the Drezmians with peace and light is the Solraes Imperium. The empire of light." Atlas once again stepped forward. "Our home world, our solar system, and your home once as well have been at war for thousands of years," Atlas said. "At times, it has slowed, and even a cease-fire for 150 years, but we have been on the defensive the entire time. Growing, learning, waiting for the right time, and unfortunately losing," Atlas said, pausing. "Our enemy is from the dark side of our galaxy; they are very technologically advanced. Their system has a dying red star, providing little to no light. A black hole lies at the very edge of the system, sticking out into dead space. This has caused them to expand and look for more stars to harvest for energy. They are the Voidreavers. Evil, vile creatures."

The screen turned black again. Drake realized he had been holding his breath; he breathed in. How could any of this be real? he thought. Drake looked over at Thatcher. She had a completely blank expression. She was scared. She looked tough, but Drake could see the fear on her face. The screen revealed a humanoid-looking creature, but it was far from it. The creature looked pale; Drake assumed that trait arose from the lack of any real light source on the planet. The creature was completely hairless and had a very boney-looking face. Definitely not pleasant to look at, but still not terrifying.

They had gray irises and longer-looking legs and arms. At least 6'4" in height and not bulky.

"Meet the Voidreavers," Aziel said, and everyone stared at the figure on the screen. No one spoke for a few moments. Drake broke the silence.

"What is the state of the war? Are they attacking the Eclion system?" Drake asked.

Atlas smiled at Drake. "Admiral, it's so nice to finally meet you," Atlas responded. "And not yet. They haven't made it that far into the system. We've been able to keep them at the edge of Eclion for a while now. But we know they are working on something and have been for a long time… We aren't sure exactly what, but we assume they are getting close," Atlas paused for a moment. "But they didn't know we were raising an army," he said, smiling.

Thatcher interrupted. "Raising an army? Are you talking about humans?" Thatcher asked.

The three men in the middle stood silently. Corbin spoke up this time with a soft voice. "Yes, Thatcher. That was the purpose of Earth. The Drezmians needed to raise an army out of the eye of the Voidreavers. They found Earth and planted the seed. Our civilization grew, and now they have come back for their people," Corbin said, trying to answer as best as he could.

Thatcher raised her voice. "Our people are weak. Earth has been dying for years. The time to get an army has passed. You'd be sending weak, frail people into war," Thatcher said.

Drake agreed in his heart. They all knew that the dying Earth had made a fragile species with no food, disease, and catastrophic weather. Drake spoke up; she was right. "We will be sending our people to the slaughter; the Earth has made humans frail," Drake said, siding with Thatcher.

Corbin walked forward. "My friend, the Drezmians are capable of many things; they have enough food and medicine to make our population healthy."

Atlas raised his voice slightly. "I promise all will be explained. Just let me continue." The man said, stepping forward again. Corbin stepped back, and Drake leaned back in his chair.

Atlas turned and looked at all of Drake's men, and then he stopped on Drake. "You must understand that you are Drezmian; you come from us. You have as many rights as any other on this vessel or back on Tyradis. You weren't raised for slaughter," Atlas said, showing some compassion in his eyes. "But yes, the plan was for anyone who was able to be, can be in our military at some position."

"How is that remotely humane?" Thatcher said, still arguing back. "We aren't your property; why force us into your war?"

Atlas glared at Thatcher, then over to Drake. "Admiral, I recommend you converse with your men and Corbin to get everyone on the same page," Atlas said. "This will go much smoother that way." His demeanor was still calm, but you could see his frustration. "And to answer your question, Ms. Fiona, how," he said, sounding almost degrading. "It's humane because we are saving your population from the world your people destroyed," Atlas said. "You are our blood; we set things in motion as soon as we saw the degradation on your planet," Atlas said as some slight realization played over Thatcher's face. "Dismissed," he shouted as he walked out. Aziel followed him closely. The rest of their men walked out the door, leaving only Drake's crew and Corbin standing before them.

They all sat in silence for what felt like an hour. Drake released the rest of the men except Thatcher and Jason. Corbin pulled up a chair from the other tables and sat in front of the three.

"I need you guys to focus," Corbin said in a severe voice. The joking, relaxed man was gone now. "First, we have no choice in this matter; it will go forward no matter what," Corbin said.

Drake took a deep breath. He knew his friend was right. They had no choice. "He's right," Drake spoke.

Thatcher looked over at him with a sad look. Drake met her eyes. "This is the path before us," Drake said, trying to be reassuring. "We have to walk it out." Drake saw a weight almost roll off her shoulders. It surprised Drake how much his reassurance soothed her.

"What was that email about?" Drake asked. He had forgotten to bring it up earlier, he had been in too much shock.

Corbin halfway smirked at this. "So you got it, then?" Corbin asked.

"We did," Drake responded. "The entire message didn't play. I had honestly chalked it up to an older emergency message," Drake said to him.

"Yeah, sorry about that. Everything was sheer chaos for a solid week," Corbin said. "The Drezmians had contacted me roughly a year before and told me they planned to get us soon. I sent you a message on the only server left working in IEC headquarters when people were being loaded into ships and I was leaving my office. The signal was weak, and I rushed; I was told to activate Bethany; I did the best I could to warn you we were coming without telling you anything," Corbin said, trying to explain.

Drake didn't react; he barely knew what to think anymore. "Why?" Drake asked, "Why couldn't we know?" Drake asked, wanting more clarity.

"Marcus, this goes beyond me, beyond you, and beyond any of us. No one knew except me, some higher-ups at the IEC, and a few world leaders," Corbin said. "The order had always been to build, train, and advance ourselves to space. The IEC was for advancement but also to build a few critical ships out of the Voidreaver eye. They knew they would get as many as they could off the planet. We were for a different purpose," Corbin said, taking a breath for a moment. "And we just followed orders as asked. That's why I made many decisions that didn't always make sense," Corbin said, looking at Drake.

Thatcher scratched her head. "Where are the others? The other ships, I mean," Thatcher asked.

"The Andromeda and the Valiant are all with transport ships; they have been briefed about most of what I'm telling you."

Drake tilted his head slightly. "So Bartus and Clovis know everything?" Drake asked him.

Corbin looked at Drake reassuringly. "I will tell them everything else when they arrive tomorrow; they are working on final adjustments with passengers and crew. Their ships are undergoing renovations similar to those on the X-Caliber," Corbin said.

"Tomorrow?" Thatcher asked, surprised.

"As I said before, they are way beyond us technologically."

Jason sat back. "How far ahead are we talking?" Jason asked stone-faced.

"They have something called QLP or Quantum Lattice Pathways." Again, everyone sat in silence and shock. "Like bending space and stuff," Corbin said with a smile forming.

Drake almost thought he saw a smile on Jason's face at this news.

"Why did the message in the email sound so frantic?" Jason asked.

"Because of the riots," Corbin said, frowning. "Some, a lot actually, stayed behind. We couldn't give much info. As much as they needed," Corbin responded.

"Do you blame them?" Thatcher asked. "They were probably scared out of their minds."

Corbin looked at the ceiling, searching for words. "It was expected, and they were given the choice. Stay and die with Earth, or come and have a chance," Corbin said, still looking at the ceiling.

"How many?" Drake asked, still taken aback.

"The Drezmians have some pretty massive transport ships. About 10 in total. We were able to take 4 million, but everyone else refused. Along with the ten thousand on the Andromeda from Mars and one hundred on the Valiant, the last of the humans," Corbin said.

Thatcher leaned forward. "How about the two hundred thousand soldiers you have frozen on The Caliber?" she asked, taking a shot at Corbin.

Corbin stared intently at her, but not with anger. "I understand how you feel about this. I really do, but nothing you or I say will change anything. It's out of my hands. They've already started the growth process on the Seraph," Corbin said, responding to her shot at him. "That's all we can discuss now, friends. Everything is linked from the X-Caliber to the Seraph, so tablets and all communication lines will work. We will discuss phase 2 of this when the other ships arrive tomorrow." Corbin stood and walked towards the door. "Drake, meet me in my office later. Call Zyrex, and he will escort you to it. See you all tomorrow, get some rest," Corbin said as he stood to walk away.

Drake and the others watched as Corbin strode out the door. For a man Drake called his equal, he seemed towering and powerful when he walked away. Drake wasn't afraid; it was just a feeling of distance towards him. He seemed so much different than the Corbin Drake had always known.

Thatcher, Jason, and Drake sat in silence for a few moments. Thatcher was the first to speak. "That's a lot, just a lot," she said as she laid her head on the table and choked back a cry. Drake reached over and grabbed her hand. She held it tight without looking up. He could tell she was silently crying. Jason made a concerned face at Drake, and he nodded his head.

Jason pulled out his tablet. "Looks like all the preparations are done," Jason said.

"For what?" Drake asked.

"For Private Manson's Spaceman Burial," Jason responded.

Drake steeled himself, feeling every single emotion hit him simultaneously. On top of it all, he had still lost a man a little over a week ago. He breathed hard and held back the tears. "Call the crew," Drake said.

Jason began to send a message to the crew of the X-Caliber. "No," Drake said calmly, "call everyone."

Jason's eyes got big. "I don't know if they will listen," he responded back.

Thatcher raised her head still with tears in her eyes. "If we are blood as they claim, they will be there," Drake said, holding Thatcher's shoulder before walking towards the door and calling Zyrex. "Take me to my ship, please."

A man with a deep voice came back through the tablet. "Of course," he responded. "I'll be there soon." The man had an almost abnormally deep voice.

Zyrex met him in the hallway. The man was in a black uniform, like Aziel's. It had a red marking on the side of the completely blacked-out helmet. It must be a marking to signify rank, he assumed. He motioned for Drake to follow him and led him through the black halls toward the X-Caliber.

20

CHAPTER TWENTY

Drake showered and shaved off the stubble that had grown on his face. He made food before getting out his Admiral's uniform. Drake hated it. He didn't like dressing up for anything. But he ironed it and put it on anyway, for Manson, he thought. A while later, he walked through the halls and headed to level 1, where the launch bay was. All through the halls, he saw open panels and tools. Wires being run, and systems being worked on. He knew Corbin would tell him later, but he had no idea what they were doing with his ship. It had to be good. Might even get one of those sparkling yellow shields, he thought, trying to lighten his own mood. The halls were empty as Drake walked through, making it deathly silent except for the hum of the ship; everyone was already on level 1. Drake put on his cap as he entered the elevator and rode up. There was no way they would come, he thought, thinking about Atlas's men, Corbin maybe, but not the others. Right as he had that thought, the door opened, and he walked into the other airlock. As it opened, all the eyes turned to see him. Drake stepped through, and a loud voice came over the PA. Drake looked up to see Langston, and he nodded a respectful nod. Drake walked towards where Thatcher, Jason, and the rest were standing, and Langston spoke in a deep tone.

"Attention on deck… ADMIRAL MARCUS DRAKE."

At that moment, all 497 members of Drake's crew snapped to attention and saluted as he stepped into the middle. When Drake looked over, he saw the other side of the bay. It was the entire crew of the Seraph, with Atlas, Aziel, and Zyrex all standing in the front, all bowing in respect. Drake looked over to Thatcher and saw Corbin standing there, saluting him. Drake's emotions swelled. His men, his family. He scanned the room. He saw Nan, Liam, Amelia, Louris, Jackson, and even RJ standing there in his uniform; they all did. Drake slowly walked towards where Manson was lying. It was customary to salute him first. He approached the side of the bed and touched his arm. The cold feeling sent a shock through his hand and arm. He steeled his mind. Drake slowly saluted Private Manson. He turned to his crew and saluted them. They did the same. Drake then turned to the Drezmians and saluted them, and they bowed with respect. Drake stood behind the Private and spoke, stoic in his voice and commanding in his presence.

"Private Manson gave his life for the greater good, for the mission. We will always remember him as brave and steadfast in the face of certain death; he was a good friend and an even better man," Drake said in a booming voice. He continued. "We may be asked to take on the same fate in the days and trials ahead. For your fellow brother, for the future of our race. For the future of all of us. For the future of all Drezmian kind."

Drake looked over at Atlas when he said that last part. Atlas bowed his head and shouted, "For the greater good."

Drake looked over at Corbin. "Until the very end, my brothers," Corbin said as he also bowed his head.

Drake saw Thatcher looking at him. A hint of fear but also trust in her eyes. She stepped forward.

"For the greater good," she said as she bowed in respect.

Drake saluted. "FOR THE GREATER GOOD," he shouted. All the crew of both ships started cheering and chanting. Drake reached over and pushed the red button to his left. The platform raised, and Manson was lifted into the airlock. Drake pushed the other button, sending Manson to his Spaceman's burial. He saluted one last time to his fallen comrade as a tear ran down his cheek.

Most of the day was somber, and the two crews intermingled, with some returning to their duties. Some obviously avoided the Drezmian, choosing not to accept what was being told to them. But they were loyal to Drake and the ship, so they kept their mouths shut and kept on their way. It didn't worry Drake, though. It would shake out over time. Drake walked around and talked with his crew. There were food tables that Louris and her team had prepared, so it was also a celebration of life. Drake spotted Corbin in his IEC uniform, which fit Corbin's muscular physique just right. Corbin saw Drake approaching.

"Marcus, my boy!" he exclaimed. "Beautiful speech. You helped bring people together, and it's lovely," Corbin said as he looked around with his usual big smile.

Drake tried his best to put on a smile, but the smile didn't look genuine to Corbin. Corbin's smile faded slightly.

"Marcus, talk to me," he said with a concerned tone.

Drake looked at Corbin. "Can we talk?" Drake asked.

"Always, brother," Corbin responded.

They walked over to the far side of the launch bay where all the parts for the probes were stored, not needed anymore, and had previously been planned to be repurposed before the last few weeks had transpired.

Drake puzzled his brow as he stared at the floor leaning on the wall. "I'm with you; I always will be. But you and I both know Manson didn't have to die," Drake said in a serious tone.

Corbin's usual soft expression became stiff. "Are you sure?" he responded. "Don't you see, Marcus? Look at the bigger picture here."

Drake stared right into Corbin's eyes. "I see that one of my men died because you deemed it necessary to steal our probe," Drake said, getting annoyed.

Corbin shot back quickly. "Because you put him in mind banking."

Drake stepped forward. "The bigger picture I saw was the mission I dedicated my whole life to falling apart, and I did what I had to do to save the integrity of our mission, the one you made, Corbin," Drake said in a soft voice filled with fury and passion.

Corbin looked off towards the hanger, still teeming with people moving around. He looked back at Drake.

"Look, Marcus, I know this was thrown at you, and much more is about to get dumped on you." Drake wondered what Corbin meant by this. "But we needed a way to get your men to trust the others. And a massive show of respect for a fallen comrade is a pretty good way to do it," Corbin said in a very calm tone and demeanor. "We didn't know exactly how it would go, but probability suggested there would be a ninety percent chance someone would perish trying to retrieve memories from the mind bank." Corbin paused again while Drake stared at him expressionless. "We were willing to take that risk," Corbin said, pausing. "Marcus, sometimes in war, sacrifices must be made for the greater good, and this is not the only life that will be lost in this. Marcus, I need you with me."

Drake tried his hardest to look Corbin in the eyes; he forced himself to as he breathed out heavily. "Corbin, I've been with you since the beginning, and you know that," Drake said as he shifted his weight and stood up more straight. "But not a single soul on this crew asked for this war; we aren't soldiers."

"No, you aren't," Corbin said, interrupting. "You are the Admiral and the crew of one of the most technologically advanced and vital ships in the IEC, as well as the entire Imperium navy after the upgrades and fabrications."

The two men sat on crates that were nearby. They sat unspeaking for a while as people passed by them.

"So, there was always another purpose behind its design?" Drake asked with a half smile.

Corbin grinned big and chuckled. "Brother, there is a different purpose for everything we have ever done at the IEC."

Drake's mind raced back to his time at the Corp., all the tests and training. Corbin leaned forward as he sat.

"Listen to me, buddy," Corbin said in a kind voice. "A purpose for everything. I was selected because of my intelligence; you are smart, yes, but not to my level."

Drake knew this was true, but it still stung on the inside.

Drake chuckled. "Still holding our first aptitude tests over me, huh?" Drake said with a smile.

Corbin just looked at him with a smile. "I never held it over you. But it showed them exactly what they needed to see to put you in the spot they were missing," Corbin said.

"What was that?" Drake asked.

"A tactical genius, a man who sees things others don't," Corbin said, "your will and spirit are unbreakable, and a true leader and a warrior," Corbin said to Drake. "They needed their guy, and they found him. That's why they tested you when they met you out there."

Drake grimaced, remembering the decision to fire the limited weapons selection upon the glowing yellow orb.

"You were a little trigger-happy, but they saw what they wanted to see," Corbin said, pausing momentarily as Drake sat in silence. "A man who was willing to do what others wouldn't do. A man who wasn't afraid to stare death in the face and do what had to be done to protect the ones he cared about."

CHAPTER TWENTY-ONE

THE NEXT DAY

The X-Caliber vibrated as the new shield systems were tested. Drezmians and humans alike floated around the ship, working on the inside and the outside. Progress was moving smoothly, according to the reports pouring into Drake's office, as he worked through learning new systems, rewriting protocols, and reassigning roles around the new mandate Corbin and Atlas had been sending over from the Seraph. Drake pored over charts and paragraphs of weapons systems. A message popped up on his screen; it was from Jason. The message read:

"Hey, boss, Atlas and Corbin are calling a meeting at 3 pm over on the Seraph. They want the council and me to be there. The Andromeda and Valiant will be here with the transport vessels in 4 hours."

As Drake read, he heard a knock at his door. "Come in," he shouted, and the door slid open. Thatcher walked in and immediately ran up to Drake and hugged him. Drake didn't expect it at all, but he hugged her back. He'd never seen this side of her. It's like all the walls were down. It's not like Drake minded it. Just new for him. She stepped back and straightened her shirt.

"Sorry," she said. "I just thought you were dead after they boarded the ship, tears welling in her eyes. We didn't know anything for a day or two; everyone was so scared, but Lucian and I kept them calm, and we were able to maintain order."

"Thanks, Thatch," Drake said with a genuine smile. She smiled back, and they both sat down. They discussed the data pouring in and all the new upgrades for a while.

"Are we gonna talk about what's happening between us, Marcus?" Thatcher asked him. This caught him off guard. He knew exactly what she was talking about but didn't know if he was ready to feel this again. His wife flashed in his mind; he saw her face. Then the dream flashed in his mind, what she had told him… "Lean on her…"

"Drake? MARCUS?" Thatcher yelled as Drake snapped back to where he was. He stared at her, and she had a concerned look on her face.

"I'm sorry, we can wait to talk about it another time," she said as she stood to leave.

"No, Fiona, wait," he responded. "I just, I just…" Drake stuttered. "I haven't felt this in a long, long time."

She looked at Drake with knowing eyes. "I've never felt this before, Marcus. It's scary for me too." She looked at the wall where a picture of Drake's family hung. She smiled and laughed.

"Drake, I could never be her; I could never replace your Carmen. But you have to let yourself feel again, and if you feel what I feel in my heart, then this has to mean something." As she spoke, Drake saw the passion in her eyes, and he knew she was right. She would never be Carmen, and he didn't want her to be.

"Fiona, I don't want you to replace Carmen. No one ever could," Drake said softly. "I need you to be who you are. For me, for us, for this crew." Drake closed his eyes. "Because I want whatever this is, whatever it becomes. I want it." She smiled and nodded slightly.

"When I was little, my father would always tell me that someday, a prince would come and carry me away from him," Thatcher said, using a wistful tone. "He passed away when I was 15… I never dated, though. No one ever caught my eye throughout middle school, high school, and even into IEC. My father always told me that the man willing to die for you is worth keeping." She grinned. "He scared away any boy I ever liked," she said, laughing and wiping away a tear. "But when you were telling me to blow level 17 that day," she paused, and Drake could see hurt in her tear-filled eyes. "It shattered my heart, Marcus," she said as she wiped away more tears. "It made me realize how I really felt about you."

Drake leaned forward. "And I realized I could never do that to you, even if it meant the ship went down," he responded.

They sat silently for a moment, the weight of what had been said hanging heavy in the air.

"I didn't know your dad had passed; how did you survive?" Drake asked softly, breaking the silence. This was hard for her. She never opened up like this to anyone, not since her dad.

"I um… I was in foster care for 3 years," Thatcher began, her voice filled with pain. "As can be imagined in our day and age, growing up in the system almost broke me. Ten different homes in 3 years. They all hated me. Foster care wasn't like before, where you would choose to do it. You were forced, too. And they had to feed and clothe me from their rations," she sighed. "But it helped make me strong and who I am today," she said, forcing a smile through the memories of hardship.

Drake felt not just the pain but the callousness in her voice. "To go through all that and still be who you are today is admirable," he said sincerely. "And I like who you've become."

They sat silently for a few moments, each lost in their thoughts. Thatcher broke the silence, her voice hesitant.

"Sooo um, about what we were talking about?" she asked.

"Oh yeah!" Drake exclaimed, breaking out of his thoughts.

"We are smart, Thatch," Drake responded. "I'm not one to rush in. You know you have me, and I have you, and we will walk this out."

Thatcher stood out of her seat. "I couldn't agree more," she said in a kind voice. She extended her hand awkwardly for a handshake. Drake laughed at her awkwardness, shook her hand, and pulled her in for a hug. He felt safe, and he allowed himself to openly feel this again for the first time in years.

Right then, a man cleared his throat at the door. Drake and Thatcher whipped around. Drake felt his face burn, and he felt like a teenager again. Corbin was there with his arms crossed, and he chuckled. "Could have seen that coming a mile away," he boomed as he laughed loudly. Thatcher straightened up, and her stonewall personality came right back up. She looked at Drake with a grimace.

"See you guys at the meeting," she said as she left the room quickly. Drake leaned forward on the desk, smiled, and laughed with Corbin. Corbin stepped into the room.

"Hey brother, I know it's a bad time, and we are already throwing a lot at you, but we need to walk and chat," Corbin said, leaning on the back of the chair. Drake turned off his computer, and he walked towards the door.

"Hey, what's more on my plate?" he asked sarcastically.

"Where are we headed?" Drake asked as they walked out in the hallway.

Corbin kept silent as they walked towards the elevator. Drake waited for him to pick a level, but he didn't expect him to push the button. He did. The level 15 button was lit up as the elevator descended into the ship's belly. Corbin looked up at Drake.

"We need to talk about Bethany."

Drake had forgotten; how could he forget? It had haunted his dreams and mind. Drake remembered what his wife had said in his last dream... "I AM BETHANY." Drake looked up from the wall, holding all the level buttons. "You told me in your message to complete Bethany," Drake said.

"I did, my friend," Corbin responded, looking at Drake intently.

"What did you mean by that, Corbin?" Drake asked. "You said you hoped I never knew."

"That's true," Corbin said, leaning up against the metal sides of the elevator.

Drake raised an eyebrow at him; he was never this short with him. He could see the panic and stress in his eyes. "What aren't you telling me, buddy?" Drake asked with sympathy in his voice.

"I'll let you know when we get there," Corbin said as he turned away from Drake toward the door.

The elevator stopped with a thud, and both men entered the dimly lit hallway. The lights flickered on like they usually did. Rowan stepped out of the door of his office when he saw Corbin and Drake. Rowan looked worse for wear. Like he hadn't slept in a few days, the bags under his eyes and the growth of stubble on his face showed that pretty well.

"Hey fellas," he said, sounding very tired. "We are almost done here. I just left what you told me to leave," Rowan said as he turned back into his office. Drake and Corbin followed. As they entered the room, Drake noticed that most of the shelves were completely bare except for one. Rowan led the men to the same table with four chairs Drake had sat at not too long ago. Rowan scrolled on the monitor in front of him, landed on the shelf inventory, and turned it around.

"As requested, most of the shelves have been activated and moved to the Seraph," Rowan said, looking down at his hands.

"Good, we are on schedule then; thank you," Corbin responded.

"Why are we starting the embryos?" Drake asked.

Rowan looked over at Corbin, not wanting to be the one to talk. Corbin stood up. "Rowan, can you give me and Marcus some time?" Rowan stood and walked out without saying another word.

Drake felt uneasy. He knew this was his best friend, but things still felt off after four years and the recent events. They walked around the room, looking at the empty shelves, still cold from the cryo. All the shelves were lit green, meaning they had been activated. Drake didn't know the process after this, though. That was Rowan's department.

"We moved all of them onto the Seraph," Corbin said as they walked toward the back of the room. "They have the infrastructure and know-how to begin raising the children."

"How long does it take?" Drake asked. "I mean, is it like an average child?"

"Not exactly," Corbin responded. "They have ways to speed it up." He paused for a really long time. Drake saw hesitation in his eyes as if he wanted to say more.

They had reached the very back of the room. The men stopped in front of the only shelf left in the room.

Shelf 01: Bethany

22

CHAPTER TWENTY-TWO

rake's mind raced as he waited for Corbin to speak. The metal shelf sat there humming. Corbin pressed some buttons on the panels beside the shelf. It slid out, revealing a growing embryo. Drake looked at it, not knowing what to say.

"Do you remember anything about Project Bethany?" Corbin asked.

"Very little," Drake responded, wondering if he should tell him about the dreams he had been having. It was Corbin; Drake knew deep down he could trust him. "It's weird, though; ever since I got the email, it's been appearing in my dreams. Some bizarre and trippy dreams." He searched Corbin's face for a response but did not find one. Drake could see a knowing look on Corbin's face; he knew more than he was telling.

"Marcus, I told you this is much closer to you than you know, remember?"

"Yes," Drake responded. "You never expanded upon that, so I forgot about it."

Corbin stroked his beard. "I realize now that we should have told you from the start, but we can't change that now," Corbin said, pressing the button on the panel to close the shelf. Corbin turned to look Drake in the eyes. "Project Bethany was made long before we were born. The goal was to create and make the most effective, competent, and strategically sound leader possible. They tried over and over again. Cloning wasn't the answer, so they knew it would have to be a natural birth."

Drake's head swirled as he put the pieces together, but he was still not sure. Corbin continued, "The predecessors of the IEC were tasked with completing this project. But there was no progress until they met Carmen."

Drake instinctively took a step back. The dream of his wife flashed in his head … "I AM BETHANY"…

Corbin reached out and steadied Drake. "What does any of this have to do with her?" Drake asked with desperation in his voice.

Corbin's eyes were soft as he looked at his best friend. "Bethany was Carmen's life work."

"She worked in systems and infrastructure," Drake responded.

"Yes, she did, but her main objective was this," Corbin said, pointing at the metal shelf. "Drake, I'm gonna tell you something you aren't gonna want to hear."

"Probably not," Drake whispered.

"When Carmen gave birth to Sadie, she got sick; she knew her time was running out." Carmen, being ill on the hospital bed, played in Drake's head; the thought hurt his heart. "She was taking a lot of medicines. But not the kind that would make her better," Corbin said as he took his hand off Drake's shoulder and started pacing. "She had been working on genome injections that exponentially increased brain development and rapidly accelerated the growth process from 18 years to just 5. And it worked," Corbin said with a smile. "There were numerous successful tests on the injections, with many subjects reaching full maturity. Zyrex is one of them," Corbin said with enthusiasm. Drake remained silent. "But the genius side of it is after 5 years, the accelerated growth just stopped and slowed way down."

Corbin's smile faded, and he looked away as he continued. "But it had a side effect, it killed the mother."

Drake's world felt like it would shatter at any moment. All he knew felt like it was falling around him. Drake leaned on the wall and slid down to the floor. Corbin kneeled beside him. Drake shook his head back and forth, not able to form words. "No," was all he could muster.

Corbin moved closer. "She was 1 month pregnant when the injection took her. We had to perform emergency surgery to save the child."

All Drake could do was look into the eyes of the man who let his wife die. "You knew," Drake squeaked out. "You knew, and you didn't say anything or do anything to stop it," Drake said, pushing Corbin away and standing up. Anger swelled in him. "You let her put this project before her own life."

Corbin stood and faced him. Drake hadn't felt this angry in a long time. He knew he needed to calm himself; this anger wasn't him. He breathed deeply.

"Marcus, I need you to know this was her choice; we gave her every opportunity to step away. But when the idea was presented, she never looked back; she knew the risks. Yet, she still gave her life for the greater good."

"Why couldn't it be someone else?" Drake choked out. "If it was successful on Zyrex, why not go with him?"

"Because my friend, no one has ever had the genius Carmen possessed, and no one has ever had the heart you possess. They reassured me over and over again that it had to be her and it had to be you. The only problem is that you are two separate people. Project Bethany is Carmen; Bethany is you, Marcus. Project Bethany is your son… The one who's gonna save the Drezmians. The one who's gonna save us all."

The world shifted around him. The lights seemed foggy, and his heart raced. The weight of what he had just heard pressed on his chest with a million tons of force. It couldn't be true; none of it could be. Drake blinked several times. Breathe, just breathe, he thought, attempting to bring himself back to reality. As he took a deep breath, Corbin came back into view. Drake saw that he was moving his mouth, but he heard no words escaping his mouth.

"What?" Drake asked, sounding almost half asleep.

"Are you okay?" Corbin asked.

Drake's thoughts refocused. He narrowed his eyes on Corbin. "You let this happen," Drake said. The pain was evident in his voice. Corbin stood, walking towards one of the empty shelves beside the one they had been standing at. The cryogenic shelf still froze the air around it.

"I did, buddy. I did it because I had a job to do. Carmen did as well." He pulled out one of the chairs from a desk and sat on it facing Drake. "I know you will need some time, and you might hate me, but at the end of the day, I had no grounds to stop it. It goes far above you and me."

Drake's mind twisted at the thought of hating him despite hearing the news he'd just received. This was his closest friend. The closest thing to a brother he'd ever have. Drake pulled himself up and started for the door. Corbin stood and tried to keep pace after him.

"Drake, wait!" Corbin exclaimed.

Drake turned around and got in his face. The only person who could ever do that and not suffer consequences. "I recommend you give me space, Huxley."

Drake only used his last name if he was super put off, and Corbin knew that. He stepped back. "Okay, okay, I'll give you space," Corbin responded.

Drake turned to leave and peered at the shelf again as he walked, the growing child flashing through his mind. Corbin called after him again. "Don't forget about our briefing."

Drake didn't want to think about anything like that at the moment, but he knew he'd soon have to put off any of these feelings and do his job. He would; he just needed some time.

"And one last thing," Corbin shouted almost out of earshot as Drake pressed the button to call the elevator. "I left you something in your room."

That was Corbin, always trying to lighten the mood, no matter the circumstances. Drake stepped into the elevator without saying anything. When the door closed, he immediately pressed the button for his floor. It rose momentarily before Drake punched the side of the elevator and screamed at the top of his lungs, leaving behind a dent and a small cut on his hand. He leaned his head on the metal walls. It felt cold against his skin as he began to cry. The emotional toll of the last few weeks poured out of him. Drake reached over and pressed the override button to stop the elevator. He slumped down to the floor and pulled his legs to his chest. He knew he'd have to pull it together soon, but he had to let this out.

All that he knew about Carmen felt like a lie. How could she never share this? How could Corbin never share this? His head hurt. He just wanted it to all go away at this moment. His mind flashed to all the times Carmen had deflected questions about work, all the times she had large projects that required overtime. Drake never questioned it. They worked in the same building, after all. But she loved him. So why would she ever keep this from him? More and more questions filled his mind. But the answers would have to wait.

The last thing Corbin said still rang in his mind.

"Bethany is your son..."

"Son," he thought. Drake couldn't wrap his head around this. That he'd be a dad again. So many questions raced in his mind. Would he raise the child? Was it even fair to put the pressure the IEC and the Drezmians wanted to on him? Was it okay to force this life on him? Drake felt sick. This wasn't right. None of it was. He sat there for a few moments with no answers. Drake couldn't fully grasp what any of this really meant.

"Father, help me see a way through this," Drake prayed. He knew he had to be strong and find a way to keep going. Drake stood to his feet, feeling resolve flood back into him. No matter what he felt. No matter how much this weighed on his soul, he had to be strong. For his crew, for Fiona and Jason. Drake had no idea what lay ahead for them. He didn't want to know. But he knew he would do everything he could to keep the ones he loved safe. Drake took a few minutes to wipe his tears and blood off his hand. He pushed the button for the elevator to resume its course. The elevator dinged, and he stepped into the bustling hallway. Crew members rushed back and forth. Drake smiled as he saw his people, his family. He walked and smiled at his crew. He stopped briefly talking with a few of them on his way back to his quarters. Drake reached his door. He resolved in his heart. He would be strong for his son. A final gift from Carmen. No matter the circumstances behind it, it was still a gift. He typed in the code for his door. As the keypad beeped, a bark could be heard from behind the door.

Drake puzzled his brow. He hadn't heard a noise like that in years. "What the heck," Drake said out loud as the door opened. Before Drake could move, a brown fur ball knocked him onto his back and licked his face. The busy hallway grew silent as the crew members looked at their admiral on the floor. Some tried to run over. Drake fought the creature momentarily before he realized. Drake grabbed the face of the dog, and it stopped for a brief moment.

"CODY!" Drake exclaimed as he hugged the dog tighter than he had ever hugged anything before.

CHAPTER TWENTY-THREE

The dog jumped and licked over Drake as he struggled back to his feet. He was laughing and couldn't believe his eyes. Drake saw all the crew members gawking at them.

"We are okay," he said with a chuckle as he and Cody walked back into his quarters. As the door opened, Drake was greeted by the gift Cody had left him. The dog had found and helped himself to his entire supply of toilet paper, much to Drake's disappointment. It was ripped up and scattered everywhere. He sighed as he looked down at his friend.

"What a way to welcome me, bud," he said, patting the panting dog behind the ears.

Drake spent the next bit picking up all the mess, and Cody stuck by his side the entire time, a little slower than he used to be. He was older now, and it showed. Cody peered up at him with foggy eyes. It reminded him of home, though, how Cody would religiously follow him around the house and yard. He only left his side when the girls would throw a ball or offer food. It made Drake smile, picturing the girls playing with Cody as he and his wife sat on their back porch. The gray sky above and brown grass below their bare feet. Not much green grass, if ever, was grown. The dying planet couldn't afford such luxuries. But it was what they had, and it was enough.

Drake had left Cody in Corbin's care when he left for the missions. It hurt letting him go. It felt like he was leaving behind his last family member in exchange for a new one. It was a somber day for many people as they left what remained of their families. Drake sent a picture of Cody to Thatcher and Jason. They both immediately responded, saying they were on their way.

Drake, Thatcher, and Jason all had lunch and just talked. Cody ran around the kitchen's center island, trying to grab any scraps that made their way onto the floor. They talked about the previous weeks and the weeks ahead. It felt like it was back home around the holidays, all the family together. The last few weeks had definitely brought them closer together, closer than he had been to anyone else on the ship. But he knew he had to tell them what he had just learned. He trusted them, and maybe they would have advice. But Thatcher... Drake thought to himself, how would she take his news?

Drake threw Project Bethany around in his head as they all spoke. They had moved to the living room and were all sitting around. Drake shared the old brown leather couch with Thatcher and Cody while Jason took the recliner. Drake leaned forward and spoke up.

"Do you guys remember that message I received a few weeks ago from Corbin?" Drake asked.

"Yeah, of course," Thatcher responded, and Jason nodded his head.

Drake rubbed his hands on his chin. "Corbin told me everything about Bethany," Drake said, pausing. They both sat in silence as Drake explained everything. He went through it all, from the experimentation to Carmen's involvement and his son. Drake tried his best to not look at them as he spoke. He tried to explain it as best he could, but his head was still foggy. When he finished, he looked up. Jason sat there with a completely blank expression.

"How deep does all this go?" Jason asked, still staring at the wall.

"I don't know. I don't even know what this means for me," Drake responded. He looked over at Thatcher. A single tear rolled down her cheek.

"You have a son," she said, wincing with disbelief in her voice. Drake had no idea how she felt at this moment. He didn't know how he would feel if the roles were reversed.

"I guess so," he replied with uncertainty in his voice.

"Congrats," she said, standing and starting for the door.

Drake stood and walked after her. "Fiona, wait up," Drake said, trying to stop her.

She stopped at the door and turned to face him. "Marcus, I don't know anything that's going on anymore. None of this lines up," she said, crying now. "I can't be what you are gonna need."

Drake reached up and wiped the tears now streaming down her face. "I don't need you to be anyone but yourself."

She closed her eyes as she pushed the button to open the door. "I can't do this right now; I'll see you at the briefing," she said as she walked out.

Drake sighed as he turned back to see Jason, a look of confusion all across his face. "What was that all about?" he asked.

Drake walked over and sat down in his previous seat on the couch. "Where do I start?" he asked himself as he began to explain the long story to Jason.

There were two distinct thuds as Drake and Jason walked towards the Seraph, right on schedule.

"Those must be the other two ships," Jason said.

Drake had never expected to see anybody from the other two missions again. The ship was electrified. The crew was excited about seeing long-time colleagues from the IEC again. They had all trained together for years before getting their assignments aboard the ships. Drake was excited to see Clovis and Bartus again. He had trained closest with them at the IEC, along with their second in command. Thatcher had trained closely with all of them. His heart ached at the thought of her. He knew she was hurting, but he also knew not a soul would know it at the briefing. She'd have her brave face on and her walls built up as usual.

Drake straightened his old Yankees hat on his head, trying to shake the thought of her out of his head. He had other things to worry about. The hat wasn't the most professional thing in the world, but Drake rarely, if ever, dressed professionally. He preferred joggers, a T-shirt, and his old ball cap. Then again, most on the ship did as well. "No need in the middle of space," he always said. They made their way past the airlock and into the docking hallway. The stark change from gray walls to black announced the transfer into the Seraph.

Zyrex was waiting on the other side of the docking hallway in his usual black armor. Drake's heart felt like it stopped when he saw him, remembering what he really was. "Still human," rang in his ears as he remembered what Corbin had told him. Drake choked back his emotions. Zyrex bowed when Drake got close. Drake decided he wouldn't let this affect him in the slightest. He held out his hand. Zyrex tilted his head slightly in confusion.

"You shake it," Drake said with laughter.

Zyrex stretched out his hand, and Drake shook it.

"Good to see you, Admiral, Jason," he said, nodding at them. Jason just raised his eyebrows at him in response.

"If you'll follow me, I'll take you to the amphitheater," Zyrex said in his soft, deep voice.

"Not the briefing room?" Drake asked.

"Not enough room," Zyrex responded.

"How many people?" Jason asked.

"A lot," Zyrex responded, looking forward. "All the officers from each ship, including all the transport vessels. So a lot."

Drake searched for any emotion in the man's voice but found none. He had no idea what to think about him even if he was human. He was a genetic miracle, and it freaked him out. They walked for a while in silence through the black hallways. It surprised Drake how bright the halls felt despite the lack of color. They arrived at a set of large sliding doors. Zyrex stepped up and pressed the scanner with his wrist, and the doors slid open silently. Drake and Jason walked into the massive room full of people, all walking around, talking, and finding their seats. Drake and Jason made their way towards the front. Jason stepped off into the crowd with the rest of the people. Drake saw countless others he knew; he stopped to greet a few and hugged some old friends. Drake eventually made his way to the front, where the higher-ups sat.

Drake looked up to see a curly-headed woman walking over. "Mrs. Clovis!" Drake exclaimed as he fast-walked over to her. Her long hair seemed longer than it had four years ago, which was a stretch.

"How've you been?" Drake asked.

She smiled sincerely at Drake. "Oh honey, I've been good," she responded. "The ships have been getting redone the same as yours."

Drake always viewed her as a mother figure the entire time he knew her. She held compassion for everyone. But when she flipped her switch, she was more commanding than even Drake could be at times. Bartus walked over. Drake reached out his hand. Bartus looked him in the eye and shook it. He held the handshake for a little too long.

"Hey there, Drake," Bartus said.

"Hey Bartus, good to see you. How have the last few years been treating you?" Drake asked him.

Bartus mumbled under his breath as he turned back to his seat. Drake looked over to Clovis; she just shrugged at him. At that moment, the lights dimmed as Corbin and Atlas walked onto the platform. The room grew silent as the men stood in the center. Atlas stepped forward and spoke with a booming voice.

"Thank you all for coming, and welcome aboard the Seraph. Let's get to work."

24

CHAPTER TWENTY-FOUR

Atlas's voice rang out through the amphitheater. "We would like to welcome all members of the IEC." There was applause from the crowd. Corbin looked over and met Drake's eyes. The two men nodded at each other. Drake still felt anger, but that was for another day.

"We know you have all been through a lot the last few weeks," Atlas continued. "Unfortunately, I cannot promise it will get any easier, and we appreciate the patience you have all had during this process. From all of us, we apologize for all the secrets. But it was required for the success of this mission."

Atlas stepped back, gesturing to the wall behind him. "Firstly, I'd like to update you about the changes made to the three vessels made for the missions."

The gigantic black wall behind the two men turned on and displayed the three IEC ships. The screen spanned the entirety of the wall behind them. The Andromeda popped up first. The ship filled up the screen with a more boxy look than the other two ships. It could fit twenty X-Calibers inside. Mostly designed as a humanitarian vessel, it had lots of room for people and families to live and be transported.

"The Andromeda," Atlas spoke. "The largest ship out of the three. Its main purpose will be military transport, the transport of small fightercraft and land vehicles, and mostly the transport for our troops to and from war zones."

Clovis straightened up, looking proud at her child.

"We have added our latest generation shield generators." A yellow shimmer appeared around the ship, the same one they saw the day they first saw the Seraph. Atlas continued, "Along with that, we made major changes to all the transport bays to be fitted with our current fighter ships and transport vehicles and ships. We've also added basic weaponry, but the main purpose of this ship is to stay out of the fire as much as possible."

The screen moved, and the Valiant zoomed in on the screen.

"The Valiant," Corbin said, stepping forward from behind Atlas. The sleek and slender body of the ship moved around the screen. Tiny in comparison to the other two ships. "This ship was designed for one purpose: to be fast and to be stealthy. We will explain why here later." Bartus moved in his seat, his concern playing all over his face.

"The same shielding system, albeit on a much smaller scale, was added." The same yellow shimmer appeared around the ship. "We've also added a cloaking system to make the ship almost completely invisible. Only possible on a ship of this size," Corbin said. "Allowing it to slip behind enemy lines when needed. Plenty of powerful point lasers were also added."

Atlas moved forward again. "The X-Caliber." Drake felt eyes on him from around the room. The sword-shaped ship moved onto the screen. The ship was long and deep but still small enough to be maneuverable. The aggressive design of the ship Corbin insisted on all made sense now.

"Our forward command ship," Atlas said. "Designed to go into battle and be our forward operating center along with the Seraph in the heat of battle. We have heavily upgraded the weapons aboard this vessel." The screen panned around, showing various turrets and laser arrays.

Atlas continued, "Contrary to the other vessels, this ship was designed for battle, and the crew selected it with that in mind." The same yellow shimmer appeared around the ship, showing the shielding. "All of the ships have been equipped with weapon dampers to prevent this from happening," Atlas said as he pointed to the video wall.

A video played, showing the X-Caliber firing upon the Seraph, the turrets, and missiles, causing the ship to go off course and flip its nose upward. The crowd laughed. Drake knew it was funny, but he had no other choice at that moment. But it did look pretty comical, seeing what it caused the ship to do. No weapons testing was ever done in space because it wasn't needed. Those systems will make sure that doesn't happen again.

"Lastly, we have installed QLP drives on all three ships; Quantum Lattice Pathways move space backward as we move forward, allowing us to move through space as we please. Allowing faster-than-light space travel."

Atlas looked over at Corbin, who spoke up. "At the conclusion of this briefing today, the new assignments for your crew members will be allocated, and we will roll through training protocols for all the new systems on your ships. Most of the controls will be the same, but the upgrades need to be tested, and we need your crews to have as much training as possible before the times ahead." Corbin turned and walked off the platform, leaving just Atlas in the middle. His gold uniform, somewhat like armor, shimmered in the lights.

"Thank you, Grand Admiral."

Drake tilted his head at this. He had never heard that term used before in the IEC, but it made sense that Corbin would be bestowed a position above him.

The screen once again shifted, displaying a bunch of charts and words that made no sense to Drake.

"The mission," Atlas boomed with seriousness in his voice. "Our mission is to get home in one piece. Tyradis, our home, sits in the middle of the Eclion system, far to the west of our galaxy."

The screen panned around, showing Tyradis. It had beautiful blue oceans and vast land masses. The size was incomprehensible when it sat next to Earth on the screen. No wonder they had advanced the way they did; they had basically unlimited resources, Drake thought.

The screen played videos of the planet's surface, a mosaic of towering mountain ranges, vast plains, deep valleys, and sprawling forests that stretch far beyond the horizons known to Earth. Its oceans are deep and wide. Gigantic cities sat atop this beautiful giant. It was like nothing they had ever seen before. The screen moved out, showing the planet's seven moons. Then it panned out again, showing the Eclion system with fifteen planets. Drake assumed they were inhabited by the Drezmians.

"Our home system holds fifteen planets," Atlas said. "Ten of which are inhabited," Atlas said as the screens moved.

The screen moved out again to show a video of a beautiful galaxy. The colors colliding and mixing together. It reminded Drake of the sunsets before the sky was always gray. The name Infixus Spiral played on top of the screen. As Atlas spoke, the screen zoomed in on a specific part of the galaxy, showing the Eclion system and its location.

Atlas cleared his throat as he continued. "The issue is how the Infixus and the Milky Way rotations have lined up." The screen panned out again. "The current position of this galaxy has us jumping into the complete opposite side of Infixus. Into the east side of the galaxy." Atlas paused as the screen zoomed into a system at the galaxy's edge. A bright mass with an empty void stood at the edge, distorting everything around it. A fading red star sat in the center. Atlas looked at the screen, obvious discomfort in his voice.

"The black hole makes any other jump point impossible. It will pull us out of jump space the second we get near it."

The Maw of Abaddon played above the video of the black hole. "It means a place of destruction, the heart of darkness. We are entering into Infixus through the Obsidian void, the home of the Voidreavers."

Whispers erupted all around the room. Atlas stood motionless like he had expected this reaction. Drake peered over at Thatcher. She was already looking at him. Drake saw the fear plastered on her face; she was trying to hide it, but he saw it as clear as day. He felt it as well. How could he not? Someone stood up and started shouting.

"Why should we put our lives on the line for your war?"

Drake searched for the source of the voice, and to no one's surprise, Helks was standing two rows back, face beet red, and a look of anger as he shouted at the golden man on the platform. A few others from the other ships joined in. They were losing control of the room. Drake understood their hearts and where they came from. But they had no choice; the last thing they needed was a mutiny. Drake rose to his feet.

"SILENCE!" he shouted, authority pouring from his voice.

The room once again fell silent.

"Show the man some respect. We're all scared, but that doesn't change anything," Drake said as he finished and sat down.

Atlas met Drake's eyes. "Thank you, Admiral," he said as he bowed. He continued, "I understand the fear you all must feel. If there was another way, we would take it. But this is the only option we have." The room kept silent as the screen faded and moved around again. "But we have a plan."

25

CHAPTER TWENTY-FIUE

The ten transport ships appeared on the screen, smooth ships that didn't seem to have any weapons. Drake didn't know how it was possible, but they were even bigger than the Andromeda.

"These are one of our top priorities," Atlas said. "Making a path for them to jump out of the system as fast as possible."

The screen panned out again, showing a dark planet. "You need to know the absolute mess we are going against here, and the reason we've never attempted to attack the Voidreaver homefront." The screen zoomed in on the planet.

"This is Vorterra, homeworld of the Voidreavers."

A video played, showing more details of the planet. Engulfed in storms, located at the edge of Abaddon. The gravitational forces at play have created an environment of extreme conditions and bizarre phenomena, making Vorterra a place of complete disparity. The planet's surface is riddled with vast, storm-swept deserts of dark sand, towering spires of rock that emit strange, harmonic frequencies, and oceans that boil during the day and freeze over at night due to the erratic climate caused by the black hole. In this chaos, the Voidreavers have built their citadels and research facilities designed to harness the unique energies and materials found only on Vorterra. These structures are feats of engineering, capable of withstanding the planet's gravitational distortions from the nearby black hole.

The Voidreavers study the anomalies caused by the black hole. The screen panned out again. Atlas turned from the screen.

"The Voidreavers have found ways to harness energy in ways we can't comprehend at the moment. Abaddon should have destroyed them, but they found ways to use it for advancement. I tell you this to let you know this species is unlike anything you've ever known."

The only other species they had ever known, Drake thought.

A piece of machinery appeared on the screen. "In fact, the QLP drives were reverse-engineered using the technology we recovered from a fallen Voidreaver craft. A lot of our advancement has come from them."

Atlas paused for a moment, collecting his thoughts. "I don't believe in degrading the enemy. That portrays weakness. And our enemy is not weak. But neither are we. We've been building, waiting, for the right time. And that time is now."

Atlas smiled. The giant wall moved again as the system as a whole came into view. At the northeast end of the system sat Abaddon. Four different planets could be seen spanning between the edge and the dying star. Atlas walked all the way to the front of the platform, getting close to the crew.

"Here's our plan," he said as the screen moved closer to the black hole's edge, showing a broken field of rock, ice, and debris. "Remnants of a planet torn apart by the black hole's tidal forces. When we jump, we will enter right behind the Shattered Remains. This will block us from any immediate fire from ships deployed in this region. The good news is that," the image moved to show the front of the sector, "the moment we jump in, the Zion fleet will have engaged the enemy near the planet of Ferrum. The Zion fleet is one of our main offensive fleets with over thirty various carriers, command ships, fighters, and medical vessels. One of the best in the Imperium."

It zoomed in on the planet, playing footage.

"The innermost planet, Ferrum, is a metallic world with a surface scarred by colossal valleys. These chasms result from intense gravitational forces, revealing rich veins of precious and rare metals. Automated Voidreaver mines dot the landscape, dark structures matching the color of their citadels on Vorterra."

"Once Zion is engaged, we will have ten minutes to push past the shattered field and into the territory of planet Graith. If it goes according to plan, it will draw a considerable mass of their fleet to the front of the system. We have to be as far into the system as possible before jumping. That allows us to be clear of most of Abaddon's pull. By the time we are clear of the debris field approaching the innermost planet, we will more than likely be heavily engaged by the enemy. The first planet we will pass is the gas giant Graith."

The screen showed the planet, sitting at the edge of habitability, the furthest planet in the Obsidian void, with rings composed of ice, rock, and debris pulled from interstellar space by the black hole's influence. Graith's atmosphere is a rich tapestry of colors, hiding within storms larger than planets. The screen zoomed out, showing the moons all spinning around the planet.

"Its many moons contain Voidreaver outposts and research labs that study the gravitational anomalies from the black hole's accretion disk. Without a doubt, we will face opposition around this planet," Atlas said with determination. "This is their religious center, where they study their deity, Abaddon. This is where the fight really begins. The Seraph and the X-Caliber will head this front; we will attempt to destroy as many vessels as possible to get the transport ships through. The Andromeda will not leave the front of the transports, acting like a shield while also dishing out as much firepower as possible. The Valiant, you will be heading up the rear, cloaked and picking off any ships that get too close."

Drake sat there baffled, hearing all of this. The way Atlas spoke. It all felt too simple. Too much was left on the table. There had to be more variables at play here. Drake wanted to chalk it up to the fact that the Drezmians had only ever known war. But it felt like Atlas spoke too freely about this. It was obvious people would die here, but Drake kept his mouth shut for the moment. He would have his time.

Atlas continued, "As we pass Graith, the Zion fleet will also be moving in, collapsing in on them. Our goal is to push through as fast as possible. We can't possibly take on the fleets stationed around these planets with our numbers. So, we will do our best to meet up with the Zion fleet as soon as possible."

"What if we can't?" A hand shot up from beside Drake. Thatcher sat there with her hand up.

"Excuse me?" Atlas asked, looking at Thatcher.

"What if we can't get past these ships? I imagine this being their base of operations, and we will be met with heavy opposition," she asked what they were all thinking, Drake thought.

Atlas showed composure as he responded. "Nothing in war is ever guaranteed. We would wait it out, but we don't have the luxury of time. I cannot lie to any of you. Some of us here might not make it. But this gives us our best chance of survival."

Thatcher slouched back in her seat, concern still all over her face. The screen turned back on, showing the Eclion system. It panned over to the edge of the system, showing a massive fleet of twisted and mangled-looking ships.

"The reason we are confident is this right here." It zoomed in on the fleet. "The Voidreaver fleet has been amassed outside of our system. A substantial portion of them. We have set a blockade preventing them from pushing through."

The screen once again zoomed even closer to the ships, showing the anatomy of the vessel. The dark metal ships had sleek, angular shapes with sharp edges and points, mimicking the jagged spires of Vorterra. The design was both functional, reducing drag and disturbances from cosmic storms, and intimidating, projecting strength and aggression. The ships emitted a distinctive energy signature reminiscent of the bioluminescent creatures of Vorterra. This glow was most visible along the edges of the hull. The color of the glow shifted depending on the ship's operational mode, from a deep, menacing red during combat to a subdued, eerie green while flying through space. It also acted as a shield for the vessel.

"This gives us a fighting chance," Atlas said, putting some optimism in his voice. The Obsidian void returned onto the screen. "The most significant opposition will come when we pass by Vorterra. But we have a plan for that as well."

The ten transport ships popped up again. "Only nine of these ships are actually occupied. The tenth is filled with a particle bomb that will put a big dent in their main fleet," Atlas said with a smile. The screen showed the transport ship moving towards the planet as the others flew by. It exploded and showed a bunch of ships getting blown up by the ship.

"Hopefully, this works as intended," Drake thought.

"This will allow us to move towards Thalassia, where we will meet with the Zion fleet." The screen showed the white planet. Gradual loss of light and heat caused Thalassia's once warm and vibrant oceans to cool and stagnate, eventually freezing over completely. The global ocean that covered most of the planet has transformed into a hardened shell of ice, beneath which lies the silent, preserved remains of Thalassia's aquatic civilizations and ecosystems. Once thick with water vapor, the atmosphere has thinned, leaving the surface exposed to the harsh and unforgiving space environment. The screen showed the Zion fleet and the IEC fleet converging together near the planet.

Atlas spoke up again. "The Zion fleet will move past us, holding the line as we jump out of the system. It will take a few moments to get those systems ready. But the star will help us as its gravitational pull will help us jump out of the system."

The red star came into view. Solis Obscura sat in the far west region of the system. The star cast a dim, crimson light across its few remaining planets. The star's light struggled against the gravitational pull of Abaddon, creating haunting shadows and elongated twilight zones on its planets. The planets never revolved around the star, locked in an eternal struggle between Obscura and Abaddon. The final screen played as Atlas spoke.

"We will then jump out of the system and head home. Should be simple enough," Atlas said with a smile.

26

CHAPTER TWENTY-SIX

T he room sat silently as everyone tried to take in what had been said. "Does anyone have any urgent questions before we break for systems testing?" Atlas asked. His calm demeanor was almost unsettling after what they had talked about.

No one spoke for a few moments. Drake stood from his seat. Someone had to, he thought. Atlas turned to him and bowed. "Admiral, what's your question?" he asked.

Drake stood tall and unmoving, trying his best to project confidence. "I believe I speak for the entirety of the IEC, but you must understand not a single one of us has ever fought in a battle, let alone an all-out conflict. My people aren't ready for this war."

Drake knew people were scared. And it was the truth. They weren't prepared for this. No matter the amount of upgrades shoved into the ship.

Atlas smiled a knowing smile. "Admiral, I speak for all of the Solraes Imperium when I say this plan has existed for thousands of years. You're an accumulation of all of it. You all are," he said as he gestured to the room. "Every test, every trial, everything you've been through has prepared you in one way or another."

This answer didn't settle anything at all. But Drake knew the decisions were already made. He would go into a real battle where death was a possibility. Then again, it wasn't that different from what he was born to do. Do whatever he could to protect the ones he loves.

Drake furrowed his brow. "I hope the Imperium is right about this, or a lot of innocent people are gonna die," he said as he stared Atlas directly in the eyes.

Atlas reached up and moved the white straight hair out of his eyes. "You have my word. We will do everything in our power to get everyone home safe."

Drake sat once again. Atlas walked back to the middle of the stage. "We jump in one week. One week to prepare and train. One last thing, my friends.

If we are to succeed, we must be one and united," Atlas said, looking strong and confident. "So, effective immediately, the IEC will be disbanded."

People looked around the room, trying to see if he was serious. "You will be reassigned based on rank and job role within the ships. It shall go as follows."

The screen lit up again, showing a list of colors and ranks next to them.

Gray: entry-level enlisted personnel or non-commissioned officers. Gray, being neutral, represents the possibility of anything.

Blue: for intermediate officers, representing them taking a step into more responsibility.

Tan: for experienced officers below the highest command. Drake looked at Thatcher. He assumed that would be her color.

Black: for the elite or special operations units directly under the Admiral or for a specialized rank that signifies the execution of the most critical and confidential missions. Aziel and Zyrex both wore this color. It made sense. They seemed like the type.

Red: for admirals commanding the entire military or significant portions thereof. Drake had always loved red, so this color didn't upset him one bit.

White: worn by the grand Admiral, symbolizes strategic brilliance. Corbin's color. And the highest rank you could achieve by merit alone.

The screen faded and then showed the last color.

Gold filled the screen. The highest ranking color. Reserved for the Commander of the Imperium, Emperor, and Empress, representing the pinnacle of authority.

The screen lit up, showing a portrait of a man with white hair down to his shoulders. The gold armor shimmered. The man's aged stoic face looked familiar to that of Atlas and Aziel. The same sharp jawline and pointed nose. The gray eyes are what showed through the most. Those eyes weren't naturally occurring on Earth. Maybe it was on Tyradis? Drake thought.

"This is our Emperor," Atlas boomed.

The tension was palpable in the room. Kiaus Vantari…the Ruler of all of the Solraes Imperium, of Tyradis, of all Drezmians. Atlas paused, taking a breath. "The Emperor… My father."

This realization didn't shock Drake, but it seemed to take everyone else in the room by surprise. He looked like him, the same face. And Atlas exuded royalty. Not in a prideful way. More like the power he held and possessed. He used it for the good of his people. The Emperor looked powerful, but the kindness in his eyes shone through.

The screen panned out, showing a beautiful woman sitting behind the man. Her long golden dress almost intertwined with her long white hair. Even for her age, her beauty was remarkable. Her face glowed as if kissed by the sun itself. The same gray eyes as the others. "The Empress of the Imperium. Aurelia Vantari, my mother," Atlas said, evident pride in his voice.

The screens faded again. "On behalf of the Vantari family, I'd like to say welcome to you all. You are our blood, as you know. Different upbringings, but still Drezmian all the same. You'll find your new wardrobe in your quarters before training today." He paused, looking at everyone in the room. Taking his time. "We all fight together. For this family. For the Solraes Imperium. The Empire of Light."

Atlas walked off the platform as the lights in the room came back on, and people began to talk and move around. Drake stood from his feet, trying to soak in the last 20 minutes. It was a lot. He tried to stuff it down and move forward. They would all have to. Looking around, Drake saw different emotions and reactions. Some people were smiling, some looking down at the ground. Others laughed, some cried. All of their lives were changed forever. Drake just hoped it was for the better.

Drake walked around, seeing more people he hadn't seen in years. While talking with some of his people, he tried his best to comfort everyone or calm the nerves of others. Clovis and Bartus walked up to Drake as he spoke with one of his department heads. Clovis had a sad look on her face. Bartus showed no emotion, as usual.

"This is all too much, baby," Clovis said. "This isn't what we signed up for," she said as a tear rolled down her cheek. "My one job was to keep those people alive. Now, we are shoving them directly into harm's way."

Drake pulled her in for a hug, trying his best to comfort her. "All we can do is train and do what's right at the moment," he said.

Clovis wiped the tears and nodded. "You are right, baby."

Bartus sighed and shook his head, looking at Drake intently. "I hope we all make it out of this."

Drake gave a slight grin. "We will, my friend," he said as he extended his hand to him again. Bartus shook it with more emotion than he usually did.

Drake took this as a small win. Over Bartus's shoulder, Drake spotted Thatcher speaking to the other Commanders. He knew she didn't like any of them. Especially Cyrus Seraven. He was Admiral Clovis's second in command. He had a thing for Thatcher since day one, and everyone knew it. Drake saw him chatting up a storm, leaning close to her and making a lot of gestures with his hand. Thatcher looked over and caught Drake's eye. She mouthed the words "HELP ME." Drake chuckled and pretended he didn't see anything. He knew he would pay for that later.

As Drake walked out of the room, he thought about everything. The plan, his son, Thatcher, Corbin, the Imperium, his crew. What did all this mean for all of them? Drake had been willing to risk his life for the ones he loved once before; he knew that wouldn't change for him. At the end of the day, he would lay his life down to save lives. Who would raise his son if he died? He thought as he passed the crew of the Seraph, tan, black, blue, and a lot of gray passed him by. The new uniforms would take some getting used to, but it wasn't a bad thing. Unity would be of utmost importance; this was a start.

Drake passed back into the halls of the X-Caliber, where he was greeted by familiar faces. He grinned at them as he passed. All of them, donning their new colors and uniforms. It looked good on them, he thought, equally worrying about having to actually wear a uniform that wasn't joggers. But he had no choice, he assumed. He had to lead by example.

Drake entered his room and was greeted by Cody. It seemed like it was the first time Drake had seen him all over again. The dog went wild and ran around the room with the utmost ferocity. After getting him to calm down and sitting with him for a minute, the dog fell right back asleep. Drake looked in his closet for the new uniform, but it wasn't there. He searched all around, and it wasn't in his quarters. His door opened as he was in his bedroom. Drake peered out of the room to see Corbin with a box with a red uniform sticking out.

"There it is," Drake said as he walked over.

"Yeah, sorry about that, buddy, I made them go back and add some things to it to make it more your style. Not as rigid as the others and some personal touches," Corbin said with a sincere smile.

"Thank you," Drake said as he pulled out the uniform. He hadn't actually touched the Drezmian clothing yet. It felt so different from anything he was used to. It felt like it weighed nothing. Even the metal pieces of the chest plate and shoulders were like the weight of a shirt. Drake laid it back into the box and looked at his friend.

"I hope you realize how crazy of a mess you've put all of us in," Drake said, letting some subdued emotions emerge.

"I know," Corbin said with his lips pursed.

"People are going to die," Drake continued.

"And I know that too," Corbin responded again. "Marcus, how about we start moving forward by not putting all the blame on me. I never asked for this, same as you. They chose me. Like they chose you, like they chose Thatcher, like they chose Carmen," Corbin spat back at him.

Her name felt like acid to Drake's ears. "Don't talk about her," Drake said, getting in his face.

Corbin looked at him, his expression blank. "I know you are afraid, Marcus," Corbin said as he stared at him. "You are gonna have to pull your heart out of things and start acting like a man."

Drake felt something snap inside him, and he shoved the man in front of him. "You think me having feelings about my best friend and dead wife lying to me for most of my life makes me less of a man?" Drake said as he stepped towards Corbin again. His shove had caught him off guard. Corbin shoved Drake as hard as possible and almost sent him flying back into the wall, but Drake caught himself.

Drake certainly wasn't as big as Corbin, but he was undoubtedly strong. Cody was barking at the two men. Corbin walked fast over towards Drake, rage seeping out of his face. Drake ran at him, catching him off guard and spearing him onto the island in the kitchen. Corbin yelled as he grabbed the neck of Drake's shirt, throwing him hard onto the ground. The wind left his lungs as he struggled to see straight. Corbin leaped towards Drake as he swept his leg under him, sending him flying onto the ground.

Drake sprang up, leaping onto the 250-pound man before he could get to him. Corbin was fast, though. A punch landed directly with Drake's left eye, making him see stars as he felt his neck snap back. But the adrenaline kept him focused. He returned the favor as he sent a punch directly into Corbin's nose.

Corbin held up his hands as blood streamed down from his nose. Drake stood to his feet and walked over to the kitchen, leaning on the granite and breathing in deeply. His face and hand throbbing. Corbin did the same, getting to his feet as blood got on his white uniform. He laughed as he put his head on the counter.

"Three to five," he said as he chuckled.

It took Drake a minute, but then he realized what he was talking about. This was their eighth physical altercation. Drake has won three times now. Drake laughed, grabbing a rag and running it under the water. He handed it to Corbin, and he wiped off his nose.

"You're catching up, my friend," Corbin said with a smile.

Drake grinned back at him. They had fought before. They had hurt each other pretty bad. But this was his best friend and always would be. He was hurt in his heart. And it would take time. But for the moment, they had worked it out in their own way.

Corbin cleaned up his face and got the bleeding to stop. "I'll see you on the bridge," Corbin said as he walked out of the room.

Drake walked into the bathroom. His eye was swollen and turning blue. This was gonna be fun to explain to Thatcher, he thought. Drake brought the box from the kitchen to the bedroom, and he put it on. It was solid red; the pants fit well with red metal plates on the shins and quads. The upper half is what was different from the other uniforms. On the left of the chest was his name and rank in black letters: ADMIRAL M. DRAKE. The other side had the crest for the Solraes Imperium: a star with a spear through it. His left arm had words printed on it. The IEC mission statement: FOR THE GREATER GOOD. The other arm had print on it as well: TILL THE ROAD RUNS OUT.

Drake smiled at this. It was what his pops always told him. The fact that Corbin remembered and had it put on his uniform made him feel bad for punching him in the face. But it would be okay. They had fought many times before today. The uniform did fit well. It felt like he wasn't wearing anything. But it felt sturdy, and Drake couldn't help but think he looked cool. The red cape almost touched the floor. It almost felt like it was too much, but he would try it out. It wasn't like traditional uniforms. He could definitely get used to it. The uniform had a helmet next to it. The same one all the other crew wore. What he had seen Aziel and Corbin wear when he first spoke to them. Drake reached over and grabbed the Old Yankees cap sitting next to it and put it on. They don't control me completely, Drake thought as he walked out of the room towards the bridge.

27

CHAPTER TWENTY-SEVEN

The doors hissed as they opened for the Admiral. His red robe flowed behind him as he stepped onto the bridge. "ATTENTION ON DECK." The crew bowed all around him. Drake looked up from under the brim of his hat. This scene reminded him of just a few weeks before when it was pandemonium. The contrast was stark but refreshing. It felt different to have them bow instead of salute. But that was the custom in the Imperium, so that's what they would do. Drake bowed back at them. "Let's get to work," he shouted.

The crew went back to their duties. The bridge had definitely changed in the last week. The one window at the front had been expanded; it almost spanned the entire bridge, giving a full view of the vast open space in front of them. Many of the monitors and systems they had in there previously had been ripped out and upgraded. Translucent panels replaced a lot of the control panels and monitors. It baffled Drake how they got this done in a week. The middle of the bridge now held the command station that once sat on the second level of the balcony. Drake looked up there and saw engineers in gray and blue uniforms on what used to be the command deck.

Lucian walked up to Drake, his blue uniform looking sleek and clean. "Hey boss, good to see you," he said with excitement in his voice.

"My friend, good to see you too," Drake said, still looking around the bridge. Lucian walked over toward the middle, where the new command station was. Crew members sat at stations in a circle around the two chairs in the middle.

"Where's RJ's seat?" Drake asked.

"Oh, he got reassigned to the Seraph. Not sure where," Lucian responded.

Drake frowned. "They didn't say we would be splitting crews," Drake said, sounding displeased.

"Just a few here and there," Lucian responded. Even though RJ never did a single productive thing, it still made Drake slightly sad. He was still family.

"Any other reassignments?" Drake asked.

"Yeah, they moved Helks over to the Seraph as well."

"What?" Drake exclaimed. "He's one of my commanding officers. Who will oversee his job?"

Corbin walked up behind Drake and put his hand on his shoulder. Drake turned to see Corbin. His nose looked swollen and bruised around the eyes. "It's not broken, by the way," Corbin said with a smile. "How's that eye doing?" he asked.

Drake lifted his hat, showing the bruised eye. "Not as messed up as that nose of yours," he said. Both men laughed.

"We thought it best for Helks to be on Seraph so we can have a close eye on him," Corbin said.

"That makes sense," Drake thought. Especially with him being prone to throwing fits.

"We are stationing Aziel and Zyrex on the X-Caliber. They will both be overseeing weapon functions and shield systems. They've already been working with Langston this past week to get him up to speed, along with the crew we've reassigned to that department."

"That's great," Drake said as he surveyed the crew members in black uniforms stationed by the windows. Their stations ran along the windows to give them a better view of what was going on outside the ship, providing a faster reaction time than the monitors might afford. "So that was the plan all along?" Drake asked him.

"All of this?" Corbin said, motioning to the newly redone bridge. "Yeah, mostly. I knew from the beginning this ship would be a battleship. That's why, at every turn, I insisted on this aggressive design and some weaponry. But I had to be as inconspicuous as possible not to make it obvious to anyone," Corbin said, smiling slightly.

"I think you did a good enough job," Drake said. "Hopefully, we designed it well enough for what it needs to do."

"I have no doubts," Drake said, patting Corbin on the shoulder. "I will be on Andromeda for testing, so I'll see you later," Corbin said as he turned to leave.

"Good luck," Drake shouted after him. Drake walked around the deck checking in with people. Most seemed super optimistic. Drake looked back as a woman wearing a shiny tan uniform walked in. Her slick back bun sat tight to her head. She exuded confidence as she walked in. She walked straight to the command center and started working on her console. Drake walked over. She looked up at him and smiled.

"Red looks good on you, Admiral," she said softly, meeting his eyes.

"You don't look too bad yourself, Thatch," he said, returning the smile.

"What happened to your face?" she asked him.

Drake tried his best to cover. "Corbin and I just had a small disagreement."

Thatcher laughed as she looked down at the console again. "Looks like it was pretty small," she said as she got silent. The silence felt heavy. Drake walked around and sat in his chair, looking over the new controls and options available to him. He'd have to get used to them in a very short amount of time.

"Hey, I want to apologize," Thatcher said, leaning over towards him.

"For what?" Drake asked.

"For getting upset about something you have no control over," she responded. "I know you are under substantial pressure right now. And the last thing you need is for your…" she stopped. He knew what she wanted to say, and it made him grin. He wanted that too. And it would come. Just not right then. She tried not to laugh as she continued. "The last thing you need is for me to let my emotions dictate my actions."

Drake looked at her with compassion. "Your emotions don't bother me. I'm not scared of them."

She smiled, looking back down. "Thanks," she said. "It's just been a long day."

"It has been," he responded. "Let's get through these drills, and you can have dinner with me tonight."

She smiled and nodded her head. The bridge doors opened, and three men walked in. Langston sporting his new black uniform. The other two men followed. Aziel with his helmet off and Zyrex with the red streaks across his helmet. They walked by, taking their seats in the outer circle of the command center. Langston nodded at Drake as he sat down. Jason walked in wearing a gray uniform.

"I never thought I'd see the day, my friend," Drake said, smiling at Jason. He didn't look bad at all, and Jason knew that.

"Oh, these things? Just something I threw together," he said with a dead serious face. He took his seat on the outside circle directly beside Drake. All the crew members had stopped and were looking to their leaders in the center.

Drake stood. "Welcome to our first day of testing. Let's try not to kill ourselves, alright?" Drake asked with a grin. The crew members smiled back. Thatcher grabbed the intercom.

"Crew of the X-Caliber, to battle stations. New systems testing in five minutes."

The alarms wailed as they sat in their seats. Atlas appeared on Drake's console screen.

"I'm going to walk you through some scenarios if that's okay with you," Atlas said.

"Copy that," Drake said as the screen filled with data and all the earpieces connected.

"Bridge command checking in," Thatcher said.

"Weapon systems checking in," Langston said.

"Engine systems checking in," Lucian said.

"Shield array systems checking in," Zyrex said.

"Comms and data systems checking in," Jason said.

Drake took a deep breath, letting the nerves roll off of him. "Admiral checking in," he said with confidence. "We are a go for launch."

There was a thud as the ship unlatched from the Seraph. The ship floated for a moment in silence. Then, there was a boom as the newly upgraded engines fired to life. The ship shuddered under the strain of the new engine.

"Stabilizers, engaging now," Aziel said over the comms. The ship steadied out as the new stabilizer systems kicked in.

"Alright, Admiral," Atlas said. "We need you guys to get used to your vessel's new speed and movement. Try some different maneuvers."

"Copy," Drake said as he cleared the screen. "Alright, Lucian, let's see what the engines can do," Drake said.

Lucian held up a thumbs up. "Roger that, boss."

Drake gripped the sides of his seat as the ship roared and surged forward. The stars bent beside them as they raced faster than that ship had ever gone. It felt like Drake was sucked deep into his seat. He strained against the force. The only people on the bridge not affected were Aziel and Zyrex.

Atlas appeared again. "Good, I see the engines work correctly."

Drake looked around at everyone, trying to stay calm. They weren't used to this yet.

"Don't worry, Admiral. It gets easier. Try some directional movement," Atlas said.

"Lucian, let's do some direction changes."

"Roger," Lucian shouted as the ship flew upwards. The g-force got more manageable as they flew more. The ship started dipping down as it turned. The back end flipped up, and the ship started flipping.

"Lucian, what's happening?" Drake screamed.

"I don't know, boss." The ship flipped twice before it was stabilized. It was now facing the rest of the ships.

Drake spoke up as everyone tried to catch their breath. "Okay, everyone. This is good. We learn by failure."

Atlas came back onto the screen. He chuckled. "That looked like a fun time, Admiral. But try not to make that a habit."

"Yeah, for sure," Drake responded. "Fly back here in one piece, and we will do some weapons testing."

"Copy that," Drake said as the ship flew back to join the others.

The Andromeda also flew around, testing its new engines in the distance. The rest of the ten transport vessels all sat around the Seraph. The ship had almost made its way back when a ship suddenly appeared in front of the bridge. Everyone on the bridge screamed as the Valiant uncloaked itself. Looking through into the other bridge, Bartus was actually laughing. The Valiant was the fastest thing they had ever seen before. It disappeared without a trace on any radar or sensor. The ship stopped in front of the others, waiting. The Andromeda made its way back over, and the Valiant stopped right over the top of the X-Caliber.

Atlas appeared again. "Alright, friends, to get you a little more used to the ships, we will put you through some live-fire training sessions," Atlas said. "These will make up most of the training. Today, the laser turrets will be set to 10 percent power, with no chance of injury. By the end of the week, we will have you at full power. With some twists and turns along the way."

Thatcher looked at Drake. "We are going to shoot at each other?" she asked with concern on her face.

Drake turned back to Atlas on the screen. "Are you sure? What if?"

Atlas cut off Drake. "Admiral, this is the only way," Atlas responded. The belly of the Seraph opened up as 20 small fighters flew out at breakneck speed.

"We start now," Atlas said as the screen turned black. The fighters immediately began firing upon the ship. White laser bolts flew past them, some slamming into the metal of the ship.

"Zyrex, initiate shielding systems," Drake yelled.

"On it," he said in his deep voice. The white lasers sent sparks off the metal siding of the ship. The yellow shielding collapsed around the ship, enveloping it in its protection.

"Langston, return fire. Set to ten percent power," Drake yelled as he prepared to engage them.

"Yes, sir," Langston yelled.

"Lucian, get us out of here." The ship lunged forward, speeding over the top of the Seraph. The other two ships split off, dealing with their problems.

"Five ships on us," Thatcher yelled over the chaos.

"Langston, where's my fire?" Drake yelled, standing up now.

"Right here," he said with a smile. The ship rumbled as the laser turret burst to life, sending white lasers at the pursuers. The ships were very agile, dodging the fire with ease.

"Have to narrow in that fire, Langston," Drake said, looking at the video feed behind the ship as the ships waved around the laser fire.

Langston was yelling in his comms to his men. "Switch weapons typing. Half lasers and give me some guided munition," Langston yelled. Some of the men in black switched over to guided laser missiles. The green beams went everywhere, locking onto the ships as they split off, avoiding the fire. Some ships flew past the bridge windows, trying to outrun the streaks of light. One of the green streaks caught up with a fighter and exploded in front of the ship. It was a vibrant green explosion. The fighter's yellow shimmer was gone. It turned and flew back in the direction of the Seraph.

"Four to go," Drake yelled as the remaining fighters streaked around the ship. They continued to lay fire into the X-Caliber, sending yellow sparks flying off the shielding. He knew it wouldn't do anything to the ship at this power, but it was still intimidating. Drake watched for a moment. There was no pattern to their flight. They just flew around and shot, trying to get a break in the shielding layers.

"Langston, try to get them all in front of the ship," Drake said. "We're gonna get them cornered."

"Yessir," Langston yelled as his men fired more guided laser missiles. The green streaks pushed them from behind the ship. A green explosion happened on the side of the ship, sending another fighter back to the Seraph. The three remaining fighters burst from behind the ship out in front of the X-Caliber. The white lasers, still firing at the fighters, getting slightly more accurate as some of the shots hit their mark.

"Fire now," Drake screamed. The frontal quantum laser spit out a white beam. Sparks flew off the beam as it hit the first ship, pushing past into the second ship. A green laser flew past the explosion and into the last ship. A green explosion sent flames out of the ships. The fighters onboard fire suppression kicked in. The fighters were completely disabled.

The bridge sat in silence as they waited. "Atlas, Atlas come in," Drake said into the comms.

"I'm here, Admiral," Atlas responded calmly.

"Are they okay?" Drake said, panicked.

Atlas laughed. "Yes, they are okay. A little angry you beat up their fighters so badly. But a few days in the bay will have them up and running again. I'm glad I started you on ten percent," Atlas said with a smile. "Good work. Congratulate your crew for me on a job well done."

"Thank you, Atlas," Drake responded.

Atlas bowed on the screen. "Come back to the Seraph and re-dock. But be warned, that was only the tip of what was to come." The screen went black. Two larger ships flew by and tethered to the three damaged fighters out in front of them, bringing them back to safety.

The bridge was buzzing with excitement as people high-fived and hugged each other. Drake knew this was only a piece in a giant puzzle. But it was a victory they desperately needed. He joined in on the celebration with his crew.

The leaders on the bridge stayed behind after they docked back with the Seraph for a debrief. Atlas and Corbin joined in on the big monitor.

"So, how do you think today went?" Atlas asked.

"As well as it could have," Drake said, pausing. "I thought we killed those pilots."

Corbin cleared his throat. "We made sure the power of the weapons wouldn't kill anyone. At least not for the first day," Corbin responded to him.

"That's good," Jason said sarcastically.

Atlas spoke again. "You fared better than the other two ships; despite Corbin being on the Andromeda, they suffered some hull damage by not getting the shields up fast enough," Atlas said, disheartened. "And the Valiant's cloaking systems got damaged in the firefight. But overall, all three of the ships defeated the fighters. You managed to do so without suffering any hull or system damage, so I congratulate you all." The leaders looked around at each other and smiled. "But I'm warning you," Atlas said, firmness in his voice. "This was only the beginning. And even the training we give this week won't be enough to prepare you for what's out there. But Admiral, I commend you," Atlas said with pride. "You made concise decisions today. That's what we will need out of you."

Drake bowed. Atlas and Corbin did the same. "See you tomorrow, my friends," Atlas said. The screen went black again.

Drake thanked his crew again and sent them to bed. Thatcher and Jason stayed behind with him. They sat around and talked for a while. Jason stood and turned to leave.

"I have to do some check-ins before I hit the hay, so I'll see you guys in the morning."

They both said their goodnights, and then it was the two of them sitting in the command center. Drake sighed, taking his ball cap off and scratching his head.

"So, about that dinner?" Drake said.

She smiled. "You remembered?" Thatcher asked.

"Of course I did," Drake responded. The bridge door opened, and Louris walked in, holding two plates from that night's dinner.

"Thank you, ma'am," Drake said as he hugged the older woman.

"Anything for you, Drake," she said, giving him a kind wink.

Thatcher laughed as Louris walked out. "Might have to watch out for her," Thatcher said with a big grin.

They ate their food and discussed life, what was to come, family, and the mission. Drake felt happy. Genuinely happy. After what felt like one of the most emotionally draining days of his life, Thatcher made him feel like everything would be okay. She made him feel right again.

28

CHAPTER TWENTY-EIGHT

The week seemed to drag by, and the days stretched into nights as they circulated the planet of Pluto. They had tested out the engines long-term on the final stretch to Pluto. What would take them six months took two days—stopping halfway to do more live fire drills and upping the firepower to twenty-five percent. The Andromeda had fixed its hull, and the Valiant's cloaking system had been repaired.

It was more drills, with more of the fighters on day twowo. Double the amount. Two ships out of the forty actually got destroyed. One is by the laser turrets of the Andromeda, and the other is by the frontal quantum laser on the X-Caliber. Thanks to the suits the pilots wore, they weren't seriously injured. Atlas made sure to reiterate that they signed up for these drills. They knew what they were getting into. It still made Drake uneasy. And that was only 25 percent. The last thing he wanted was to have his own men's blood on his hands. But that was the cost of war, they kept saying.

Day 4 had them fighting at fifty percent power. The booms of the laser turrets felt more solid as the laser bolts slammed into the sides of the ships. The shields hadn't been tested at total capacity yet; Drake figured that wouldn't be the case for much longer. He made sure to stay after each day and have a meal with Thatcher when everyone had left the bridge. It was comforting for both of them. The stress kept piling on, and the drills got harder. It would be all-day drills to simulate the long-windedness of actual battles. The transport ships would even join in sending fire from outside the battlefield. The bridge became a well-oiled machine. It was intense, but everyone knew their job and operated the ship well. Atlas was content with the progress up to that point. X-Caliber had managed to sustain only light hull damage throughout the week, the shields only being knocked out briefly when some laser missiles slammed into the side of the ship. They showed some weak points, but the shield generators were upgraded.

The fifth and sixth days were rough for everyone. All-day drills that tested the will of all the men aboard. The turrets glowed red as the continuous fire rained from the ship, laser missiles whistled by in every direction. Langston had gotten good. Being able to direct fire where it was needed, Drake made adjustments, and Thatcher called out positions. Jason helped by making adjustments to weapons, typing, and cycling overheated turrets to help the ship continually lay down fire. He wanted to contribute more than just IT, so Aziel trained him on how to do his job. The battlefield spanned all around Pluto. A hundred fighters in squads ebbed and flowed, absorbing fire, making ways for other ships to push through and drop payloads directly onto the ship. They were far more effective than on day one. The power of the weapons was set to seventy-five percent. Enough to kill if shields were not activated. Zyrex managed the shield systems well, directing power where it was needed. The Andromeda and Valiant worked together as they would in the mission. The X-Caliber was by itself. They would have the Seraph, but in these drills, they were alone. It allowed the crew to sharpen their skills as much as possible.

The X-Caliber had been allotted 25 fighters to be deployed. The pilots for the fighter craft had been given as much training as possible in the last few days. Drake hand-selected the men to fly these attack craft. He chose Aziel to lead them as he had the most experience out of anyone in the Imperium flying these craft. He had even helped design them. Sleek and fast. A light steel color. The ship had a decent amount of firepower and as much shielding as they could manage to stuff into a small package. The Signet of the X-Caliber, a shining gold sword, was printed on the side of the ships. A new addition that was also added to the X-Caliber itself. Something Drake liked very much. The signet was added to all the uniforms aboard the ship; it was something to bring them all together.

"Aziel, how are we doing out there?" Drake yelled into his comm over the sound of constant turret fire and missiles exploding.

"As well as we can," he said, the sound of his engine firing in the back. "We haven't lost any fighters yet."

"We need to figure out a way to get these fighters separated," Langston said as he looked over to Drake.

Drake looked at his monitors, trying to see any data or pattern he could break. He had realized that this week. As trained and skilled as these pilots were, they all had a pattern. The silver blurs flew all around as Drake focused his mind. He never had any formal training in being a battle tactician. But Drake's mind excelled in these situations, seeing things unfold on a map in his mind. Drake's eyes opened.

"Lucian, punch it," Drake said calmly.

"Roger that," Lucian said as the ship fired forward. The crew on the bridge handled it much better than they had the days before.

"Aziel," Drake said as they started moving away from the battlefield; four squadrons of fighters followed the ship, maintaining fire on the vessel.

"I'm here," Aziel responded as the X-Caliber moved, turning right.

"Get to the back of those squadrons," Drake yelled.

"Sir, that leaves you with no fighter coverage," Aziel pleaded.

"I understand that," Drake responded calmly. The fighters with the golden swords flew away from the vessel, heading towards the back of the fighters in pursuit. The ships were all flying around at incredible speeds.

"Lucian, when I say, move port side towards the fighters," Drake said.

"You got it, boss!" he yelled as he communicated to his crew.

Drake knew their weakness, and this would expose it. "Langston, let's hit them with something old school," Drake said with a smile.

"Copy that," Langston said excitedly. The familiar thud of the 50 cal turrets sounded as the fighters flew right into their path. At that moment, a wall of green escaped the X-Caliber as a wave of targeted lasers hurtled toward the fighters, moving in quickly. That was their weakness. They moved in too quickly, not giving them enough time to respond.

"Now," Drake yelled as the fighters got close enough for the 50 cal turrets to do some damage. Unlike the laser turrets, the physical munition was left un-dampered. So the ship rattled as the 50 cals roared to life. The steel-cased lead-cored pieces of Earth hurtled toward the squadrons. Aziel's fighters corralled them like cattle. The fighters tried to break off at the last second, laying as much laser fire into the ship's side as possible.

"Zyrex, how are those shields holding up?"

"They are holding," he responded, sounding slightly panicked. This didn't make Drake feel very confident. The bullets slammed into the shielding of the fighter craft, sending yellow sparks flying in every direction. The fighters that split off were met with a wave of green lasers. Drake leaned forward. He knew he had them trapped. Fighter after fighter's yellow shimmer disappeared as the turrets ripped through the shielding, and the missiles took care of any of the pilots trying to escape. At least half of the squadrons had been taken out in this one attack.

"We won," Drake thought in his mind. Drake reached for his console and called Atlas to come pick up his disabled fighters. "Incoming," Thatcher yelled as Drake saw three large vessels approaching.

Atlas appeared on his screen. "Not bad, Admiral," Atlas said with a smile. "I commend you for getting out of a tough situation." He paused, "but you must learn to deal with someone your size."

The Andromeda approached along with two other transport vessels. Clovis came over to the comms. "Hey Marcus baby, I'll try not to hurt your ship too badly," she said in a mocking tone.

Drake looked back at Atlas. "I can't fire at the transport ships. What if I blow up the ship?" he said in a panic. The three ships were moving in closer. Atlas spoke again.

"I know this is scary, Admiral. But emotions must be left out of it."

Drake disagreed. But again, he didn't have a choice. Drake closed the screen, cutting off Atlas. He turned to Lucian. "Get us out of here," Drake tried to say as calmly as possible. The crew on the bridge turned to look at Drake.

"What's going on?" someone asked on the bridge. Drake looked out at them.

"Trust in each other; you know your job, we work together, and we will succeed." The ship fired to life again as they shot back over the top of the three gigantic ships in front of them.

"How are shields?" Drake asked Zyrex, who was running around to the crew members in his row. He looked up and walked over. His black reflective helmet shone off the lights on the bridge. His deep voice resonated from behind the mask.

"The shields are holding, but they are very depleted; they can't take much more," Zyrex said. "They are having a hard time keeping up. If all these ships are firing on us, they might give in," he responded.

Drake rubbed his stubbly face as he processed this information. He had been letting his beard grow out this week after it had been clean-shaven. Looking out the windows, seeing the stars move around them as lasers shot past the ship, Drake looked over at Thatcher as she scanned her monitors and shouted info to her crew. She was made for this; her cool, calm composure made for an effective leader. Drake didn't feel calm; he felt like he was running out of options. He didn't like running into a corner. It hit him.

"If I'm in a corner, just go up," he thought. "Lucian, move the ship straight up and get behind them," Drake said to Lucian.

"Langston, full weapons package at them. Activate the laser cannons," Drake yelled.

"Copy that," they both responded as the ship rocketed upward. The laser cannons fired behind the X-Caliber at the pursuing ships. The transport ships were not as fast or agile as they were. But their shielding was heavily upgraded, making the weapons fire half as effective. But the laser cannons were huge weapons shooting huge energy bolts that slammed into the shielding, sending large sparks flying off the yellow shimmer.

The Andromeda proved to be faster than they expected, having twice the engine power and unloading every single weapon aboard the ship on them. The X-Caliber leveled out, trying to get behind the ships. The Andromeda moved up earlier and cut them off.

"Pull up," Lucian shouted. The ship strained as it leveled out right before hitting its sister ship. The transport ships had managed to get behind the ship. Drake looked at the radar. They were surrounded and keeping pace with them. The Andromeda below, one of the transports directly behind and the other keeping pace on the starboard side. All three ships sent heavy fire into the ship's shielding. Yellow sparks were flying off the shield all over the ship. The X-Caliber fired back as much as it could. The turrets glowing red hot, the missile bays firing as fast as possible, and the 50 cal guns shooting as fast as they could muster, the laser cannons rocked the ship as the fifteen placements fired constantly. It looked like a white and green glow from the ship as all the weapon systems fired off simultaneously.

Aziel and his squadron had been doing as much as they could, but they were ineffective against the hulking vessels. They were just trying to keep the smaller remaining fighters away from them. A big explosion sounded off to the port side, giant flames expelled from a giant hole in the side of one of the transport vessels. Drake's heart sank.

"Cease-fire," he shouted. The turrets turned off as Drake saw the ship lag behind.

"How did we break their shields?" Drake asked, sounding panicked.

Langston looked all over his monitors. "There must've been a lapse in the shielding with all the munitions."

"A lapse that caused the death of probably thousands," Drake said to himself.

Four ships from the Seraph raced over, helping put out the flames and looking for any survivors who got sucked out into space. The rain of fire from the other two ships did not cease. Drake tried desperately to get Atlas back online. He didn't pick up. Drake yelled and punched his console. Thatcher looked over at him, concerned. No one else heard him scream because of how loud the firefight was outside. He just shook his head, looking down as he leaned on the broken screen in front of him.

"Shielding at critical," Zyrex yelled.

Drake breathed in deep. He still had a mission, and he'd deal with Atlas later. "Can we revert power from anywhere else?" Drake asked as he walked down from the command center over towards Zyrex.

"No, sir, we are gonna lose shielding if we don't do anything."

Drake ran back over to Langston. "Give them everything we've got," Drake said.

Langston nodded his head as the ship's weaponry came back to life, returning fire. The ships circled each other, exchanging fire into their precious shielding. After a few minutes, the yellow shimmer unveiled itself from around the X-Caliber. The alarms wailed on the bridge, alerting them to what they already knew.

"Shielding compromised," Zyrex yelled. The full force of the laser turrets slammed into the ship as it ripped into the metal siding of the ship.

"We're exposed," Thatcher yelled.

A big explosion rattled the entirety of the ship and sent its back end flipping upright.

"Sir, we have no control over the ship," Lucian said, trying to regain control. Through the broken monitor, Drake could see the shield-compromised light, and down below it, engine failure flashed on and off. The laser fire slammed into the ship for a moment longer, ceasing as the ship spun and flipped aimlessly.

"We have no way to slow down or correct ourselves," Lucian said, sweaty and panicked. Drake looked out the window as the stars swirled around them. Drake sat down as the chaos ensued around him. How would they survive an actual battle with aliens who actually wanted them dead? They couldn't even defend themselves against three ships that just wanted to rattle them.

The ship stopped abruptly, throwing some people onto the ground and others straining to keep their balance. Drake's body flew out of his seat towards Thatcher. She had had the brains to buckle herself in. He slammed into the side of her seat. She grabbed his hand.

"Are you okay?" she asked, genuine concern in her voice.

"Yeah, I'm okay, Thatch," he said, getting to his feet.

"Sir, the rescue ships have tethered on," Lucian said as he inspected his panels.

Drake looked around, assessing his bridge. They looked defeated. This was a new low for them. They had been so successful the last few days. Now they were completely dead in space.

CHAPTER TWENTY-NINE

The fire alarms sounded, snapping Drake out of his gaze.

"The engines are entirely disabled," Jason said, running back over from the weapons front. A video feed appeared from the back of the ship, flames pouring from the main engine. A rumble could be heard as a ship flew by the front of the ship. The Seraph had raced over. The transport ships joined in at the back of the X-Caliber. The video feed showed the ships putting out the fire at the back of the ship. The fire alarm stopped, and Drake took a huge breath.

Drake went through each floor and made sure everyone was okay, especially back in the engine rooms. The damage was heavy and would take some time to repair. Luckily, none of the engine structure was damaged, just some of the mechanical parts. At least a week for repairs, they estimated. Good thing they had all the resources of the Imperium to hopefully speed that up. He was just glad no one on his crew was injured. People called into the bridge to see what was going on. Thatcher made a general announcement, letting everyone know the situation and asking them to report if further issues arose. Drake was internally furious as he waited for Atlas and Corbin on the bridge. They had told everyone else to clear out, leaving him alone on the bridge. The Seraph managed to dock back onto the ship with no issues. After ten hours of constant firefighting, Drake was happy to give his men some much-needed rest. His mind wandered back to the transport vessel. Were they all okay? The hole looked massive, and the explosion wasn't a small one. Those were humans on that ship. His people. He couldn't bear the thought that he had killed them. He wasn't looking forward to seeing the two of them. He was going to have to hold his tongue as best as possible. Drake walked the length of the bridge's windows over and over. He had removed his cap and the outer layer of his uniform shirt. A skin-tight red shirt clung to his skin. Outside the window, the transport with the hole in its side had ships flying all around the opening. They had already started repairs; Drake assumed they had done the same for the X-Caliber.

The doors on the bridge hissed as two men walked in. Atlas led as Corbin followed him in. Drake stared at the men as they walked over to where he was. Drake walked up to them, arms crossed. His anger showed on his face.

"First off, there were no injuries aboard your ship, so that's a win," Corbin said.

"What about the transport?" Drake asked, looking at Atlas.

Atlas didn't move his gaze from Drake's face. "Sixty-eight, sixty-eight casualties," Atlas said quietly.

Drake turned, looking back at the transport being worked on. He screamed, not caring what he looked like at that moment. He turned and walked past the two men to the command center, sat in his seat, and put his head on his lap. The two men followed and sat around Drake. They all sat in silence for a few moments. Atlas spoke up again.

"It might not help, but the deaths are not in your hands."

Drake didn't say anything.

"There was a faulty power cell in the shield generator. It only took half the fire that it should have taken," Atlas continued.

Drake looked up at Atlas, meeting his eyes. "It was my ship that fired the shots."

"Yes," Atlas responded. "You did because you were defending your ship."

Atlas kneeled down, getting close to Drake. It was weird, Drake thought; this man was royalty, his father an Emperor; why would he be kneeling down to my level? Atlas put his hand on Drake. "My friend, you must realize the cost of freedom."

"Innocent lives shouldn't be the payment," Drake responded to him.

Atlas smiled and leaned back. "You couldn't be more correct. But sometimes, the cost of freedom requires sacrifice. Sacrifice doesn't always make sense in the moment," Atlas continued, standing again. "It's painful, it hurts, it will rip your heart open. Their deaths don't make sense, but in the big picture, they have helped water the tree of freedom."

Atlas leaned on the smashed monitor. "After a time, with enough watering and nurturing, the tree will grow and be strong, yielding fruit. It won't be easily toppled over. Our tree has been growing for many years now," Atlas said, meeting Drake's eyes.

Drake sat back in his chair. As much as he didn't want to be here in this place, what Atlas said made sense. Atlas paused, looking out the window.

"The accumulation of blood spilled repeatedly is pushing us into a better future. One full of peace and growth. And you, Drake, are right where you need to be. We didn't make a mistake when choosing you." He turned back to Drake. "I was wrong earlier when I told you to leave emotion out of it." Atlas smiled. "Admiral, it is one of the things that makes you strong. Your heart is stronger than the willpower of any mind. Don't ever let that break."

Drake smiled slightly. Still struggling to accept what had transpired. He felt the deaths on his hands. But he was starting to understand.

Corbin walked forward. "Logistically speaking, this setback helped us take major steps forward. Seeing these weak points before we do the real thing is crucial, so it was imperative we push your crew and ship to its limits. And on the human side, they had to see that defeat was possible and that we aren't invincible. It will make them sharper," Corbin said.

Drake did agree, the means to get there was extreme. But he still agreed. Atlas bowed to Drake.

"Admiral, take the rest of the day off," Atlas said. "Repairs should only take a day or two. We will do one more test before we jump."

The thought of still having to jump into a real battlefield where they actually wanted to kill them still didn't set right. Now, only a few days away. "I'd meet with your crew tomorrow if I were you. I'll be there if you'd like," Atlas said to Drake respectfully.

Drake just nodded his head. "We will meet soon," Atlas said as he turned to leave, Corbin following close behind. Atlas stopped and looked back again. "Admiral, please remember we chose you for a reason." He turned to leave.

The doors hissed closed, leaving the Admiral sitting in his seat. The bridge was a mess. Broken monitors and a disabled ship. Drake leaned his head back into his seat. He let himself drift off, alone with his thoughts.

The cry of a baby echoed throughout the room. Drake got up from his bed and walked over to the crib.

Drake's eyes felt heavy as he walked through the room, searching for the crib. That's odd, he thought. The crib was always on Carmen's side. It wasn't there, though. Drake wandered throughout his house, looking for where his daughter's crying was coming from. He didn't know which one it was. It could be any of the three. They all seemed to cry the same. Drake chuckled as he dragged himself through the house. He felt like he had checked every single room, even outside. But the baby was still crying. Drake remembered they had a garage. It was the kids' playroom. Why didn't he think of that? He walked closer, and the crying got louder. He opened the door, and there was the crib, which was in the dead center of the room. That's really weird, Drake thought. Why would Carmen put the crib in the garage?

He walked closer. The baby was still hidden by the sides of the crib. He got closer and peered over, sleepily grabbing the child and soothing it. The baby immediately quit crying. "It's okay, Sadie," he said instinctively. That was his baby girl, after all. Drake looked down to kiss his daughter. He moved back the hood covering the child's face. When he did, the baby opened its eyes. Fierce gray irises shot right into Drake's soul.

He breathed heavily, feeling his body roll out of the chair he was sitting in. The dim lights of the bridge came back into focus. The cold floor shocked him awake. Drake dragged himself back into the seat he fell from. He looked around for what had made him wake up in the first place. Drake almost jumped out of his seat again when he turned to his left and saw Thatcher sitting beside him, trying her best to hold back a laugh.

"Fiona!" Drake exclaimed, seeing her.

"Hey, Admiral," she said in a laughing voice. "What are you doing up this early in the morning?" she asked him.

Drake tried to avoid the question. He didn't want to admit he had never left in the first place. "The better question is, what are you doing here?" he asked, trying to play it cool. Even though the massive crick in his neck was probably giving it away that he had slept in that chair all night.

"I could barely sleep. So I came to look at the stars and try to tire myself out that way," she said as she walked past him towards the front windows of the bridge. Drake just now noticed, but she had her hair down. He couldn't remember if he had ever seen her with her hair not in a tight bun behind her head. Even in social gatherings, when she could be more casual, she would always have her hair put up. But her hair was long, and it was gorgeous. The long blond hair hung around her face. As she turned back, looking at him.

"Care to join me?" she asked, motioning towards the windows.

Drake walked over. The soreness in his body was prevalent now. Sleeping in his command chair didn't do his body any favors. They sat on the floor, peering off into the vastness of the stars and galaxies. She smiled, looking out.

"I wonder which one is our new home," she asked, wrapping her arms around her legs.

"Maybe that one," Drake said, pointing at a bright red spot.

She smiled. "I think it'll be that one," she said, pointing at a bright blue star in the distance.

"Why that one?" Drake asked.

"I'd like to think everything is blue there," she said, still grinning as if imagining the blue waters of Tyradis.

Drake turned to look at Thatcher. "Why don't you ever let people see this side of you?"

"What side?" she asked, confused, still looking out the window.

"The side that allows yourself to feel. And I've never ever seen you with your hair down, Thatch. It's beautiful. People would love this side of you," Drake said sincerely.

She didn't speak for a moment. She took a deep breath. "Marcus, I had to be perceived as tough from a young age. Like I was untouchable to survive. I tried a few times when I was a teenager, but I got bullied like there was no tomorrow."

"What happened?" Drake asked.

She laughed. "It's silly thinking about it now. Back then, my hair was impossible to manage. I would try different hairstyles, but I had no idea what I was doing, and my father was way out of his depth in that area. Paying a professional stylist was out of the question, and there was no woman figure in my life to help me. So, school was pretty brutal in that regard. That was the one thing I could ever use to express myself," Thatcher said. "We didn't have money for makeup or nice clothes. But I could fix my hair. Safe to say, I was a hot mess in that regard," she said, laughing, looking at Drake. "But one day, I spent an hour in the morning trying to make myself look like all the other girls. I put on my mom's old shirt and skirt, showed up to school, and tried to be myself. I was in my art class that day." She smiled again. "I loved that class so much. Seeing all the beautiful colors truly made my heart happy. But all the girly girls were in that class. The ones from the wealthier families. They had all the nice things, and most of them had mothers. They were messing with me all class long. Over and over, calling me names and picking at my hair. Calling me ratty and dirty and a lot of other names I won't repeat again," she said, looking out at the stars, almost like they were comforting her. "It ended when a girl threw paint in my hair. So I let myself be what they thought of me, and I beat her up really bad. I had never fought before, and I didn't know how. I just kinda punched and kicked till I was dragged out of the classroom. She had a broken nose that would heal in a few months. But something snapped in my heart that day," she said with a frown.

Drake could see how hard this was for her to talk about. She didn't want to let anyone in. Her walls made her feel safe. She struggled to put her words together. "It wasn't the first time. But that was the final straw for me. When they finally let me back into school, I had my hair up in a bun, and I wore jeans and my dad's old denim jacket," she said as she looked over at Drake, a tear in her eyes. "That's the day I put my walls up."

Drake reached over and hugged her. He felt her melt into her arms. She cried silently, trying to hide it from him, but he felt it. He hugged her tighter as they sat there for a while. She leaned back, a big watermark on his shoulder. She looked up at him with obvious tears still in her eyes.

"I think you leaked water on your shoulder," she said, looking at him with a serious face.

"That was you, ma'am," he said, raising an eyebrow.

"I don't cry, Drake," she said, wiping her face and turning away.

He laughed and pointed at the spot on his red shirt. "This says otherwise."

She looked at him; "shut up," she said as she punched him in the arm.

This made Drake laugh harder. She started laughing with him. They just sat there for a while, feeling safe in each other's presence. She leaned onto Drake's shoulder, still gazing out the window.

"What were you doing here at three am?" she asked.

"Is it three in the morning?" Drake asked, surprised.

She nodded her head. "Yes, it is, and we left the bridge around eight pm." She looked concerned. "Have you been here the entire time?" she asked.

"Yeah," Drake responded.

"Why?" she asked him, looking around the bridge.

"I don't know; I was hoping I could find answers," Drake responded.

"To what?" she asked.

"Any of this, Thatch, just any of it. How we got to this point." He pointed down towards the ship. "I mean, like right here at this moment," Drake said as he felt the day's emotions flooding back into him. "Did I tell you how many we killed today?" he said, trying to hold back the tears.

Thatcher looked at him knowingly; "how many?" she asked softly.

"Sixty-eight lives. We took sixty-eight lives today, Fiona."

She looked down at the floor. "And I'm having a hard time accepting that we can just move on from that," Drake said in a pained voice.

"Marcus, you know it's not our fault," Thatcher said, placing her hand on Drake's knee, trying to comfort him. "Atlas filled the higher-ups in on what happened. It was an engineering failure. It would have happened out in the field if it hadn't happened here," Thatcher said.

Drake nodded, knowing she was correct. "I know, and it will probably save a lot more lives. A sacrifice that will water the tree of freedom," he said, breathing in and steeling himself. He allowed himself to have these emotions around her. He knew he had to be steel-hearted around his crew. To show their leader wasn't afraid. But deep down, he was. He didn't want to fail. To let all the people he loved down. He didn't want to let her down. Drake looked over at the woman with her head on his shoulder. He leaned his head back onto her shoulder. It didn't feel wrong anymore. He felt like he had truly let go. He knew how he felt about her. He would do whatever he could to keep her safe. No matter the cost.

They stayed there for an hour before Thatcher got up. "We should get some rest before tomorrow. Atlas will want to test the ship again when the repairs are done."

"Sounds good, Thatch. I'll see you tomorrow," Drake said as he followed her to the door.

"Thank you for being a safe place for me, Marcus," she said as they reached the door. She leaned in and hugged him. He hugged her back and smiled. She stepped back and looked him in his eyes. She leaned forward and kissed him on the cheek before walking out of the bridge towards her room. Drake stood there for a moment, smiling. It was a feeling that he really enjoyed. Drake walked back, grabbing the rest of his uniform before he walked out the door and headed towards his quarters.

He got back in and greeted Cody, who was fast asleep on the couch. Drake fed the dog and took a long shower, letting the day wash off of him. He got into bed, and Cody joined him. Drake closed his eyes to rest, knowing the days ahead would be some of the most challenging days of his life. But his mind was set, and his heart was resolute. He would rage against the void, the darkness that lay before them.

30

CHAPTER THIRTY

The leaders all sat around the table with Drake at the head. The flash drive of Manson's recovered memories was still inserted into the slot on the table. Manson's worried face played in his mind as he saluted Drake. The fear he must've felt. Drake grabbed it and put it in the pocket of his uniform, trying to get the memory to go away. Drake looked around at each of the people at the table. They were talking to each other quietly, waiting for Atlas. Thatcher sat next to Drake. Jason, who usually sat on the side of the room, now had a seat at the table. He had taken RJ's seat since he was now on the Seraph. Drake insisted that he was a part of the inner circle.

Thatcher looked like she always did. Her stone-faced expression complemented by her tight bun. Drake noticed there was a small braid slicked back into her bun. She had never done that before. It made Drake feel better seeing that. It was a small thing, but it seemed like she was opening up in her own way.

Rowan sat at the opposite end of the table, and it was apparent he tried to avoid Drake's eyes. He brushed it off as Rowan just being weird again. Tony sat beside him, taking his hat off. All the other leaders were there. Helk's seat was filled by Aziel. Zyrex stood in the corner with his arms crossed. Drake had offered his seat, but he only shook his head at him. He was still a mystery to him. He still hadn't even seen the man's face. One thing at a time, he told himself.

Jason leaned over, getting closer. "I need to show you something," he said in a whisper. Drake looked over at Jason's tablet that he had pulled out. A list of messages appeared on the tablet as Jason scrolled, looking for something. He stopped on a folder and opened it. More messages that have been archived. "Our database logs all messages sent on its network. For security purposes," he said, still whispering.

"Do we monitor conversations?" Drake said with a concerned face.

"We always have. Just never needed to look at them when it was just the crew of the X-Caliber, but now, with the mass amounts of people aboard all of these ships, we receive logs of just about all of them," Jason said.

"So, what do I need to see?" Drake asked.

Jason clicked on a specific section of messages and handed the tablet to him. Drake scrolled through about fifty messages. Every single one expressed hatred and distrust not only in the Imperium but with the disbanding of the IEC. The worst of the messages stated that Drake was a murderer for what the X-Caliber had done to the transport ship. Drake sat back in his chair.

"How widespread is it?" Drake asked him.

"It's not far yet, but it's spreading. That's why we need to talk to Atlas about it." Drake agreed with him, but it would have to be the right time. "We will," Drake responded. "Before we jump, we will talk to him about it."

Jason leaned back into his seat. "Your funeral," he said, as he closed the tabs on his tablet.

"Glad to see you are being an optimist today," Thatcher said from across the table.

Jason shot her a look, and she shot one right back at him.

"Let's simmer down there," Drake said. Still keeping his voice down. "Can we make it to tomorrow in one piece?" He asked them.

Jason smiled. "For sure, I'd rather be killed by the aliens anyway," he said with a blank expression.

"Gotta have some hope there, buddy," Drake said, patting him on the shoulder. He just raised his shoulders and leaned back into his chair. Drake looked back over at Thatcher with his eyebrow raised.

"Don't look at me," she said, leaning back in her chair as well.

Drake breathed, doing the same thing, leaning back in his chair.

It felt like forever before Atlas showed up. He eventually did. This time, he was out of his usual gold uniform. He was in a white shirt that hung low, and a golden chain hung from around his neck. A button was pinned to the collar of his shirt; it had the crest of the Solraes Imperium. He had on black pants with black boots. It was odd seeing him out of his gold attire. It always made him seem so mighty and untouchable; maybe that was the point. But underneath, he was still just a man like the rest of them. He had a tattoo on his right forearm in words that Drake couldn't read. It looked like some sort of ancient writing. Corbin walked in a few minutes later. The doors shut behind them as Atlas moved to the other end of the table opposite Drake. He looked over all the people in the room.

"First, I'd like to say thank you to everyone in this room for making it through this week. I know it was not without hardship," Atlas's face turned sad as he spoke. "The incident yesterday during one of our final training drills saw transport ship 3's main shield generator fail right as a laser cannon bolt slammed into its siding, ripping a hole in one of the lower crew quarters. Sixty-eight was the final number killed. And we shall give them their proper respect and burial when we can; you have my word," Drake nodded at him as he paused. "The good news is this."

The screen behind them showed an engine diagram of the X-Caliber engine bay. "No major engine components were damaged, and the hull integrity remained primarily intact. Repairs throughout the night and early into the morning saw us through, and we are about to wrap up repairs."

"That's impressive," Drake responded.

"I know," Atlas said, smiling. "Some of the best engineers are with us on this mission. It was all hands on deck. We have one final training before we jump tomorrow, and we will talk about it then. But please know that you were born for this time. Every single one of you," he said, smiling as he intentionally met everyone's gaze in the room. "I must explain one last thing before our final drill."

The screen faded as the words PROJECT BETHANY appeared on the screen. Drake sucked in hard, feeling his stomach drop. It felt like such a private thing. And to have it displayed on the screen like that didn't feel right to him.

"As you may all know, the two hundred thousand embryos were offloaded from this ship. The fertilization processes have begun on them, and we have distributed them among all the ships in hopes of preserving as many as possible in case ships go down," Officer Locust raised his hand. "So you are expecting ships to go down tomorrow?" He asked.

Atlas puzzled his face as he thought of the words to say. "Unfortunately, we will inevitably lose ships tomorrow. Along with that, the precious lives on board." The room grew silent as Atlas stopped talking for a moment.

Drake spoke up. "We will honor their sacrifices by doing whatever it takes to get as many people out of the system safely as possible," he said resolutely.

"Thank you, Admiral," Atlas said as he moved some of his hair out of his face. "But this right here." He said, pointing to the screen. "This will be left on your ship for you to safeguard and protect. Nothing is more critical to this mission than this."

"What is it?" Another officer asked.

"Not all answers give clarity," Atlas responded as the screen faded to black. "Whatever it takes to get this vessel to Tyradis in one piece should be your concern. Let me clarify a bit," he said, leaning on the edge of the table. "What you are bringing from Earth is very important to the Imperium. Trust me when I say that."

Most of the officers nodded.

"That's all for now," Atlas said; "please report to your stations and prepare our final drill and testing."

Everyone got up and started for the door. Drake stood with the rest of them, turning to leave. Atlas had turned and was talking to Aziel. Atlas looked over at Drake.

"Marcus, stay behind, please." Atlas said to him. Drake looked at Thatcher as he turned around and sat back in his seat. Everyone else cleared out of the room as Atlas spoke for a few more moments with Aziel before he also left to join the others on the bridge.

Atlas walked over and sat next to Drake in Thatcher's seat. When his brother had left, and it was just him and Drake, he let out a huge sigh. Leaning heavily back into the seat as his head tilted back. He looked over at Drake.

"I'm tired, my friend," He said with a slight grin on his face. "That engine failure set us back more than I'm comfortable to admit."

Drake frowned at this. "Why do we have to jump tomorrow, then?" Drake asked.

Atlas leaned forward again, tapping on the wooden table. "Because the Zion fleet will be there at a specific time tomorrow. We have to be there to set off the plan, or a lot of my men will die tomorrow."

"I think a lot of men are going to die tomorrow, no matter what," Drake said.

"That's probably true," Atlas responded, "but hopefully, we take even more Voidreavers with us," he said, looking at the grains in the wood. "Alot is going to change when we get back home, Marcus," Atlas said. "Tyradis is a beautiful place, and you will have a safe home where your son can grow over the next few years."

Drake had forgotten he would grow to 18 in only 5 short years. "Almost doesn't seem fair, you know? like we are taking away his childhood," Drake said to him.

Atlas just nodded slightly with a knowing look. "A sacrifice that will allow a trillion others the luxury of a safe childhood… You're a big-picture kinda guy, aren't you?" Drake said.

Atlas looked up at him. "In my position, you have to be. Inward focus will often lead to a lot of deaths. I know from experience," he said, frowning at him. "It doesn't mean you can't care or see what's right in front of you," Drake responded.

Atlas nodded, almost giving a smile. "I try my best, but it's hard to be in the present moment, the here and now when the entire Imperium military rests on my shoulders."

Drake felt sorry for him. He saw a man who just wanted to help his people and save lives. His entire life was a sacrifice for his people.

"How long have you been doing this?" Drake asked him.

"The military or my current position?" Atlas asked.

"Both," Drake responded.

Atlas leaned back. "Being the firstborn of the Emperor in the Imperium comes with a lot of weight. When I was twelve, I was enrolled in the military academy. I first served as a fighter pilot when I was sixteen. It consisted of non-stop deployments and missions for two years; my uncle was the Commander of the Imperium at that point, the highest position besides being the Emperor. The missions took me all over Infixus, different sectors and systems. Almost died on more than one occasion," Atlas said.

"When I was eighteen, we were on a deployment further into the east of Infixus than ever before. About ten systems away from the obsidian void. We were planning to liberate one of our research stations that had been taken over by a Voidreaver attack. We jumped into the system, but our intel was wrong, and they had an entire fleet there. We were outnumbered ten to one. It was a massacre; I should've died that day."

Atlas paused. "My uncle died on his capital ship. He was a good man; he helped raise me in the academy. Helped mold the man I am today."

"He sounds like a great guy," Drake said.

"He really was," Atlas said, breathing in deep. "When I returned to Tyradis, I was next in line for the position. I wasn't ready at all, and honestly, I was completely torn apart by my uncle's death. But I didn't have a choice. I had a duty to the Imperium. So I stepped up. I became the youngest Commander of the Imperium in our entire existence. And that's been my life for the past fifteen years; it's been rewarding and painful simultaneously," Atlas said solemnly. "I've learned over the years what the weight of responsibility can and will do. At the end of the day, I've realized that it's meant to crush you. In hopes that in that death of one's self, you find renewed life that is not reliant on one's own abilities but on the wisdom and strength that comes from it," Atlas said.

Drake rolled that thought around in his head. "It's meant to crush you," it felt counterproductive to his goals. But Drake knew what Atlas meant by it.

"But we have renewed hope now," Atlas continued. "This war has raged for far too long; it has to end at some point. I just hope I get to see the end of it," he said as he smiled at Drake.

"You will," Drake responded.

"Nothing in this life is guaranteed, you know that Marcus," Atlas said, as he looked at Drake knowingly. "Again, I'm sorry about your wife and the secrecy behind her mission. Her death was a loss to all of us."

"You knew her?" Drake asked, sitting up in his chair.

"Never in direct contact. But I kept a close eye on all of you throughout the years. She was a great woman with an even brighter mind," Atlas said.

"She really was," Drake said, looking down from his gaze.

"You know, my friend, I've been thinking a lot about legacy," Atlas said, changing the subject.

"What do you mean?" Drake asked.

"I mean, if I die tomorrow, what legacy will I be leaving behind?" Drake thought about this for himself in the moment as well. He hadn't ever really thought about it in this context before.

Atlas held up his right forearm, showing his tattoo. "This is writing in the ancient language of our people. An ancient version of English that you know today," Atlas said as he moved his arm around. "It translates to ONLY THE BOLD DARE DEFY THE VOID. It's very common amongst people in our military to get this tattoo after you've survived your first mission," Atlas said, admiring the tattoo. "It's a motto, I guess you could say. Something we have held onto all these years. It reminds us of our enemies but also of our strength and resolve to defy them."

He paused to think. "It unsettles me to think my legacy will be linked to this war. It's all my people have ever known. I believe legacy should be what you leave behind, what you have built. Not to be remembered as a great warrior or leader, but that I built something worth protecting."

Drake smiled at him. "You have," Drake said to him. "I see what you've built here, Atlas; these people revere you. Not as a brutal leader, but as a sound council and a trusted leader," Drake responded.

Atlas thought for a moment. "Thank you, Marcus. The greatest honor for our people is to be remembered as someone who fought for the light. If I die tomorrow, I guess that's all I can ask for. Someone who fought the darkness till his last breath."

Drake nodded at him. The thought of his newfound acquaintance, maybe even a friend, dying didn't sit right with him. But he was right. Nothing was guaranteed.

Drake looked off into the room as he spoke. "I've always believed in following the road laid before you until it runs out. Something my pops would always say."

Atlas grinned at this. "You and him were close?" Atlas asked.

"He's the reason I'm here," Drake replied. "He would tell me that all the time. Marcus, follow that road until it runs out. If it's God, it'll keep going. If it's not, it'll run out."

Drake laughed; "I guess it hasn't run out yet."

Atlas smiled at him again.

Drake continued, "I guess I just want to be remembered as someone who fought for something higher than myself. I don't need my name written about or celebrated; I just want to create real change and keep the people I love safe," Drake said, looking at Atlas.

"I believe you will," Atlas responded to him.

"Are you close to your father?" Drake asked him.

"Our whole family is very close," he responded to him. "The Vantaris always have been, at least in my lifetime. My mother has always made sure of it. We have a fairly large family; they all serve in various capacities in the Imperium. My father is busy, but he makes time when he can."

"That's good," Drake responded to him, Remembering his own grandfather. "I wish I got to see my pops, even one more time, to tell him thank you," Drake said, trying not to let emotion take over.

"I'm sure he is proud of the man you've become. And of the man you will become," Atlas said to him with kind eyes.

Drake nodded at him.

"Well, my friend, we have a big day today. I'll let you in on a little secret," Atlas said, standing up.

Drake stood with him.

"Oh, how exciting," Drake said jokingly.

"We aren't just doing live-fire drills today. We are jumping out of this galaxy to test out your jump drives. We are saying goodbye to the Milky Way galaxy."

CHAPTER THIRTY-ONE

Drake walked through the halls. It felt different this time. There was expectancy in the air. No one knew they would jump today, not into Infixus, but into another galaxy. But no one knew. No one except Drake. He had returned to his room, and a fresh uniform had been laid there with a note next to it. - I figured you could use a fresh set after the week you've had; ps helmet is required for jump travel - Aziel. Drake frowned. He didn't like the idea of his face being covered by the helmet. It looked cool, but Drake much preferred his old Yankees cap. He walked with the Yankees cap still on his head and the helmet in his left hand. He had made sure to secure Cody on his way out. He had never jumped before. No telling how bumpy it would get.

Even though Drake didn't know what lay ahead for them, he held himself with more confidence than he had previously. He had resolved to himself that he couldn't guarantee anything, so with that fact, he wouldn't let anything faze him. Thatcher had already announced earlier to let everyone know the final drill would begin soon and to either lock down or get to battle stations. An eerie quiet hung all over the ship, especially since yesterday. There was tension in the air. No one wanted to be in a room that would have its walls ripped off by a laser cannon.

As he reached the bridge level, he walked towards the door. He stopped in front before he pressed the button to walk in. He took a deep breath. He took off his Yankees cap and put on the red helmet. The visor slid down and sealed in place with a slight hiss. An electronic HUD appeared in front of Drake's eyes. A lot of info started appearing on the screen. Almost too much to keep track of. A diagram of the ship's status was on the bottom left. A small radar was in the top right with a bunch of other weapons and shielding info. This would help him have an edge. Even if he hated wearing it. The doors opened, and Drake walked onto the bridge with his crew, standing ready and at attention. They were prepared to get to work.

Drake stood in the center of the command station. Everyone around him had on their helmets as well. "I see all of you got the memo," he said, looking around to his crew. "Yesterday was hard. Very hard for all of us, this entire family. But it has only made us stronger," Drake said with confidence. The crew nodded around him. "If we are going to be successful, we must leave yesterday behind us and only look at what's right in front of us." Drake was talking to himself as well. Letting go of past things was hard for him to do. But he knew in order to grow, he had to let go. "The lives lost will be mourned. But we have a job to do. Let's prove to ourselves we belong here," Drake exclaimed. The crew yelled in agreement. "Battle stations," Thatcher yelled under her tan helmet.

He looked over at her. Drake couldn't see her eyes, but he could tell she was looking at him as well. "Alright, officers, check-in," Drake said as he pressed buttons and pulled up data on his repaired console sitting in front of him.

"Fighter squadron checking in," Aziel said from the launch bay.

"Radar and operations checking in," Thatcher said.

"Engines and Jump drive, checking in," Lucian said as the ship undocked from the Seraph.

"Weapon systems checking in," Langston said.

"Onboard systems checking in," Jason said, looking up at Drake.

"New and improved shield systems are checking in," Zyrex said.

"Admiral checking in," Drake said, all systems go.

Drake reached over and pressed launch as the repaired engines roared to life. They felt smoother and had more power behind them. "Feels like we got an upgrade," Drake said, looking over at Lucian.

He laughed, "seems like it, boss," he responded.

The ship flew around for a while, testing out the repaired engines. Drake watched the data feeds roll in on his monitor. Everything was running as intended. "Lucian, how hard are we running the engines?" Drake asked.

Lucian looked at his monitor's 60 percent boss. He responded. "Move it to 90," Drake said.

"Are you sure?" Lucian asked.

"I need to know that they are gonna work when we need them," Drake responded.

"Copy that, boss," he said as the ship moved faster. The engines roared as the ship propelled forward. "There we go," Drake shouted as the crew cheered. "Glad to see she can still move Admiral," Thatcher said.

Drake nodded at her. She couldn't see him smiling, but he was grinning underneath the helmet. A beep sounded in his earpiece. Drake looked around his HUD, seeing if there was a malfunction. Another beep sounded as Drake spotted where it came from. In the radar, a large red dot was behind them, moving very fast.

"Thatcher, you seeing this?" Drake asked.

"Yeah, I see it," she responded. Moving around her station, trying to get intel. Zyrex instinctively put the shields up. The yellow shimmer enveloped the ship. Atlas appeared on Drake's monitor.

"Hello Admiral, good to see your ship is in working order," he said, smiling. "All its functions are going to need to work properly for this."

"For what?" Drake asked him, confused.

The X-Caliber shook as laser fire slammed into the rear, sending sparks flying off the shields. "For us," Atlas said. "Do whatever you can to avoid us."

The monitor turned off, and Drake turned to Lucian. "Do whatever you gotta do to avoid the Seraph," he said.

"You got it, boss," Lucian said as he turned, screaming at his crew. The ship started trying to outmaneuver the Seraph. It was a game of cat and mouse as the less prepared X-Caliber tried its best to keep out of the fire of the Seraph. Atlas was skilled at directing his bridge almost flawlessly as the ship followed the X-Caliber, perfectly laying fire where it needed to go.

The X-Caliber pointed back at Pluto. "Lucian, get us there as fast as we can," Drake yelled. He nodded at Drake, focused on getting the ship out of the Seraph's incoming fire. Drake knew what was at stake. He had to keep the ship from getting damaged. They had to jump to another galaxy today. He couldn't afford any damage to any of the systems.

"Langston, get weapon systems ready," Drake yelled.

"Copy that," Langston shouted as he ran to the bridge's windows to get the weapon operators ready. Drake looked over at Thatcher. "We can outrun them; we just gotta get onto the back side of Pluto; we can meet them head-on for a fight."

"Are you sure?" Thatcher asked, they have at least double the weapons we do.

"The last thing Atlas expects us to do is to face them head on," Drake responded. "They have most power routed to engines and weapons. Their shields are weak," Drake said, looking at energy readout from the Seraph.

The X-Caliber approached Pluto. "Lucian, get engines back up to ninety percent. Can you handle the steering at those speeds?" Drake asked.

"I'm gonna try my best," Lucian responded. He increased the speed of the ship as it shot forward. The Seraph reacted late to the change in speed. Didn't see that coming, did you? Drake thought to himself. But he knew Atlas was intelligent. He would react swiftly. The Seraph fired forward, attempting to match the speed. Drake was thankful at this moment for the sleek design of the Xcaliber. Allowing it easy maneuverability. They started to lose visibility of the Seraph behind them on the horizon of Pluto. The red dot on the radar went away slowly. The bridge drew silent as the proximity alarms silenced.

"Start moving us around," Drake said, looking out the window. Lucian moved the ship's port side. They are gonna expect us to turn. Drake thought. "Move up and out of the gravity of Pluto." The ship lunged back upwards, away from cover.

"Turn it around," Drake yelled. The ship turned, facing Pluto.

"Langston, direct all weapons to the front side and get ready for them to crest over either the top or bottom." They sat there waiting for what felt like forever. Drake tried his best to slow his breathing. Was this actually working? He thought.

A beep sound in Drake's comms. "North over Pluto," Thatcher said as Drake looked up from his monitors. The Seraph crested over Pluto. Drake didn't have to look at the readout. He could see every single weapon was pointed right at them. "FIRE NOW," Drake yelled.

It might have even been beautiful if there wasn't enough energy and firepower to wipe out an entire army back on Earth. It reminded Drake of the fireworks they would light off every freedom day, adding more smoke to the already gross and polluted air. But at least the colors were beautiful. It was a time for people to get together and celebrate. His girls loved Freedom Day. They didn't know what it represented. Most of them didn't. It had been in place for what some people estimated a thousand years. Nonetheless, people enjoyed the day. The massive horde of laser turrets, cannons, and laser beams with streaks of green missiles headed right toward the Seraph was beautiful and scary at the same time. The Seraph didn't see it coming when the full ship crested over the horizon. The entire payload of weaponry slammed into their shielding. Yellow sparks flew out almost as brightly as the lasers. The Seraph immediately returned fire frontwards at the X-Caliber. It felt like two titans duking it out as each dealt more and more shots at each other. The shielding of the X-Caliber was spewing yellow sparks in every direction as it absorbed the incoming fire. Drake just hoped their shields would last longer.

"Fire the frontal quantum laser," Drake yelled over the sound of the vibrating ship.

Langston looked back at Drake. "Sir, if their shield gives, we could destroy their ship."

Drake knew he was right. But from the readout, their shields had just enough left. "Do it," he said. Authority poured out of his voice.

Without question, the quantum laser shot out in a beam and slammed into the Seraph. An explosion of light made Drake's heart sink. Had he overestimated their shields' strength? The light dissipated along with the yellow shimmer around the Seraph. There was no damage to the front of their ship.

"Ceasefire," Langston yelled. The Seraph ceased its fire as well. The crew erupted into a cheer. Drake looked over at Thatcher, laughing. She hugged him. He hugged her back. Atlas came over the big screen on the bridge.

"Well done, Admiral," he said with a grin. "That shot took some guts. And nice call using Pluto to get out of our eyesight."

Drake removed his helmet with a hiss. His hair was wet with sweat. He smiled at Atlas. "Just glad to see you in one piece, my friend," Drake said, bowing towards him.

Atlas bowed back. "And to the rest of you, I wanna say a fantastic job this week. You all adapted and learned well. We can only hope it translates to the battlefield. We will talk soon."

Atlas sat back as the screen faded. The crew cheered again. Drake looked around at them, feeling proud. He looked at Thatcher; she had taken her helmet off, and her face also glowed with sweat.

"We might have a chance," Drake said, smiling.

She smiled back and hugged him again. The crew all walked around and talked on the bridge for a while. One by one, the other ships started joining them. All the transport ships, the Valiant, the Andromeda, and lastly the Seraph. After a while, Atlas came onto the screen again, addressing the entire fleet. The whole crew stopped to listen.

"Hello to all of you. If you have yet to see me, my name is Atlas Vantari. Son of the Emperor and commander of the Imperium. Not everyone knew who he was on the transport ships. None of this had been explained to them yet. They must be so scared and confused," Drake thought.

"I know answers have been lacking here lately. And I'm here to put all your minds at ease and warn you simultaneously. Firstly, we have your best interest at heart. And all the details will be explained once we get to our destination." Drake could only imagine how the people were reacting on the transport ships. "The other side of this coin, being the road home, is a bumpy one," Atlas said, his face turning serious.

Drake saw the compassion this man held for everyone in his care. "We will do everything in our power to get you home safely." Atlas paused for a moment, pressing some buttons. "Ok, commanding crew, only you can hear me now," he said, turning back to the monitor.

"In order for us to have a viable jump point into Infixus tomorrow afternoon, we need to change our position. We are jumping to another galaxy." The crew looked around at each other.

"We will be jumping into the galaxy you know as the Black Eye Galaxy. Known for its unusual black band in front of its brighter inner bands. It is 17 million light-years away, so our jump today will take an estimated 1 hour and 23 minutes." How they achieved this level of speed was way beyond Drake's comprehension.

"We have already uploaded the coordinates into your jump drives. The transport ships will jump first, followed by the Andromeda and the Valiant. The Xcaliber will jump right before the Seraph does. We will jump behind everyone in case of any engine failures. We can jump out of space with you to hopefully repair the engine."

None of it felt real. Were they really about to do this? Was all that went through Drake's mind. "I know this is all a lot right now. But this is what must be done. We jump in twenty minutes." Atlas said, looking down with sadness. "It's time to say goodbye to your home, the galaxy that offered you so much."

Atlas looked up and slightly grinned. "Even though it's a hard goodbye filled with fear of the unknown. We look forward to what comes next."

He paused one last time. "I'll see you guys in the Black Eye."

The screen turned off. Everyone just looked at the screen. Some looked at Drake. "Be brave," was all he could muster in the moment. Azeil walked up to him.

"Hey, don't worry about the jump. The first time is always so scary. But your crew will do just fine," he said to Drake.

Drake smiled at him. "Thank you," he said, meeting his eyes and just for being here with us. "I actually volunteered," Aziel said. "I wanted to be on this ship."

He said, looking around. "Something about it just called to me."

"I'm glad you listened," Drake said, patting him on the shoulder. "I'll assist Lucian with the jump procedures since it's his first time," Aziel said, looking at all the complicated equipment installed for the jump drives.

"I'm sure he would appreciate that," Drake said, chuckling. "I wouldn't be any help."

Aziel just smiled at him. "More help than you know, Admiral."

Aziel bowed and walked off towards Lucian. Jason had walked over and was talking to Thatcher. Drake walked up to join them. He sat in his chair, swiveling towards the two.

"How do we feel?" He asked them.

"I'm glad we didn't die," Jason said with a stone face.

Drake just raised his eyebrows. "Me too, buddy," he said, laughing.

Thatcher just smiled. "I can't believe we are really leaving. Everything humanity has ever known. We are just leaving it behind," she said, staring out the front windows.

"And you think I'm the downer," Jason said, leaning his head back onto the console as he sat on the floor.

"I'm being serious, Jason," she said, getting ticked off. "Everything we have ever built or dreamed is back on Earth."

Drake looked at her. "We are carrying it with us now," he said.

She smiled and nodded at him. Aziel walked up to them.

"Sorry to interrupt, but we will jump in five minutes."

CHAPTER THIRTY-TWO

The crew watched as the first transport ship jumped into thin air. Almost like it just vanished. But as Aziel had explained in a concise rundown, jumping into a Quantum Lattice Pathway was basically, in layman's terms, bending the space towards you at an unregistrable speed while the jump drive propels you through at an insanely high speed. Allowing you to move through space like it was a Sunday drive to grandma's house. The space directly in front of the ship almost bent into the ship as it disappeared. All the vessels disappeared in succession, one after another. The Valiant disappeared. Corbin got on comms before the Andromeda jumped. "Marcus buddy, have a good trip; see you in the next galaxy." Drake laughed and wished his friend a good trip. Atlas spoke into Drake's earpiece.

"Are you ready?" he asked.

"As I'll ever be," Drake responded, looking out over the bridge as his crew moved around. "Coordinates set," Lucian said, evident nerves in his voice. Aziel held his thumb up towards Drake, giving him the green light.

"See you on the other side," Drake said to Atlas as he pressed the green jump button on his console.

In the blink of an eye, the space in front of the ship bent backward as the X-Caliber disappeared from the Milky Way galaxy. Over 17 million lightyears away from a distant galaxy. This was an impossibility on Earth, and now that Drake was seeing it with his own eyes, he felt a tear run down his cheek. Everyone had the same reaction. It was beautiful. As the stars bent inwards, the ship rocketed into what seemed to be oblivion. At first, the feeling was incomprehensible. Like a million tons of pressure immediately slammed into you. But it very quickly went away. The ship groaned as it settled into the new stress it was placed under. Space compressing into the metal hull of the ship. Drake sat on the edge of the seat, his heart racing. He was halfway expecting the ship to rip apart at any moment.

Aziel walked up to him as the stars in front of them almost seemed to crash into the windows. "Beautiful, isn't it?" he asked Drake as he leaned on the console next to him. "I know it's kinda freaky the first time. Traveling faster than the speed of light can cause you to question every nut and bolt on this thing," he said, patting the console he was leaning on.

Drake smiled at him. "It's beautiful. The fact that we are literally going to another galaxy right now is mind-blowing to me," Drake said.

"It was my first time out of the galaxy, as well," Aziel said. "Atlas has been out many times. Visiting other galaxies in hopes of finding something, anything that could help us," Aziel said.

"Have you ever found any other civilizations?" Drake asked him.

Aziel shook his head; "not since before your ancestors were placed on Earth."

"So, there are other beings out there?" Drake asked him, pressing further.

"Supposedly, there were. They had met in a faraway galaxy. There are legends of them told down from one generation to the next. But we haven't ever seen them or heard from them," Aziel shrugged, so who actually knows.

Drake resigned himself to that answer for now. He had enough on his mind.

A crowd had formed at the windows as the crew stood in awe of the crazy spinning colors and lights in the space in front of them. Aziel walked back over to Lucian to talk about their flight path. Drake sat back in his seat. Resting for a while, the crew milled around the bridge. They had opened the bridge doors, allowing the rest of the crew to come in and see the view from the front. People came in and out for a while.

Drake's monitor lit up in front of him. Atlas appeared on the screen. "Marcus, my friend, it's good to see you. How are the crew and the ship holding up?" Atlas asked.

Drake smiled, "The crew's holding up just fine, and the ship has been handling the trip well. No alarms, so I assume that's a good thing," Drake said.

"That's wonderful to hear my friend," Atlas replied. "We are about 200 thousand light years behind you. In retrospect, that means we are about 1 minute behind you. We are about an hour into the trip and will be going through our jump-out procedures shortly. Aziel will help you through that process, of course."

"Sounds good," Drake said, bowing to Atlas. He bowed back at him.

"You are going to love your new home, Admiral. All your people are," Atlas said.

"I really hope so," Drake said, smiling softly. "I'll see you soon, Marcus," Atlas said. The screen went black.

The 20 minutes flew by as the rest of the crew returned to their stations, and the bridge doors closed. "Please prepare for jump-out procedures," Thatcher said over the intercom. Everyone sat in their seats, preparing to jump into the Black Eye.

"Here we go," Drake said. "We are approaching the galaxy now."

Lucian and Aziel were working on the consoles as the bending space in front of them started straightening out, and the stars quit stretching out. All at once, it felt as though the ship stopped moving. The space in front of them seemed to hold no light. The transport ships and two other ships sat in front of them. The pitch blackness felt ominous compared to the beautiful stars they had experienced for the last few years.

A few moments later, the Seraph appeared beside the X-Caliber; "check in X-Caliber," some random voice said over comms.

"X-Caliber checking in," Thatcher said.

"Copy that," the random voice said.

Atlas appeared on the screen again. "Everyone, I wanna welcome you to the Black Eye galaxy. We are currently sitting in the black-eye portion of the galaxy. I encourage you all to take a break for the rest of the day. Tomorrow will be one of the most challenging days of our lives. But I believe in all of you. Leaders, we will have one last meeting tonight aboard the Seraph," Atlas said. The screen turned off.

Drake stood looking at his crew. "Have a good night's rest; you've all earned it. We will dock with the Seraph; you can take the rest of the night off. See you all in the morning," Drake said as he turned to leave the bridge.

Walking out and heading down the hallway. Drake needed some space. The feeling of being here finally set in, and a knot formed in his stomach. They could really die tomorrow. His whole crew, his whole family. It felt like their lives were in his hands and his decision-making. Drake had no idea what to expect. Live fire drills could only teach so much. Moving into the unknown weighed heavy on his mind. He couldn't tell what frightened him more. The idea of death, or the idea of letting the people he loves die.

He made it back to his room. To his surprise, Cody was asleep on the couch. He expected him to be losing his mind. But he was as calm as could be. He wished he could have that same relaxed feeling right now. He walked around his room. He took off the uniform and put on his usual joggers and shirt. Cody came over and laid in his lap as Drake scrolled through his tablet. Looking up information on battle tactics and what makes a good battleship commander or war general. There hadn't been wars in a long time back on Earth. Everyone focused on surviving until the next day, so the information was limited. But he found some things here and there. Things mostly talked about World War 4. That was the last war to have ever been fought on Earth. That had been over 200 years prior. Drake couldn't believe the planet had even survived 1 world war, let alone 4. Overall, nothing stood out to him, though. It was a completely different kind of war than humanity had ever faced. Humans had been nasty enough towards each other; he only imagined what aliens would do. Drake sat back and sighed, looking at the wall. His family portrait hung there. His wife, his daughters, Cody. All of them were smiling. He would fight for a better future for them. Drake allowed himself to take a nap. He knew he would need it.

CHAPTER THIRTY-THREE

Drake opened his eyes to a knocking at his door. Cody was looking over there as well. "Come in," Drake yelled. The door slid open as Corbin walked into the room. Cody jumped up and ran over, his tail wagging like crazy. Corbin had cared for him for four years so he was family to Cody. Corbin greeted the happy dog as he walked into the living room, sitting on the recliner. The two men sat in silence for a few moments.

Corbin cleared his throat. "Who would've thought we'd end up here, huh?" He said, smiling at Drake.

Drake smiled, nodding his head at him. "Pretty unbelievable," Drake responded to him. "Those two kids throwing a baseball in the front yard wouldn't ever believe it if we told them," Drake said.

"I don't think they would have believed us if we told them they would leave Rustin, let alone the galaxy," Corbin said, laughing.

"I wonder what my pops would think about all of this," Drake said, looking down at Cody.

"He would be proud of you," Corbin responded to him. "He always was of everything you did."

Drake nodded in agreement. "I just wish I would've known that was the last day I would ever see him," Drake said.

Corbin frowned at Drake. "Me too buddy, your pops was like a father to me for all those years."

"He would be proud of you too," Drake said back to Corbin.

Corbin met Drake's eyes. "I hope so," he said with more sadness than comfort.

They sat in silence again after this. Both men, sitting with their thoughts. No matter what, Corbin always had a way of making Drake feel better. Even if the conversation wasn't positive. His presence and friendship made Drake feel better.

"What about my son?" Drake asked.

Corbin's eyes shot up, surprised. "What about your son?" Corbin asked him.

"I don't want him on this ship when we jump tomorrow," Drake said, his serious demeanor showing. "If this ship goes down, I don't want him in danger." He paused for a moment. "I want him on your ship tomorrow," Drake said. "The X-Caliber will be on the front lines, and you will be behind us. I don't want him here."

Corbin just looked at him. "He can't, Drake; he needs to be here with his father," Corbin said.

"But why?" Drake asked. "Why can't he just be on the Andromeda, where I know he'll be safe?"

Corbin leaned forward, resting his elbows on his knees as he spoke. "Trust me, buddy, I wanted the same thing. I even suggested it to them."

"To whom?" Drake asked him.

"I asked Atlas about it," Corbin responded.

"And he said no?" Drake asked him.

"He said Bethany was too important to leave the X-Caliber," Corbin responded.

"What does that even mean? If he's so important, why wouldn't we do everything we can to protect him?" Drake asked, raising his voice slightly.

Corbin moved to the edge of his seat. "Buddy, I promise you I have no idea. If I did, I would tell you, but at this point, all we know is that your son is one of the only things they truly care about on these missions," Corbin said as he started whispering. Like he was trying to be quiet.

"Project Bethany was and always will be a top priority," a voice said in the doorway.

Both men jumped up and turned towards the door. Atlas was standing there with a slight smile. "May I come in?" He asked.

Drake nodded. Atlas walked over and plopped down on the couch like a teenager. He wore the same relaxed outfit he had worn recently, his hair in a bun. He was seemingly very relaxed, considering the conversation he had undoubtedly heard.

"Please sit," he said, gesturing back to the seats the men had previously been sitting in.

Both the men sat back down, looking at the men. Atlas leaned back up. Looking much more uneasy than they had before.

"My friends, we don't have anything if we don't have trust," Atlas said, looking back and forth between the men. "You have my word; we have our reason for keeping your son on this ship with you. I know it doesn't seem to make sense at the moment, but I promise you that his staying on this ship is where he will be the safest."

Drake sat motionless; "how can you promise that when nothing is guaranteed?" Drake asked him.

Atlas just smiled at him. "Some answers will only provoke more questions, my friend. The decision is final," Atlas said to him encouragingly, or at least he was trying to be.

Atlas looked at both men again. "Tomorrow, our people will need their leaders. They will need both of you in on this plan and functioning in your roles."

Drake knew he was right, no matter how he felt about his son. He still had a duty to his people.

"Atlas, I don't fully understand this, but I trust you, my friend," Drake said.

He bowed his head at Drake. Corbin looked at Atlas with an intense stare.

"Project Bethany aside, what is the probability of survival tomorrow?" Corbin asked him.

Atlas scrunched his face as he thought intensely. "I can't lie to either of you," Atlas responded; "tomorrow will likely end with over half of the Zion fleet being destroyed."

"And what about us?" Drake asked.

Atlas breathed in deep. "If we do everything as planned and we work together, hopefully, half of our fleet will make it back to Tyradis," he responded.

Drake and Corbin both sat back. "Half?" Drake asked.

"Yes," Atlas responded. "We could save more lives if we had more resources in this area. But I'm afraid death tomorrow is certain. Jumping into their home system doesn't bode very well for our chances of us all making it out. So, by probability standards, one of us in this room won't make it out tomorrow."

Drake just shook his head. "People would have never signed up for this if they knew."

Atlas looked up at him. "Would you have?" Atlas asked. "If you knew the danger you would face, yet the opportunity for real change in front of you. Would you have still come along?"

Drake thought about this. If he knew everything this mission would cost him, what it had already cost him. "I don't feel like I could answer that in a way that would make sense," Drake answered him.

Atlas smiled; "exactly, my friend. No one could answer that because what we are walking into goes far beyond ourselves. Beyond you and I, everyone here has a purpose that has been destined for us to walk out. And we will tomorrow," He said, sounding confident.

Corbin's intense stare softened as he leaned back, looking away from Atlas. Something was off about Corbin. Drake could see it all over his face. But he didn't know if it was the nerves or if he really didn't trust Atlas and the Imperium.

"I'll see both of you on the Seraph soon," Atlas said as he walked towards the door and out into the hallway. Corbin still looked upset but did not portray anger like he had a few moments ago.

"Do you think we made him mad?" Drake asked Corbin.

He shook his head. "He doesn't get mad at much; he's fine," Corbin responded.

"What's your problem with Atlas?" Drake asked him.

"What do you mean?" Corbin responded.

"It's obvious you don't trust him," Drake said with a knowing look.

Corbin thought for a moment. "I've known Atlas for many years. At the beginning of the IEC, we had many talks and conversations," Corbin said, pausing like he was considering what he would say next.

"What do you know?" Drake asked.

Corbin leaned back in the rocker. "Not anything that should be of any concern to you right now, buddy," Corbin said.

Drake didn't like this answer, but he knew it was the only one he would get out of Corbin. The two men sat around and caught up for the rest of the afternoon until the meeting.

Drake was still getting used to sitting with the red cape behind him. It bunched up and took up parts of his seat. But he was willing to endure it because it looked cool, in his opinion; it also added to the commanding presence he already held. Only the main command of each ship was present. Drake, Thatcher, and Aziel were all there. Drake highly encouraged Jason to be there. Corbin didn't understand, but Drake explained all Jason had done for them. However, he was required to have a title to be in this meeting, so Drake promoted Jason to Chief Weapons Strategist. Jason didn't like the idea at first. He felt completely content with being the IT guy who helped out in other places. But Drake insisted that Jason had earned his spot in leadership. He now wore the officers' blue uniform. It suited him well. The new title embossed on the uniform looked good. Langston had been moved to the fighter squadron with Aziel, where he could better flex his fighting instincts. The four of them sat beside each other next to the officers of the Valiant. They all acted just like Bartus. All those years with him must've rubbed off on them. They all sat completely motionless, just looking forward to Atlas, who was talking.

"The time has come, my friends," Atlas said. He once again adorned his shimmering gold armor. His hair hung down again out of the man bun. "Tomorrow is the day that some of you are excited about and some of you are dreading. We must walk in it together no matter where you sit on that spectrum."

Everyone looked around at the people beside them. Thatcher grabbed Drake's hand under the table and squeezed it. Trying to gain some form of comfort. He squeezed back, trying to help calm the nerves he knew she was feeling.

"A few things to cover before tomorrow," Atlas said, motioning for the monitor on the wall. "Each ship is equipped with enough escape pods for the occupants of your individual ships." The screen showed square boxes that deployed wings and an engine in the back. "The pods have basic shielding and a minimal version of a QLP drive. That will at least get you out of the system if needed. We will have a ship meet at those coordinates in the event we need to pick up anyone," Atlas explained. The screen showed all the different ships and where the pods were located. The X-Caliber held its pods in the launch bay along with the fighter ships. "Our goal is that none of these pods have to be launched. But if they do, we have them for you, just in case." It made sense. It added an extra layer of security to the already tense situation.

Atlas continued talking for a while, just reiterating the plan for tomorrow. He went over flight paths and what to do if they were stranded from the other vessels. Drake tried his hardest to pay attention, But his mind wanted to wander. Just to anything other than what was going on at the moment.

"Hey, are you ok?" Thatcher whispered to him as he snapped out of it. He looked up at Atlas, still talking, then back to her. "Yeah, I'm ok," he responded. "Just trying to take it all in." She smiled slightly back at him as they both listened to Atlas.

"Lastly, our trip tomorrow morning will begin at six in the morning, and it will take roughly four and a half hours. We will be traveling 51 million lightyears into Infixus." The screen showed the ships lining up. "The Seraph and the X-Caliber will be jumping first as the spearhead of our operation. Then the Andromeda, followed by the transports, and lastly, the Valiant will head up the rear of the ships." The screen faded out again as Atlas spoke.

"My greatest hope is that I will see all of you on Tyradis, your new home. But if not, we will die fighting for the light." Atlas bowed towards everyone. "It's an honor to fight beside you all. I will see everyone tomorrow."

Everyone stood up and bowed towards Atlas. People shuffled around, leaving the room and asking last-minute questions to Atlas and Corbin. Drake got up to leave, with the other three following him. Atlas walked up to him before he left.

"Hey," Atlas said. "I just wanted to say thank you for trusting me up until this point."

Drake smiled at him. "And thank you for being a sound counsel and friend to me," Drake said back to him.

Atlas smiled bigger than he had ever seen and pulled him in for a hug. He whispered in Drake's ear. "You mean more to the Drezmians and the Imperium than you yet know."

Atlas pulled away. Drake looked at him, confused. He just smiled back at him as he walked away. Keeping his eyes on his for a moment longer before walking over to Aziel. They hugged and talked for a while. Jason and Thatcher walked in front of Drake.

"What was that about?" Jason asked.

Drake just shrugged. "No idea," he said, looking back over at Atlas.

Drake tried to clear his mind. "How about one last dinner together tonight?" Drake asked as the three of them walked out of the room back to the X-Caliber.

"Sounds like a good idea," Jason said, and Thatcher agreed. They returned to Drake's quarters and had a nice meal together. It reminded Drake of death row inmates' last meal back on Earth. Just the dread in the air. But no matter how he or they felt, Drake did his best to enjoy this precious time with his friends, his family. One last time before everything changed.

CHAPTER THIRTY-FOUR

The feeling, now familiar but alien at the same time, caused everyone to hold their breath, hoping the ship could handle another jump. The ship rocketed out of the black-eye galaxy after the Seraph, and the Andromeda was close behind them. The morning had gone smoothly. Corbin had talked to Drake for a while during the first hour of the trip. Just reassuring each other as much as they could, Corbin seemed more off today than usual, But Drake chalked it up to the nerves coursing through everyone's blood. A final weapon systems test was done on all the ships to ensure they were battle-ready. The blown-up engine had been a miracle in disguise for the X-Caliber. The shield generators were twice as powerful, and the engines worked smoother and more efficiently than before.

This was it, Drake thought to himself. They were on a set course to Infixus, and they would either die In the Obsidian void or reach the next day. Drake had found peace in this thought. Hopefully, the road wouldn't run out on him. With only a week of preparation and a vague explanation of the system they were jumping into, most of the crew felt uneasy about what lay before them. Drake had tried his best the hour before the launch to calm nerves and settle minds. It had worked for some. But it was hard to convince people of something you weren't convinced of yourself. But no matter what, they were on their way. The Seraph was barely visible in front of the X-Caliber, a shiny dot in front of them as they sped through the fabric of space. They were close. Only a few minutes of the 4-hour journey remained.

Drake stood from his seat and cleared the data sheets he was looking at. Everyone on the bridge turned to look at him. "Everyone helmets on," Drake said, his voice sounding thunderous and commanding. The whole bridge listened as the sound of helmets sealing sounded all over the bridge.

Atlas sounded in Drake's earpiece. "There you are, my friend. We are one minute out from entering the edge of Infixus. Abaddon will start to mess with your instruments."

Right then, alarms sounded all over the bridge as the X-Caliber had difficulty reading and understanding all the gravity readings from the black hole.

"Yeah, we're seeing that," Drake responded to him.

"Clear the alarms," Atlas said calmly. "The QLP drive doesn't need the instruments to function."

"Copy," Drake said as he cleared the alarms on his panels.

"Weapons online and shields ready for deployment," Drake shouted, and the well-oiled machine did its job. The ship's weapon systems came to life as the shield generators powered on.

"Hold off on shield deployment," Drake said.

"Copy that," Zyrex said.

"Everyone stand by for jump exit," Drake said.

Atlas came over the comm one more time. "Good luck, my friend," he said.

Drake could hear the compassion in his voice. "You too, brother; I'll see you on Tyradis," Drake responded to him.

The shiny dot in front of the X-Caliber disappeared as the Seraph jumped into the Obsidian void.

"Jump out in five, four, three," Drake grabbed the sides of the panel in front of him. "Here we go," he said under his breath.

"Two, one," Thatcher said as Lucian disengaged the QLP drive.

The space around them unbent as the galaxy in front of them came into focus. An endless field of rock and ice appeared before them as they jumped in next to the Seraph. Off to the right of them, the event horizon of Abaddon could be seen, and the light bent around it. Drake took a deep breath, there was no turning back now. The rest of the ships jumped in behind them. It was silent except for the small thuds the ships made as they appeared behind them.

Thatcher motioned for Drake to look down at her radar. On the other side of the ice field were about ten red dots, all spread out. It looked like they were headed in their direction.

"Atlas, you seeing this?" Drake asked over the comm.

"Copy that," Atlas responded. "We didn't account for their being patrols out in the ice fields."

Everyone sat silently momentarily, waiting to see what the red dots would do.

"Everyone, prepare to fight," Drake said as calmly as he could. The crew moved around with efficiency. The red dots had started moving into the Ice fields. Then, the first one appeared out of the ice. A huge black ship with a green glow all around the ship. It was sharp-looking and looked completely alien.

"Atlas?" Drake asked, trying to keep his voice calm. "What do we do?"

The proximity alarms were going off as the ship got closer.

"I'm not sure yet," Atlas responded to him. "Their shields haven't changed to red yet, and I don't believe they alerted any of the others."

The other nine dots continued fanning out through the ice field in opposite directions. The Voidreaver vessel stopped moving as the Seraph and the X-Caliber sat side by side, trying to block the view of all the other ships behind them.

Atlas and Corbin both appeared on the monitor. "What's the move here, Atlas?" Corbin asked.

Atlas's face looked full of darkness at this moment. "The patrol shouldn't be this close to the ice ring. All of our observations showed they never pushed far past Graith."

Atlas looked up at the monitor. "They knew we were coming," he said, rage boiling.

"What?" Drake asked, surprised.

Corbin's face looked unreadable. "It doesn't matter now," Atlas said, steeling his face and looking back towards the windows of his bridge. "It's a problem for another time," He said, messing with his control panel.

"All fleet, engage shields now," Atlas shouted.

The Seraph's shield deployed beside them. Zyrex punched the deploy button, and the X-Caliber's shield roared to life. The yellow shimmer enveloped the ship. All the other ships followed suit.

"Mayday, mayday," was shouted over the intercom from one of the transport vessels. "Shielding systems failed. I repeat, the shielding systems failed."

Drake looked back out the window. Transport 7 was the only ship left uncovered. Like a wounded gazelle asking to be killed by the waiting lion.

"Lucian, move the ship in front of Transport 7," Drake yelled.

"Copy," he responded. The X-Caliber swiftly moved. Attempting to get between the Voidreaver line of sight and the transport ship. Right at that moment, the Voidreaver vessel turned a deep red.

The X-Caliber wasn't fast enough. The Voidreaver ship shot a laser beam that was quicker than light. It slammed a hole right through the transport with ease. The transport immediately shot flames out and collapsed in on itself.

"NO!" Drake screamed as the ship exploded right next to the X-Caliber as they tried to avoid the shockwave. But they were moving too fast, trying to block the shot. The stabilizers could only do so much as the shockwave sent the X-Caliber flying sideways with its nose flying upwards.

Alarms wailed, letting them know what they already knew.

"Lucian, get us upright."

"I'm trying, boss," he called back to him.

The ship leveled out again to a scene of sheer pandemonium. The Andromeda and Seraph were firing into the Voidreaver vessel as much as possible. And the enemy ship was doing the exact same.

"Jason, when we level out, fire the frontal quantum laser."

"Copy that," Jason said as he ran back and forth between all the gunners.

The ship leveled out with its nose pointed right at the twisted metal of the black ship.

"Fire," Drake yelled.

The frontal laser fired. The white laser slammed into the red shielding of the ship along with all the other incoming fire. The enemy's ship had its firepower spread too thin, with all three vessels attacking it. And as the laser slammed into it, the red glow exploded. Leaving the black metal completely bare and vulnerable. The remainder of the fire from the Seraph and Andromeda quickly put holes in the ship as it stopped firing and was torn apart.

Drake breathed out heavily. Looking back over at the debris field and pieces of the destroyed transport ship. Parts of the ship were hitting the yellow shield of the X-Calibur and bouncing off.

"Atlas, come in," Drake said, breathing heavily.

"I'm here, Admiral. Is your ship ok?" He asked him.

"We are ok," Drake responded.

The line was silent for a moment.

"We have to move now," Atlas said, pushing through the distress in his voice.

"We are already behind schedule."

"Copy," Drake said.

Drake felt cold inside. The thousands of lives they were leaving behind. All gone in a moment. But if he wanted to save millions more, they had to go.

"Lucian, fall in behind the Seraph," Drake said solemnly.

"Copy that, boss," he responded.

The air was thick on the bridge as the X-Caliber moved back behind the other ship.

"Where are the other ships?" Drake asked Thatcher.

The radar still showed the nine other dots, but half were moving away closer to Graith. And five ships looked like they were flying away quickly.

"Probably headed to intercept the Zion fleet," Atlas said, sounding certain.

"We've lost our element of surprise. This is going to be a slug fest every step of the way to make it out of here," Atlas said.

Drake just nodded. He was right. They had planned to catch them off guard at Graith. To at least hopefully get past the planet mostly unscathed. But now they would be on high alert.

The fleet moved through the Shattered Remains as fast as possible, avoiding the massive asteroids and ice. The ships navigated as best they could, but still, some small rocks and ice slammed into the ship, sending sparks flowing off the yellow shielding.

The radar showed no hostile ships in the area, so they could breathe easily. Getting through the field was simple enough, but the quiet wouldn't last too long, with Graith's territory only a few minutes away.

As they moved through the field, Graith started to come into view. It blew Drake away that a planet could be this big. It made Jupiter look fun-sized. Its many moons were visible as they floated around the planet.

"We are getting out of the debris field and in range of communication with the Zion fleet, I'm broadcasting now," Atlas said.

A fuzzy connection appeared on the screen as the connection was established. A woman with black hair hung low, and deep dark eyes appeared. Her thin face reminded Drake of Atlas slightly. But it was more than likely a common characteristic in the Drezmian species. She wore the same uniform as Drake.

"Admiral Talis, it's good to see you," Atlas said, sounding optimistic.

"Your majesty," she said, bowing.

"Majesty?" Drake thought to himself. He was the child of the Emperor. It was still weird for him to hear him called that.

Atlas bowed back.

"How is the fleet holding at Ferrum?"

"We are ok; we've taken out a few of theirs, and they've taken out a few of ours. But we are making progress further into the system," Talis responded.

"That's good to hear, my friend. We are about to engage at Graith."

She nodded. There was obvious commotion aboard her bridge as laser fire, and shouting could be heard.

"Talis, I want you to meet Admiral Marcus Drake."

She bowed at him. Drake returned the gesture.

"Admiral Drake, it's so good to finally speak to you," Talis said, smiling.

He tilted his head, confused. "You know who I am?" He asked, confused. It also struck him as odd that she could be having a cordial conversation while they were fighting an alien race right in front of them. But again, they were used to this. It was their lifestyle. Drake hoped he never got used to this. He didn't ever want to get comfortable taking a life. Even if it was a Voidreaver.

"Of course, I know about you. The entire Imperium military does, Admiral. It's an honor to fight alongside you," Talia said.

"You as well," Drake said, bowing.

"See you guys at Thalassia," she said with a smile, "hopefully in one piece."

The screen cut back to just Atlas. The ships were still moving closer to Graith.

"Alright, my friend. Our ships up front will set the pace. The goal isn't to sit and destroy ships. That's just a happy outcome. We need to get through these territories as fast as we can," Atlas said.

"Copy that," Drake responded. They started to fly over the rings of Graith. It was quiet; it felt too quiet. Especially after all the noise they had just made behind the Shattered remains.

Drake looked over at Thatcher. "Are we filtering out Graith's rings on our radar?"

"No, not entirely; why?" Thatcher asked.

"Filter out the rings," Drake said, staring out the windows.

Thatcher messed with her console. "Uh, Drake, This is really bad," Thatcher said, trying not to freak out.

Over one hundred dots flooded the radar.

35

CHAPTER THIRTY-FIVE

The proximity alarms went crazy. "Atlas, you seeing this?" Drake said frantically into his comms.

"Seeing what?" Atlas asked him.

"Filter out the planet's rings on your radar," Thatcher screamed into the comms. The line was silent for a moment. Then their alarms went off as well. "They are trying to surround us," Atlas yelled. "Deploy all fighters and prepare to engage," Atlas said demandingly.

Drake turned to his crew. "This is it," he yelled. "Jason, deploy our fighters."

"Fighters ready," he yelled back to Drake.

"Aziel, be safe out there," Drake said.

"Will do, Admiral," Aziel responded over the comms. The launch bay doors opened, and the twenty-five fighters shot out of the X-Caliber. Fighters deployed from the Seraph, and a whole horde deployed from the belly of Andromeda.

"Valiant standby to go dark," Atlas said, and the fighters got into their flight packs.

"Copy that," Bartus said.

"All squadrons ready," Helks said over comms. As much as he was a pain to him sometimes, Drake still smiled at this. It seemed like Helks had found his place. The fighters had formed into 20 separate packs of 25 ships a piece. They were moving around the bigger vessels.

"We got movement all around us, Drake," Thatcher yelled. Drake looked back at the radar. The ships were moving out from under the rings. Atlas and Corbin were back on the monitor.

"We have no way of engaging all these ships without catastrophic losses," Corbin said, sounding panicked. It shocked Drake to see Corbin melting like this; it wasn't like him. But that didn't matter at the moment.

Atlas turned back to the monitor. "We push through as fast as we can; if we get stuck, we are all dead." In front of them, more than 30 different-looking Voidreaver vessels had pulled up from the ice. It looked like some were coming from the different moons' orbits.

"Looks like they want to give us a warm welcome," Drake said sarcastically.

"Try to stay together," Atlas said, keeping his composure.

Drake nodded at him. "Lucian, punch it," Drake yelled. The ship shot forward. The Seraph did as well, as they rocketed straight towards the enemy ships.

"Fire now!" Drake yelled to Jason. The ship's turrets and laser cannons shot to life. Catching a few of the ships off guard. Ripping holes into two of the ships as fire spewed out of them. It didn't take long for the enemy ships to catch on, returning fire with vengeance back at them. The laser bolts looked almost black if it wasn't for the white outline around the munition. They slammed into the vessel's shielding, sending the usual yellow sparks flying off. But it still felt like the lasers were hitting harder than they used to. The red glow around the Voidreaver ships did look intimidating, especially with the backdrop of the alien planet.

The fighter squadrons started breaking off, trying to fill the gaps between the ships. More ships started to rise from around the rings. The space in front of them started filling more and more with ships.

"Atlas, did you expect this many in this sector?" Drake asked him.

Atlas just shook his head on the monitor. "Maybe a quarter of this is typically stationed here; they had to have known we were coming." The fronts of the ships opened, allowing what seemed to be hundreds of smaller craft to fly out and speed towards them.

"All squadrons prepare to engage incoming fighters," Atlas yelled. The fighter squadrons moved around, shooting in front of the ships.

"Aziel, keep it tight, and don't push too far into the open space," Drake said to him.

"Copy that, sir," Aziel responded to him. Drake spotted the Golden Swords on the fighters as they sped by the ship. The enemy fire was still coming in. It looked like sheer chaos in front of the ship due to the mass of fighters converging. Laser bolts shot in all directions as the fighters met in the middle. The X-Caliber fired off continually as they pressed forward.

"Jason, when we get in range, switch all the laser turrets to target the smaller craft and, with all the other fire, focus on the main ships," Drake yelled.

"Any particular one?" Jason asked him.

Drake looked at the massive amount of ships speeding towards them. None of them really stood out. Some were smaller, and there were a few huge ships as well. The bigger ones seemed to be the ones firing the most. Drake zoomed in on the ships on his console. It looked like most of the ships didn't even have weapons. The big ones were the only ones actually shooting at them.

"Atlas, they are putting up a front; only the bigger command ships are actually shooting," Drake said into the comms.

Atlas was silent for a moment; "good eye, my friend," he responded. "But don't underestimate them. They knew we were coming, so we have no idea what they planned," he said.

The commotion outside was intensifying. The Seraph and the X-Caliber had pushed into the pack of fighters where they were dogfighting. The transports were struggling to keep up, firing the limited weaponry they had as well at the ships circling around them. It was like a swarm of bees all around them.

"Aziel, get back here and help clear some of these ships off our transports," Drake yelled.

"Copy that," he said as his squadron redirected back towards the transports. The Andromeda was laying down as much as it could at that moment, but it was hanging back more than it should have been. Drake tried to connect to Clovis, but the line wouldn't go through. The two lead ships were in the thick of it at the moment. Voidreaver ships and Imperium ships shot by the bridge at blinding speeds. There were some Imperium fighters getting destroyed, but for every 1 they destroyed, the Imperium took 5 more with them. They were highly trained in what they did, and it showed.

"Corbin," Drake shouted, still trying to get through to the Andromeda.

"Hey brother, I'm here," Corbin responded. There was way more commotion on their bridge. It seemed hectic and disorganized.

"What's going on?" Drake asked. "You guys are falling behind and slowing the transports down. We have to stay together," Drake said.

"We're trying, brother. But Clovis is having a meltdown, and the rest of the bridge is collapsing," Drake leaned in, looking at him through the monitor.

"You were picked for this for a reason," Drake said with confidence. "Lead them like I know you can," Drake said, trying his best to instill confidence in his friend, like he had always done for him.

Corbin nodded back to him. "Thank buddy," he said with a grin. Corbin walked away from the monitor. "HEY!" Corbin screamed at the crew. The comms cut off. Drake smiled; hopefully, that was the motivation they needed. A few moments passed, and it seemed to work as the Andromeda closed the gap between them.

Atlas came over the comms again. "Valiant, I need you to push ahead, cloaked. See if you can get behind their ships and cause some chaos."

Bartus actually laughed at that. "Sounds good," he said.

Even though the ship didn't show up on radar, Drake could still see his location marked on their HUD. The ship flew by at amazing speed. It was completely invisible. The technology blew him away.

The X-Caliber and the Seraph had almost reached the massive wall of ships in front of them. The scale started to set in with how many ships there were. Not all of them were firing, but they were attempting to block their way out of the sector. The ships seemed to stretch from the planet out into space.

"We are flying to our deaths," Thatcher said. Looking over to Drake. He couldn't see her face because of the helmet. But he knew her face was covered with sadness. The sheer number of ships seemed unfathomable.

"Atlas, what's our move here?" Drakes asked. Trying not to show the fear in his voice. He wasn't afraid to die at this moment. But his duty was to his men.

"We punch through like a spear. The Zion fleet is making good progress, and we have to make up for some lost time if we are going to meet them at Thalassia in time. Can the Valiant make a hole for us to get through?" Drake asked.

"Good thinking, Admiral," Atlas responded to him. Atlas went away to talk to Bartus.

Drake looked back to his bridge. Drake was glad to see his crew calm and handling what was thrown at them.

"Zyrex, how are the shields?" Drake asked, checking the ship reading on his monitor.

"They are holding well," Zyrex responded. "They are showing no signs of being overloaded."

"Good news to hear my friend," Drake said back to him. Pieces of the smaller fighter that had been destroyed smashed into the yellow shielding as they flew forward, Imperium and Voidreaver alike. Drake grimaced at this. Those broken ships represented lost lives on both sides. Drake didn't know how it would ever sit right in his soul. It was hard to see in front of the windows of the bridge because of all the fighters flying around.

"Aziel, have we lost any of our squadron members?" Drake asked, using the radar to navigate through the mess.

"Two so far," Aziel responded calmly. He was a master of the Imperium's small fighter craft. A weapon that Drake was thankful to have.

"Let's minimize those losses if possible," he said back to Aziel.

"We are trying Admiral, but it's an absolute mess out here," Aziel said.

"I know you are my friend. Atlas, where's our opening?" Drake said, getting concerned as the wall of ships got closer and closer. The shields were still protecting the ships as much as they could. But the closer they got, the more fire they started to take as the smaller ships were in range to take fire. Less effective but still taking a toll on the shielding.

"Bartus, now would be a good time," Atlas yelled. Out of nowhere, there was an explosion to the left. Drake looked over, seeing three ships get knocked out of the way from the explosion. Ten other ships fell out of line, trying to escape the explosions.

"There's our gap," Drake said, smiling. The crew cheered, seeing the Valiant destroy some of the enemy ships.

"Amazing work, Bartus!" Drake said over the comms. He didn't respond, but Drake knew he was happy about that one.

"That hole won't be open long. Admiral, we need to get these transports through," Atlas said as they redirected to where the Valiant had opened the hole. Drake looked at it through his radar.

"They are gonna collapse in on the opening," Thatcher said.

Drake looked at the hole in the wall of ships fast approaching. "Atlas, we need to block the hole on the left and right," Drake said confidently.

Atlas hesitated. "I don't know; we will go broadside for an extended period. I don't know if the shields can handle that, my friend," Atlas responded to him.

"Do we have another choice?" Drake asked. Determination in his voice.

The line was silent. "Okay, Marcus, I trust you," is all that Atlas said.

"Lucian, move us into the hole on the right side as far as we can go." Lucian was hesitant for a moment, seemingly frozen.

"Lucian, we have to move now," Drake shouted.

Lucian shook it off as the ship rocketed into the opening in the wall of ships. Drake looked over. He didn't know where it came from, but he felt a surge in himself. Confident and poised in this pressure.

"Zyrex, I need shields redirected off the left side and pushed on the right side top and bottom."

"Copy that," Zyrex said. The X-Caliber moved next to the Voidreaver ships. It felt ominous to be so close to these alien ships.

"Jason, don't quit laying down fire into those ships," Drake yelled. "We have to keep them occupied."

Jason continued to run to his men giving orders. The enemy fire slammed into the shielding, shaking the entire ship. But it held firm at the moment.

The Seraph joined them on the other side, laying fire into the ships. The combined fire of both the ships blew up the gigantic ship above them. Sending a fireball into the shielding. The blast threw the ships into the Voidreaver vessels beside them. The X-Caliber shields slammed into the ship beside them. The two different shields glowing against one another. The ships didn't cease firing.

"Corbin, you guys gotta get through now before they collapse on us?" Atlas yelled through the comms.

"We are almost there," Corbin responded to him. The Andromeda moved out of the way right at the opening. Sending even more fire into the other ships to help the transport move through.

The transports started moving through one at a time. "Hold it steady," Drake said as calmly as he could. The small fighter craft moved through when they could. The smaller Voidreaver ships were still making it hard. But they were taking way more casualties than the Imperium.

"As soon as the Andromeda is through we need to put our engines on full to get out of the sector," Atlas said.

"Won't they just follow us?" Drake asked him.

"They don't know our plan; they see the Zion fleet pushing in towards them, so they will keep the vast majority at Graith to protect their religious center."

"I hope you are right," Drake said to him.

"Me too," Atlas said under his breath. But Drake still heard him.

The last transport was flying through the opening. "Admiral," Zyrex said, getting Drake's attention. "Our shielding needs time to recharge."

"What are we currently sitting at?" Drake asked. The laser fire from the surrounding ships pelted the shielding, wearing them down.

"Readings are showing twenty-five percent at the moment."

"Copy that," Drake responded to him. "Atlas, we need to get out of range of these ships," Drake said, trying to remain as calm as he could. "We will start losing shields if we don't get out of here."

"We are in the same boat over here," Atlas said. "Looks like we are hovering around thirty percent."

"Corbin, are we clear on that side?" Drake asked.

"The last transport is almost through, and ninety percent of the fighters are through."

"Push the Andromeda through," Atlas said. The hulking ship started moving through the opening. The ship filled up the entirety of the opening. It hit both the X-Caliber and the Seraph, once again slamming them into the vessel directly beside them. There were still a ton of other small fighter craft on the other side of the wall. Some were able to get through the small spaces between ships. But most got caught in the heavy fire from the enemy dreadnaughts.

The Andromeda slowly slid through, taking forever because of its size. The Transports were bigger, but the Voidreaver vessels had started closing the gap much further.

"Lucian, as soon as the other ships are through, we need to get out of here and save some shielding," Drake said.

"Fifteen percent shielding," Zyrex shouted.

"Corbin, we've gotta go now," Drake yelled into his comms. The wall of ships had started to condense, putting further pressure on the shields.

The Andromeda's engines doubled its power. "Marcus, if we go now, then all of our other fighters on the other side are dead for sure," Thatcher said.

Drake looked at her, then straight out the window. Drake closed his eyes. "Their sacrifice will be a noble one," he said.

"We can't just leave them," Thatcher said. He could tell she was serious. But they had no other option. It was them or the fighters.

The Andromeda had just gotten clear of the path.

"Lucian, get us out of here," Drake said. Thatcher walked over. She grabbed his shoulder, getting close to him. "You are just gonna change your morals, Just like that?" She was only whispering, but Drake felt the daggers she was shooting into him.

He leaned in; "my duty is to this ship, my son, and you. Our fighter craft made it through," he said, whispering back to her. She just shook her head and walked back to her station.

"Lucian," Drake shouted as he turned back to the bridge. Lucian turned back to his console, and the ship lunged forward, escaping the opening. The Seraph followed closely behind. The Voidreaver ships were still firing, but it was way less than they had just received.

"Multiple fighter craft casualties," Atlas said on the comms. Drake looked over to Thatcher; her head was hanging low. He looked back to the windows in front of him. He shoved any emotion down. Drake knew his choosing to close that opening sentenced them to death. He only hoped that he could live long enough to honor their sacrifice.

36

CHAPTER THIRTY-SIX

Atlas had been correct. Only a few smaller ships pursued the small, tattered Imperium fleet. They weren't even firing at the ships, just staying right out of range of any fire. The Imperium fleet moved along steadily.

"Zyrex, how long until our shields are recharged?" Drake asked him.

Zyrex looked at his monitors. "The generators suffered heavy damage from all the collisions and heavy fire. They will reach total capacity in ten minutes, but only roughly sixty-two percent."

"That's not good," Drake said under his breath. "Atlas, our shields sustained massive damage," Drake said over the comms.

Atlas appeared on the screen. "Ours did as well, my friend; we must keep faith. We can make it through this, but we can't get caught up like we did last time."

Drake didn't answer back. It felt like they were slipping deeper and deeper into a hole they wouldn't be able to get out of. Admiral Talis appeared on the monitors.

"Your majesty, Admiral," she said, sounding rushed. "We've just gotten news from Gabriel's fleet on the edge of Eclion. The capital ship and main fleet of the Voidreavers have just jumped out of the system. We can only imagine they will return to the Obsidian void to block our escape."

"How did they get word so fast?" Atlas asked.

"We have no idea," Talis said.

"Can you hold them at Thalassia until we meet you there?" Atlas asked.

"We will try our best," Talis said, bowing to them. Her portion of the screen went dark.

Atlas looked defeated. "This wasn't supposed to happen, my friend. We are gonna be pressed on both sides."

Drake looked at him intently. "I'm with you till the very end if needed,"

Drake said, pride in his voice.

Atlas stood up tall, taking in a deep breath. Atlas bowed to him. "We are about a 15-minute push to Vorterra. I'm hoping the forces will be more spaced out than what we just previously encountered." Atlas said, looking at the readings on his monitor.

"The same principle applies here. We move through as quickly as possible. The Voidreavers constantly station their bigger battleships around the planet. That's what we target with the decoy transport."

"Copy that," Drake replied to him.

The screen went dark again as Drake sat in his seat. The silence was a stark contrast to what they had just encountered. Drake looked over at Thatcher; she held her head in her hands, obviously distraught. Drake switched his comms to the private channel.

"Thatch, Thatch, do you hear me?"

She glanced over at him and then away again. "I don't wanna talk, Marcus," she said. Drake could hear how agitated she sounded.

"Come on, Thatch, talk to me," Drake pleaded.

Thatcher reached up on her helmet and switched off her comms. Drake sighed, that would have to be settled later. Drake did various check-ins with the crew around the ship, making sure systems were still functioning, and everyone was safe. The X-Caliber squadron had docked back to refuel and resupply on hard munitions. Only losing two fighters in this whole mess so far wasn't terrible.

Vorterra was visible on the horizon. "Let's get ready for round two," Drake shouted over the bridge.

Everyone ran back to their stations. "Zyrex, how are those shields looking?" Drake asked over the commotion.

"They are as full as they are going to get, Admiral," he responded.

"I'll take what I can get," Drake said confidently. The shields enveloped the ship again as the weapons came back online. The Seraph pulled alongside the X-Caliber.

"Are we ready, Admiral?" Atlas asked him over comms.

"We are," Drake responded.

"Good," Atlas said. "We are going to stay as far from the center of the sector as we can. We can't handle a conflict close to the planet. If they are more spread out, we can take them on."

"What about the bomb?" Drake asked.

Atlas nodded his head. "The goal is to pull a few dreadnoughts close and send the transport directly into them. That bomb is a new technology that ignores any sort of shielding, even our own. So we must stay far away whenever that thing detonates."

"Sounds simple enough," Drake said sarcastically.

Atlas laughed at him. "Sarcasm isn't your strong suit, my friend."

Drake laughed; "It never has been."

"Alright, my friends, round two is here. Stick to the plan and get to the other side of the sector," Atlas said, addressing the entire fleet. "They will try to single us out and tear us apart individually. Together, we can survive this," Atlas said, trying to instill as much confidence as possible.

The launch bay doors opened as Aziel and his fighters launched and began flying around the X-Caliber. The transports lined up in their battle formation. The Valiant had sped ahead and cloaked in order to strike from the shadows. The Andromeda was now at the back and had released its hundred-plus fighters. The scene before them started to come into focus. The red glow of the dying star Obscura made it look ten times more ominous. The dark black planet appeared directly in front of them as if it came out of the shadows. The videos didn't do it justice. The planet not only looked dark, but it felt void of anything good or light. It all made sense in Drake's head now. He couldn't help but wonder if the Voidreavers were innately evil or if the circumstances of their surroundings made them who they were. Or maybe both.

All in front of them, glowing red ships hung like stars in front of the dark planet. The vessels all looked like warships. Not like the smaller ships surrounding Graith. Those were transport, scientific, or civilian vessels for the Voidreavers, Drake assumed. The big guns pointed right at them told Drake that wasn't the case this time. They were in their attack formations. They met the incoming small Voidreaver craft head-on. As if on cue, the dreadnoughts started firing directly at the Imperium fleet. The laser fire slammed into the ship with the most force they had felt yet.

"Everything we got," Drake yelled.

The ship shot forward as every weapon on the ship laid down fire. The Seraph was close behind. The Voidreaver ships shot forward in response to them. Drake didn't know how well the X-Caliber could dogfight, but they were about to find out. The Imperium fighters were very skilled, hardly taking any losses. They weaved and moved around the enemy ships. Drake looked over his radar for a way around the approaching ships. They all seemed to be flying in loose formations. This allowed them to be very flexible. It was smart when they had the sheer numbers that they did.

"Atlas, I don't see a clear way through this," Drake said to him over the comms.

"I'm also seeing what you are; this will be a scrap to get out of here." The first of the dreadnoughts were quickly approaching.

"Alright, Jason, let's tear them apart," Drake said confidently.

The X-Caliber shot its laser cannons and frontal quantum laser at the approaching dreadnought. The cannons slammed into the ship first, causing the dark red glow to glow a bright red. The quantum laser hit the ship. The continual beam caused the red glow to flicker. The ship shot back, and the X-Caliber had to veer off course to avoid the fire coming at them.

"The dreadnought shield is disabled," Thatcher yelled.

"Let's take it out," Drake said. Jason redirected the fire onto the exposed ship. The laser turrets and missiles fired towards the ship. They slammed into it, blowing holes in the metal siding. Flames spewed out of the holes, and pieces of the ships started flying everywhere. Small rockets started firing away from the ship back towards the planet.

"Those appear to be their escape pods," Thatcher said. "I'm getting heat signatures inside of them."

Drake knew their mission, and the Voidreavers were still actively trying to kill them, but it was hard seeing other beings fleeing for their lives. They still had life in them, probably families back home. Drake didn't know how their society worked, but killing them still felt wrong. Drake had to shove these feelings down. The battlefield was no place for second-guessing, only action. Drake looked back out to the mess in front of them. Time seemed to move in slow motion. The Voidreaver ship had started to destabilize and was about to blow up. Imperium and Voidreaver craft flew around them at blinding speeds. Four more dreadnoughts had closed in, all converging on their flight path.

Drake looked down, and Atlas was trying to connect with him. Drake snapped back to the present moment. He pressed the comms button.

"Sorry, Atlas, I'm here," Drake said to him.

"Marcus, we have to do something now," Atlas said, sounding panicked.

Drake looked at the radar; there weren't just a few ships headed their way. There were close to fifty dreadnoughts, all converging on their position.

"Can we send transport 10?" Drake asked.

Atlas looked back at his monitors. "No better time than the present," he said. Atlas turned away from the monitor, and the feed cut away. Drake didn't know for sure, but it felt like they were losing grip of this situation. Atlas continued getting increasingly flustered as the situation unfolded, but he had to trust him. He was his only hope of keeping the people he loved alive.

The Voidreaver vessel in front of them had finally exploded, sending shrapnel and debris slamming into the ship. They continued firing at the ships in front of them as transport 10 flew by them silently. The shielding was still up on the ship, but it wasn't needed. Most of the dreadnoughts ignored the transport as it flew out in front of them. They had to be at least curious, Drake thought. He knew he would be if a random civilian vessel approached him in the middle of a battle. They were still fighting off ships on all sides of them at this point. Drake could barely keep up with the other ships around them. He had no idea where the Valiant or the Andromeda were. All Drake could see was right in front of him.

"Drake, do you copy?" Drake heard in his comm.

"Yes, I copy," he responded.

"We have an issue with the bomb on the transport," Atlas said.

"What do you mean?" Drake asked.

"We are locked out of the ship. The Voidreavers are jamming any remote detonation or access into the ship," Atlas said.

"Do we not have a workaround?" Drake asked him.

"No, we don't," Atlas responded. "It was a safety measure. But we've never been locked out of anything before."

Drake thought back to when the Seraph had taken over his entire ship. How helpless he had felt at that moment. A complete loss of control. Atlas

   DYLAN CARRIGAN

didn't seem to be used to losing control. Drake tried to calm him.

"There has to be a solution," Drake said, checking his monitors to see if he could tap into anything.

Both men sat in silence as the battle raged outside. A ping on the monitor lit up; a smaller fighter was trying to communicate. Drake pressed it, connecting them to Atlas and Drake.

"Hello, who is this?" Drake asked.

"Hello Admiral, this is Helks;" explosions and lasers getting fired sounded in the background.

"Helks," Drake said. "Happy to hear that you are ok, my friend."

"We are losing a lot of men out here," he said. The signal cut in and out. "We are trying to get the transport to detonate, but we are having issues," Drake said.

"Well, it needs to happen soon. We've already lost two transports." Drake caught his breath. They were getting torn apart at the moment.

Atlas came onto the line. "The only way to detonate is a manual override, but that's a death sentence," Atlas said.

The line was silent again.

"I'll do it," Helks said.

"No," Drake shot back immediately. "I can't let you do that, there has to be another way," he said frantically.

"Drake, I haven't contributed to this cause one time. I haven't amounted to anything my entire life," Helks said, holding back tears. "If I do this, at least, I'll be saving lives. I would rather die fighting than die running," he said resolutely in his decision.

Drake held back tears in his eyes. "Copy Helks, but don't ever think you've amounted to nothing; you are family to me," Drake said.

"You are to me as well, Marcus; now go win this war," Helks responded as his line cut off.

Drake put his hands on his head, holding back a scream. They were slowly losing themselves. He didn't want to be in this place. He wanted to run, but he couldn't. If he ran, they would all die. Helks words rang in his ears, "I'd rather die fighting than die running."

Helks ship shot past them towards the transport. His ship passed through the shielding and into the hanger bay. A few grueling minutes passed. They were still defending themselves from the other vessels still approaching. It felt like a fence was getting put around them, and they were getting stuck in the middle.

Helks came on the comms one last time. "Don't let this be in vain," he said, pain staining his voice. "I'll see you guys on the other side. FOR THE GREATER GOOD," Helks screamed.

Drake closed his eyes. He didn't wanna see his friend die right in front of him. The transport seemed to collapse in on itself first; the ship mushed itself into a ball half the size of what it had been. Then, all at once, it was released. The shock wave went out. It decimated all the ships in its close proximity. Over twenty Voidreaver ships were reduced to scrap instantly as the shock wave hit them and quickly dissipated. A smaller wave hit the X-Caliber and the rest of the Imperium. The bridge sat silent as the path in front of them cleared. Drake opened his eyes. One moment, they were there. The next moment, they were gone. Helks was gone in an instant.

Atlas came onto the comms. "We have to go right now," he said.

The broken Imperium fleet moved forward as fast as they could.

"Incoming from the Zion fleet," Thatcher said.

Talis appeared on the monitor with Atlas, Corbin, and Drake. She sounded panicked. "Change of plans, we are pushing to meet you over Vorterra."

"What?" Atlas asked concerned. "We can't just leave this sector; the black hole will still interfere with our coordinates," he said, trying to quell his swelling anger.

"We don't have any other choice, Your Majesty. We just got word that the capital fleet of the Voidreavers has entered the Obsidian void, and they are headed right for you," Talis responded.

Atlas closed his eyes. "This wasn't supposed to happen this way," he said. The pain was so evident on his face. Disappointment and sadness crossed his face. "Talis, you have an order to jump back to Eclion. If you get caught up in this mess, the entire Zion fleet will be doomed," Atlas said to her.

"I can't just leave you behind," she said back to him. "I have a duty to..."

Atlas cut her off. "You have a duty to the Imperium. The war won't be won today," Atlas said stoically. "That's an order."

Talis bowed towards Atlas as her screen went off. "We have to try a jump from here," Atlas said, his face now void of any emotion. "It's our only shot at surviving. We can't possibly take on the capital fleet. We may be off by a few systems, but at least we will be alive," he said. "There's a slight possibility that Abaddon will rip the ships apart when we jump, but it's a risk we must take," Atlas said. "Let's get the jump drives ready."

"Copy that," Drake said hesitantly. "Lucian, get me a clear jump to Eclion. We have to go now," Drake said, walking towards the front windows and looking out into space. Thatcher followed him. She put her hand on his shoulder. They didn't say anything to each other, but Drake knew they would be ok. There was fear on the bridge. No one wanted to die that day.

"Jump is ready," Lucian yelled.

"Ok," Drake said, "give me a jump of five, four, and three."

The Valiant began its jump, shooting off ahead. All at once, there was a giant explosion in front of them. The Valiant had run into a giant ship that had appeared out of nowhere. In front of them, a ship the size of a city appeared. The Valiant's explosion seemed tiny on the colossal ship. Just like that, Bartus and his entire crew were instantly gone. The entire bridge stood in silence. No one dared to say a word. Every ounce of hope they had remaining had just blown up with the Valiant.

The giant in front of them came to a halt. So did everything else on the battlefield. The dreadnoughts stopped shooting, and the small fighter craft seemed to go back to their respective ships.

"Atlas, what do we do?" Drake asked him. He tried his best not to lose it, but it felt impossible given the circumstances.

"I have no idea, my friend," Atlas responded to him. "This doesn't look very promising for our return home."

Drake walked back to the command center. It showed that the Valiant was now offline. Along with four of the ten transports.

"Aziel, how are we doing?" Drake asked him.

"We are down to about half of our squadron left," he responded.

"I want you and the rest of our squadron to do nothing but keep ships off the transports now."

"Copy that," Aziel said.

The few remaining fighters followed Aziel back towards the X-Caliber. More and more ships continued to jump into the sector. Drake stood, seeing all of it appear in front of them.

"What are we waiting on?" Thatcher asked him through their comms.

"I think Atlas may be trying to communicate with them," Drake said. Drake looked at his monitors. It showed that Atlas was in a busy, outgoing line of communication.

"Zyrex, how are we holding?" Drake asked him.

Zyrex just shook his head. "Very poor at the moment. We only have about twenty percent of our shields left."

That would hold maybe one more engagement, Drake thought. But if even a few of the ships in front of them attacked, the shields would crumble.

Atlas appeared on the monitor again. His face was solemn. Drake couldn't quite read him, but he didn't look happy.

"They don't understand our language, but I did my best to explain that we have civilians and we aren't a war party," Atlas said, moving hair out of his face.

"Did they understand you?" Drake asked him.

"I don't know," Atlas responded to him.

The capital ship in front of them let out a low alarm sound. It sounded vile and repulsive. Drake moved towards the window. As quick as light, a beam shot out from the capital ship. It barely missed the X-Caliber, but that wasn't their target anyway. The beam slammed into the transport one behind them. Drake couldn't see the explosion, but he could feel it as the explosion rocked the entire ship.

"There's our answer," Atlas responded with no emotion.

Drake couldn't grasp this situation. Over a million lives had been lost, and Atlas seemed to stand there unfazed, or maybe he was just in shock. Drake felt himself slipping into that. He took a deep breath. He knew he had little chance of walking away from this. But his crew would.

"Jason, set all munitions to automatically shoot at the closest target," Drake said, looking straight down at his monitors.

Jason walked over. "What are you doing, Drake?" he said, cold in his expression. "We don't have any targeting capabilities, and I can't operate on the fly," Jason said, trying to get through to Drake.

Drake just looked up, putting his hand on his shoulder. "Just trust me," Drake said.

Drake turned to the command circle around him. "I want all control capabilities," Drake said. "I want all engine, radar, and shielding controls handed over to my panel."

They all just stared at him, unmoving.

"That's an order," he shouted.

Lucian moved the engine and jump controls over, and Jason moved all weapon controls over to him. Zyrex stood up, moving.

"I know what you are doing, Drake, and as admirable as you are trying to be, I don't abandon my post," Zyrex said seriously.

"You will if your commanding officer says to," Drake said to him, his voice unmoving.

Zyrex just stood there for a moment. He bowed towards him, and Drake returned the gesture. Drake looked down and saw all the ship's controls on his panel.

"I need all of you to head to the launch bay and get in an escape pod. Everyone started talking to one another. I'm almost certain this ship will not make it out of this," Drake said, taking a deep breath. "I need you all to be ready if I have to release the escape pods."

No one moved. They just sat there.

"We don't wanna leave you behind, Admiral," one of the crew members on the bridge shouted. Everyone joined in saying the same things.

Drake looked out the window, seeing the approaching capital fleet. Drake held up his hand; the bridge got quiet at this gesture.

"It's not a suggestion; it's an order. Go now," Drake said commandingly.

The crew began hesitantly running out. Lucian nodded to him as he walked past him. The Voidreaver fleet had started firing at them again. The ship's automated systems began firing back at them. Jason walked up to Drake, shook his hand, and hugged him.

"I'll see you soon," Drake said to him.

Jason just nodded and ran off toward the launch bay. Zyrex did the same. After a few moments, all that was left was Drake and Thatcher.

Drake reached up and unsealed his helmet. His head was drenched in sweat. His hair clung to his forehead, and it dripped sweat. Thatcher did the same by taking off her helmet. Her blue eyes pierced through to him. She was also sweaty, but it didn't look bad on her.

"If you think I'm leaving you, then you are an idiot," she said, walking closer to him.

"You will listen to an order I give you," he said, making his face serious.

"No, I won't. I won't let you die with this ship, Marcus," she said, tears forming in her eyes.

"If I'm gone, our people will need you to lead them," he said, wiping the tears from her cheek. "An Admiral never abandons his ship," Drake said, genuinely.

"And I will never abandon you," she said. "I can't lose you, Drake. You are my family, you and Jason." Her tears streamed down her face now. "If you make me leave, I will never forgive you," she said, sobbing at this point.

Drake pulled her in, embracing her as she wept into his shoulder. He looked her in her eyes. "Yes, you will," Drake said. "I know you will," he paused for a moment, "because I love you, Fiona."

She stepped back, looking directly into his eyes. "You do?" she said, her guard completely gone now.

"I do, Fiona. I've run from it. But at this moment, I see that I love you, and for that reason, I need you to go get to that escape pod."

She smiled slightly. "I love you too, Marcus," she said, crying again, hugging him.

He held her for a moment. His heart felt full. But his mind came back to the mission. "We will talk about it later, I promise Thatch, but you need to go."

"What if there isn't a later?" she said, getting frustrated at him.

Drake grabbed her face and pulled her in, kissing her. She melted into his arms. They embraced for a few moments. Drake let her go.

"Then I couldn't leave that on the table," he said, smiling at her.

She smiled back at him slightly, sadness still all over her face. "I love you; now go," Drake said to her.

She looked at him. "I love you too," she said as she turned, putting her helmet back on and running to the launch bay.

Drake stood in the command center by himself now. His emotions flew in every direction. He hoped he could do something about them someday, but at this moment, he had a job to do. He increased the ship's speed, matching the Seraph's pace. They were weaving in and out of enemy ships around them. The smaller fighter craft were doing their best to stay alive. The enemy had more small fighter craft than they could count. Drake had called every member of the ship to the launch bay. Everyone was in their escape pod and accounted for, according to Thatcher. Drake was satisfied knowing they were ready to go.

The shield percentage had slowly been going down. Currently sitting at 15 percent, the yellow shimmer had started sputtering, struggling to deflect the continual fire coming from the outside.

"Atlas, be honest with me. Is there any way around this?" Drake asked him.

He didn't respond immediately. Drake watched as the shields went down to 10 percent. "ATLAS," Drake shouted.

"I'm here, my friend," Atlas responded to him.

"What do we do?" Drake said frantically, "I'm about to lose shields."

The capital ship seemed to overshadow everything now. They were close enough to see that it wasn't just a ship. It truly was an entire city.

"There's only one option I see, Admiral," Atlas said. "If we can blow a hole in that ship, it will give us a break in the capital ship's fire long enough for us to jump out of here."

"How are we going to do that?" Drake asked. "We already used our particle bomb."

Atlas was silent for a moment. "The reactor on the Seraph, mixed with your nuclear warhead, will create a large enough explosion to truly do some damage."

Drake's breath caught in his throat. "You want me to launch a nuke at you?"

"It's the only way, Marcus," Atlas said.

"I can't blow you up, Atlas. I'll never be able to live with myself."

Atlas looked directly at the monitor. "Sometimes, in order to achieve our goals, the ultimate sacrifice must be made. This is not and will never be your fault," Atlas said.

Drake looked out into the absolute mess in front of them. The Seraph's shielding was starting to falter as well.

"Drake, this is no time for decisions. Forget about me being your commanding officer; listen to me as a brother," Atlas said, pain in his voice and in his face.

Drake nodded at him. "As a brother," Drake said back to him.

The X-Caliber had stopped, the shielding now at five percent; it was now or never. The Seraph floated towards the capital ship, still firing as much as possible. They had launched some escape pods. But not enough to get the entire crew off the Seraph.

"I'm going to lower the shields when we are in range. I'll need you to launch the nuke on my count," Atlas said.

Drake couldn't believe he was actually about to do this. He didn't want to. But he agreed with Atlas. It was the only way to actually get any of them home. Drake input his overrides, and an alarm on the ship sounded, letting them know the nuclear launch bay was activated and ready for launch.

"Launch now," Atlas said confidently.

Drake hesitated for a moment. A warning was displayed on the monitor. WARNING: IMPERIUM SHIP TARGETED. This made Drake's heart sink. He was about to do something he could never take back. But it was the only way. He slammed his fist on the launch button. The ship rattled as a giant missile flew from its belly.

"Intercept in 10 seconds," Drake said over the comms.

Atlas looked back at the monitor. "Thanks for being a great friend to me, Drake," Atlas said, smiling at the monitor.

Drake felt a tear rolling down his face. The shields around the Seraph disappeared as the ship crashed into the capital ship.

"Drake," Atlas said over the sound of the ship hitting the other. He looked at Drake with a look of pure peace in his eyes as he spoke. "Never forget... Only the bold dare defy the void."

The nuke connected with the Seraph. At first, the explosion seemed contained, but then a blue light shot out from the ship, and the reactor exploded with the nuke. The bright light seemed blinding. The shock wave was so intense that it knocked ships everywhere. Drake struggled to keep the ship upright. The shield alarm was going off; it showed one percent of shields remaining.

Drake heard the comms going crazy. The transports were jumping out of the system; the Andromeda had launched a few of its escape pods before it, in turn, jumped out of the system. Drake scrambled to input the jump coordinates while trying to straighten the ship. All at once, the comms went dead as the last ship jumped out of the system, leaving just the X-Caliber. As they straightened out, a missile from the capital ship slammed into the X-Caliber. The last remaining bit of shielding exploded with the shields. The yellow shimmer exploded off of the ship, leaving them completely exposed. Without a second thought, Drake slammed his hand onto the launch button for the escape pods. Drake heard over twenty engines roar to life as they shot out of the launch bay. He ran over to where his helmet had fallen onto the floor. He put it on as one last missile slammed into the glass of the bridge. The shockwave sent Drake flying back right into his control panel. The light around him seemed to bend backward. He expected to be sucked out in the vacuum of space, but instead, he was thrown to the back wall of the bridge. His head hit the metal wall hard as the world went black around him.

CHAPTER THIRTY-SEVEN

Drake had walked through a lot in his life. But he truly felt at peace now. He figured he was dead; all he saw around him was light, and it was beautiful. It didn't quite feel like he had expected. There was no one else here. Just him and his thoughts. Drake sat down as he contemplated his life, his family, and his son. Drake truly hoped his son had made it. He thought about Thatcher, Jason, and Corbin. Drake thought about Atlas and Helks. Both of them gave their lives for something greater. He figured he had done the same. Atlas's words played in his mind again, Only the Bold Dare Defy the Void. Drake had defied the void. The war he had been dragged into had taken his life, but he was content. He wasn't sad or upset with it. He was perfectly content. Drake laid down and closed his eyes again. He would just rest now.

Marcus... Admiral... someone said in a haze. He's unresponsive. Get him into the medical pod.

Drake opened his eyes, still in the space made of light; this time, a woman sat in the distance. Drake stood up and walked over to her. Carmen stood and hugged him.

"I'm so proud of you," she said, hugging his neck.

Drake hugged her back. "Where are we?" Drake asked her.

Carmen looked around. "We are where you are supposed to be," she said with a smile.

The two of them sat down together, talking and just enjoying the peace of the place they were in.

"It looks like severe brain bleeding; we need a blood transfusion right now. Marcus, we are gonna take care of you. WHERE IS THE BLOOD TRANSFUSION."

Drake straightened up in his chair as he sat in the space made of light. Catching up with his pops had been a pleasure. They shared jokes and talked about life over a cup of coffee. It was good seeing the man who raised him. His fatherly presence had always been a comfort.

"Okay, he's stabilizing... We have to get his oxygen circulating again. Man, you got banged up out there, Admiral. You are a lucky man."

Drake had been walking for a long time in the space made of light. He never got tired or hungry here. But it felt like it went on for an eternity. Off in the distance was a house made of gold. Drake ran over to it, just excited to see something different from the weeks and weeks of nothingness. Drake knocked on the door. A moment later, a man with long white hair and gray eyes opened the door.

"Ah, Marcus," Atlas exclaimed. "I've been expecting you."

Drake hugged the man tightly. His skin was golden now, everywhere except his face. Drake walked in, and they sat at a table.

Atlas poured Drake a glass of tea. "I know it's not coffee, but it'll do," Atlas said, laughing. They talked for a while, just talking about their stories of how they got to where they were.

"I feel now that you truly understand what our people are up against," Atlas said, sipping his tea.

"Yeah, now having to face it with two fewer leaders will be hard for them," Drake said, looking down at his cup.

Atlas raised his eyebrow. "Two?" he asked him. He shook his head and laughed. "No, no, only one less leader."

"What do you mean?" Drake asked, gesturing around them at the place where they were currently.

"Oh no, my friend, you aren't like me," Atlas responded. Atlas leaned forward, setting his cup on the table. "Look, my friend, you must realize something. There is far more destiny inside of you than you realize."

Atlas looked deeply into Drake's eyes. The golden walls reflected off of his gray eyes. "Being in the state that I'm in now has revealed and shown me so much more," Atlas said, smiling at Drake. "I had always suspected these things. But I see so clearly now, and it's beautiful." Atlas stood, walking over to the window in the house. "Destiny is a funny thing, my friend. Some think destiny to be constricting and a narrow path, but I see so clearly now," Atlas turned and smiled. "What had been placed in your very bones, your DNA, it's far more significant than you could ever imagine." Atlas walked back over to the table and sat back down. "Destiny is actually the opposite; the choices you make all accumulate till the end."

Atlas sighed. "My destiny was fulfilled, maybe sooner than I had thought, but I walked my path."

"There had to have been another way," Drake said.

"Perhaps so," Atlas responded. "But I don't believe in dwelling in the past. What's done is done, and I'm at peace with it. I defied the void," Atlas said, smiling.

"You did," Drake said, smiling back at him.

Atlas leaned forward. "You'll see me again when your road runs out."

Drake smiled at that.

"It's time for you to go, my friend," Atlas said. Both men stood up as Atlas walked Drake over to the door. "One last thing, my friend," Atlas said, looking at Drake with a serious face. "Don't lose yourself when fighting for the light; the pull of the dark has taken many men."

Drake just nodded at this. Atlas patted Drake on the shoulder as he walked out the door. It felt different stepping out the door. The light seemed to swallow him as he walked. He was entirely surrounded by the light.

Drake's eyes shot open, peering around a foreign room. Drake breathed in deep, and it burned. His lungs felt like they were on fire. The monitors strapped to him went crazy as he tried to stand up. A woman ran into the room, wearing a light blue dress that seemed lighter than air. It went all the way to the floor. Her black hair was up in a bun with braids hanging down her face. Her face was round, and she had kind brown eyes.

"Admiral, please don't stand; you are still so weak."

"Where am I?" Drake asked, sounding super groggy like he hadn't spoken in years.

"Oh, you are in the best medical wing in the entire Imperium palace."

"Imperium palace?" Drake asked, sounding confused. "I'm not dead?"

The nurse laughed. "No, you certainly are not," she responded. "You almost were, but we've been bringing you back. Welcome to Tyradis, Admiral," she said, bowing to him.

The room was beautiful, even for an infirmary. Decorated in gold and silver on the walls. But the actual room and medical equipment still looked super modern. Nan would love it.

Liora had been helping Drake. He had figured her name out the second day he was awake. She didn't talk much at first, but she had opened up to him. He was the only one in this room. And she's the only one who ever came in. For a week, Drake only saw Liora. She would stay for a while and keep him company while his body continued to heal. She refused to give any information about how he was found or the condition of his ship or crew.

Being off the ship and out of space felt surprisingly lovely. So Drake just sat around all day. He would do rehab when Liora asked him to. He had fractured his back, a crippling injury on Earth, but on Tyradis, some medicine and rehab fixed him up. He got better and better every day, and Liora even let Drake take his monitors off. After a few more days, Drake felt much better but still very tired. But more restless than anything. Liora came in acting very excited that afternoon.

"Mr. Drake, I have good news."

"That's good to hear," Drake said. He didn't see how he could ever truly recover from what happened. Mentally, he felt utterly fried. But he was coping the best he could. Liora helped him keep his mind preoccupied with anything other than what had just transpired. She pulled out a longer white shirt and some pants. It looked very similar to the loungewear he had seen Atlas wear.

"Here you go, Mr. Drake."

"What's the occasion?" Drake asked.

"The Emperor has requested your presence now that you are healed."

Drake's heart stopped. He had to see the Emperor. Drake remembered the video they had seen of him aboard the Seraph.

Liora bowed to him. "When you are ready, the guard will escort you to his office," Liora said. "It's been an absolute pleasure serving you," she said, smiling.

"You've been amazing; thank you for everything," Drake responded. "I'm sure I'll see you again."

She smiled and walked out of the room. Drake sat in silence for a moment before he changed. He had needed this break. But he still had so many questions, just about everything.

38

CHAPTER THIRTY-EIGHT

Drake walked alongside the guard out of the medical wing. Stepping outside felt like a dream. The cool breeze and beautiful blue sky almost brought Drake to tears. It had been so long, and even before the last few weeks' events, Drake had never thought he'd see this again; he was sure the remainder of his days would be on a metal tin can on a rock out in space. He breathed in deeply as they walked. The oxygen still burned; it was so fresh, and his body wasn't used to it yet. But it was still nice to feel. The guard had been friendly enough. He didn't talk much. He wore more general military wear. Being stationed on the planet probably didn't warrant the same uniforms they had been given on the ships. It was still gray; the sleeves were rolled up, showing a very similar tattoo to the one Atlas had on his arm. He wasn't kidding, Drake thought. They walked for a while.

The palace was huge. A gigantic white and gray building with towers and a giant structure in the middle. There were plants of all kinds and beautiful green grass planted. The guard explained they were headed to the Emperor's office, not the main throne room. That palace was more symbolic than anything these days. Most of the work was done in the office. They passed a few people here and there. They all looked very healthy. Most of them had the deep black hair that Talis and Liora had. A very stark contrast from back on Earth. It was still hard to believe this was on a completely different planet, let alone a galaxy. A few had stopped and bowed as Drake walked by them. It felt off. Did they know who he was? he wondered.

They eventually made it to the administration wing of the palace. The guard showed his ID, and the two guards opened the doors. Drake and the guard walked into a bustling and jam-packed room. There were rooms all around the walls. And desks sitting in the middle of the room. People ran around talking, some shouting. But it wasn't chaos. It was a well-oiled machine. They walked around to the back of the room, where another door sat. Most stopped and stared at Drake as they walked by. It was probably just as weird for them to see someone from another galaxy. At least it was only one for them. Drake had the pleasure of it being trillions. They came to a golden door on the other side of the room. The two guards checked the guard's ID once again. The guard that had been escorting Drake stepped aside. And bowed to Drake. He returned the gesture. Drake walked down a very elaborately decorated hallway towards the opening at the end. There were paintings of the Vantari family on the walls. Different vases and things of that sort as well. Drake reached the opening at the end of the hallway. He took a deep breath and stepped in.

The man behind the desk looked up, meeting Drake with his old gray eyes. The man smiled slightly. He looked much older than the video had shown. He looked like Atlas and Aziel combined, just older. His white hair was up, and he wore something similar to what Drake wore. Just with a lot more gold.

"Marcus Drake," the man said. "I've waited so long to meet you. Come in, come in."

The man gestured him into the room. Drake walked into the room. Compared to everything Drake had seen, the room seemed very simple. It was lightly decorated, with a fireplace in the corner with chairs around it. A large wooden desk. The wood looked like an odd grain that didn't occur on Earth. It was probably natural to Tyradis, he assumed. The man stood up, meeting Drake in the middle of the room. Drake bowed before him. The man smiled at him. He reached out his hand. Drake reached out as well and shook it; his skin was far rougher than Drake had expected.

"My name is Kaius Vantari, Emperor of the Solraeus Imperium." Kaius paused for a moment. "And on behalf of all Drezmians, welcome to Tyradis, your new home."

Drake just nodded; he didn't know what to say. He followed Kaius over to where the chairs were by the fireplace. There was coffee in a pot sitting there, ready for them. The men sat down.

"Don't worry. We have coffee here," Kaius said cheerfully. His voice was deep but also very comforting. He could, for sure, be demanding when he needed to be. "We actually sent coffee beans to Earth all those years ago. It's good to know it stuck around," Kaius said, pouring a cup for both of them.

Drake accepted it graciously. It smelled amazing. He hadn't had fresh coffee in years. It tasted even better than he remembered. The men sat in silence for a minute. Kaius sat his cup down.

"My friend, you must have a million questions."

Drake nodded, staring at the fire and then back at him. "I certainly do," Drake said.

"Well, first off, know that most of your crew survived their jumps in the pods."

"Thatcher?" Drake asked, almost a little too excited.

Kaius smiled. "They all arrived with little to no injury. Thanks to you," Kaius said, looking sincere. "Every member of your bridge made it safely."

Drake was happy to hear that. That meant Jason, Lucian, and Zyrex were all okay.

"Aziel?" Drake asked, the concern clear in his voice.

Kaius smiled. "He and the remainder of his squadron made it back; your concern for my son warms my heart," Kaius said with a smile.

"What about Corbin, and the Andromeda?" Drake asked.

"The Andromeda made it back safely, along with four transport ships," Kaius responded. "And we've been retrieving escape pods daily for the past two weeks."

Kaius paused, sipping his coffee; he seemed uncomfortable at the mention of Corbin. "As for Corbin, we believe he jumped in an escape pod and launched over Vorterra."

"Why would he do that?" Drake asked. "That makes no sense at all."

"It doesn't," Kaius said. "That's why we believe he is the one who betrayed us and somehow sent information to the Voidreavers of our plans."

Drake looked at him, confused. "There's no way he would have done that."

"The pull of the dark will make men do some things that we deem impossible, my friend," Kaius said, rubbing his face. "But we believe he is now with them on their planet."

It was hard to believe, but this man had no reason to lie to him. Drake remembered the last few times he had seen Corbin and how weird he had been acting through it all.

"We aren't certain," Kaius said. "But our intel shows us that, for whatever reason, your brother Corbin sold out our fleet to the Voidreavers."

Drake took a deep breath; how could a member of his own family betray him like that? He hoped it wasn't true and it was all a big misunderstanding.

"Time will tell all things," Kaius said sincerely. They had a thousand things to worry about. It would just have to be worked out later, Drake thought to himself. Drake looked back at the fire. It was hard to find words to say. The entire experience was flooding back into his mind.

"I'm really sorry about Atlas," Drake said, tears trying to form in his eyes. He fought them back. He looked up to see Kaius looking at him, a tear rolling down the old man's face.

"Me too," Kaius said. True pain in his voice. "But please know this, I wouldn't blame you one time in a million years for what happened," Kaius said, wiping the tears. "My son was brave and a kind soul. And I know that sacrificing himself saved so many lives. And more importantly, it saved our mission."

Drake's mind suddenly turned back to his son, the mission. "My son?" Drake asked quietly, looking at the man. "Is my son safe?"

Kaius stood up, walking closer to the fire. "Your son was able to be pulled from the wreckage," Kaius said, looking down at the fire. "We found you barely alive on the bridge. You were clinging to life." Kaius laughed. "Your helmet was the only thing that saved you; Aziel mentioned how much you hated wearing it."

Drake nodded. "I prefer my Yankees cap," he said, looking at his hands.

Kaius grinned. "It took some work, but we brought you back. Your heart stopped four separate times." Kaius walked over, standing next to Drake. "We recovered most of your ship, and we've already begun repairs and modifications. The X-Caliber will be a completely different ship next time you see her."

It made Drake's heart happy. That ship was family to him, his home, and the thing that had protected him. He was glad to know it hadn't been completely destroyed.

"When we recovered you, the boy, and the ship, we immediately took you guys back here." Kaius smiled at Drake. "He was born the day we got you guys back here. He is completely healthy."

Drake smiled at this. "Can I see him?" Drake asked.

"Of course," Kaius said, patting him on the shoulder.

Kaius punched the bracelet on his wrist. "Send him in," he said, speaking into the bracelet. Kaius walked towards the door as Liora walked in, holding a baby wrapped in a soft-looking blanket. She smiled at Drake. It was good seeing her again. Kaius grabbed the baby from her and walked over. Drake took the child from his arms. The baby was sleeping at the moment. The child looked exactly like Drake. He has Carmen's nose and ears, but Drake's face shapes all the way. Kaius sat back in his seat, looking over at the two.

Drake couldn't believe it. He was a father yet again.

"As you know, he was genetically modified," Kaius said, looking seriously at Drake. "He will be at the age of 18 in 5 years."

Drake just looked at the child in his arms. He didn't seem any different. The child stirred, crying slightly. Drake rocked him in his arms. The baby quit crying and opened its eyes at Drake. His heart skipped a beat in his chest. His son stared back at him with piercing gray eyes.

Drake's mouth hung slightly open as he fought to find the words to say. Kaius was looking directly at Drake. Drake met his eyes. Kaius just pursed his lips at him.

"There's one last thing you need to know," Kaius said, leaning closer to them.

Drake raised his eyebrows at him.

"Before you say anything, yes, he is you and Carmen's child."

Drake's heart settled for a moment. But it still made no sense to him. Kaius took a deep breath.

"It has never been explained or explored. There's no medical reason for it, but every member of the Vantari bloodline born on Tyradis has gray eyes."

This made Drake even more confused. "But my son isn't a Vantari; he's my blood," Drake said, bewildered. "You're saying that my son is a Vantari?" Drake asked him.

Kaius looked at Drake proudly. "I'm saying you and your son are both descendants of the Vantari bloodline," Kaius said.

Drake sat back, looking down at his son. "Corbin told you most of it. About your son and the mission," Kaius said, looking at the fire. "But he left out the one part that all of this rested on," Kaius paused. "He left out the part about you, Marcus."

Kaius grabbed his coffee again, sipping it before he spoke. "When the Council long ago decided we would send Drezmians to another world, it was agreed a royal family member would go with them. Your long distant grandfather, my long distant uncle. The plan was to bring them back someday, stronger, wiser, and able to lead the Imperium to the victory that has always eluded us. And here you are now, sitting in front of me. The fruition of all that planning," Kaius said, grinning.

Drake sat motionless, staring at his son. "Your long distant grandfather's name was Drake Vantari. When he got to Earth, he switched it to Axton Drake. That's actually who we named Atlas after," Kaius said, smiling at the mention of his late son. "So that's where you get the last name Drake from."

It felt so off hearing all of this, like a distant dream that was being shoved into Drake's reality. The baby cooed, looking at Drake again before closing his eyes and falling back asleep. Drake looked away from the child and back at the man.

"We were not 100% sure if your bloodline still ran with ours," Kaius said, moving a strand of loose hair out of his face. "But when your son was born on Tyradis, His gray eyes told us everything we needed to know. You are the descendant of Axton Drake."

"So that makes you my cousin?" Drake asked him softly.

Kaius nodded his head with a smile. "You and your son are part heirs of the Solraeus Imperium."

Kaius turned back to the fire, staring at it intently. "That means when I'm gone, your son will take charge of the entirety of the Imperium," Kaius said as he looked back at Drake. "He will rule all Drezmians and the Imperium and help finally bring peace to our people."

39

CHAPTER THIRTY-NINE

Drake and Kaius sat there unspeaking for a few long moments; hearing this felt off and, in his heart, didn't sit right. But he would ultimately have little choice.

"What if he needs more time to be ready when you pass, Kaius?" Drake asked him.

Kaius smiled softly, looking at the child in Drake's arms. "He will be; if I know anything about our family, it's that whenever we are called upon, no matter what, we answer that call." Kaius looked up at Drake. "Like you did," Kaius said, nodding at Drake.

The man reached over to his pants pocket, pulling out a golden bracelet. He handed it to Drake. It looked very similar to the one Kaius was wearing.

"Because of your bravery in the face of certain death, and the choice to save others, disregarding your own life, you have proven to me that you are ready," Kaius said with a serious face.

"For what?" Drake asked him.

"To take over my military," Kaius responded.

Drake just shook his head. "I don't know if I'll ever be able to put myself into that situation ever again," Drake said. "I almost lost everything that I love."

Kaius stared at him knowingly. "I promise I understand more than you'll ever know, my friend. But our duty can never rest upon what we have been through. Our duty to these people has been placed in our very bones, our DNA," Kaius paused, "I cannot force you to keep that. But you know deep down that it is your duty."

Drake looked away from the man's gaze. It was as if he had seen right into his very core. He knew what he had to do, and he was going to follow the path before him till the road ran out. Drake slid the bracelet onto his wrist. The crest of the Imperium in the middle glowed when he put it on. Kaius smiled at him.

"Marcus Drake, I, Emperor of the Solraeus Imperium, promote you," Kaius stood, Drake still with the child in his arms, and got onto one knee, "with all the power, benefits, and privileges that shall come with it. I name you Commander of the Imperium, high commander of the Imperium military force."

Drake stood up. "Thank you, Kaius," Drake said, meeting his eyes.

The man smiled back at Drake. Kaius motioned for Liora to come back into the room. "Please take the child back to infant care." Drake handed his boy back to Liora.

"He's almost released from our supervision," Liora said to Drake, "as soon as he is, I will have him brought to you in your home," she said, bowing and walking out.

Kaius walked over to his desk. "We will have a formal crowning for your position later," Kaius said, messing with some papers on his desk. "Primarily so that the people would get a first look at their new military leader. Oh, and Atlas's funeral will be held next week."

Drake nodded. "What do I do now?" Drake asked him.

Kaius just smiled at him as he sat back in his seat. "You rest for a while; you deserve that."

Drake bowed to Kaius. "Thank you, my friend," Drake said to him.

Kaius bowed back to Drake. "We have a lot of work to do, and the days ahead are uncertain. But I will always have your back. We are family, after all," Kaius said, smiling. The old man's presence was truly soothing.

Drake was walking out the door when he turned to ask one more thing. "Where is Thatcher?" Drake asked, trying to act nonchalant about it.

Kaius grinned at him. "Ms. Fiona is usually in the Hall of Light at this time of the day. I'll have one of my guards escort you there."

Drake smiled at him. "Thank you," Drake said to him as he walked out the door.

Drake tossed around everything he had just talked about as they walked, including his son, their lineage, his position, and Corbin. It felt like the end and the beginning of so many things. His life would never be the same. He was mostly okay with that. The gentle breeze was still there. What Drake assumed were birds were singing and chirping. More people walked around the palace at this time of the day. He figured it was lunchtime or something like that. This temperature was a perfect spring day back on Earth. Hopefully, Tyradis had a decent weather cycle, Drake thought to himself. In the distance, a bustling supercity could be seen with all sorts of modes of transportation. They would have to build their new lives here. Drake saw new opportunities and a new life ahead of him.

The guard let Drake into a long corridor; there were screens on the walls and what looked like artifacts all around. Down towards the end, Drake recognized two figures instantly. He ran towards them.

"Thatcher! Aziel!" Drake exclaimed as he reached them.

They turned, and they both embraced Drake, laughing and crying. Aziel let go, but Thatcher didn't; she cried into his shoulder.

"I thought I lost you," she said through her cries into his shoulder.

He held her close. He pulled her back and looked her in the eyes. "I'm not going anywhere, Thatch," he said, comforting her.

Aziel hugged them both again. "It's good to see both of you," Aziel said.

Drake stepped back, looking around the room. "What is this place?" Drake asked.

Aziel smiled. "The Hall of Light is where we commemorate our greatest heroes and most significant sacrifices," Azeil responded.

Drake looked around at the hundreds of plaques, screens, and artifacts around the room. "This is incredible," Drake said.

Thatcher nodded. "I've been coming here a lot. Just looking at everything," Thatcher paused. "And helping with this." Thatcher motioned to the portion in front of them. It was covered with a white cloth.

"Are we ready?" Aziel asked her.

She smiled at him. "I believe so," Thatcher responded to him.

They both walked forward, grabbed the edge of the cloth, and pulled it off. A giant screen turned on underneath. It showed a picture of the Seraph, the X-Caliber, the Valiant, and the Andromeda. "The Battle of the Obsidian Void" appeared above the pictures. Some videos played showing portions of the battle. It felt so surreal watching portions of the battle. At the end, it showed a picture of Atlas. "In memoriam of Commander of the Imperium, Atlas

Vantari " appeared on the lower portion of the screen. After that, pictures of Helks, Bartus, and even Manson appeared. "We thank these brave souls for their sacrifice for the light." After that, a long list of names appeared, showing many civilian names lost on the transports and other officers.

"It's beautiful," Drake said.

Thatcher smiled. "We've been working hard on it. We are working on getting some artifacts from the battle on display," Aziel said. "We are just waiting to get clearance to display some of it."

Drake smiled at the two of them. They walked out of the hall and talked for a while together.

40

CHAPTER FORTY

The next few weeks slowed down as Drake got into his new routine. The Crowning ceremony went well. The overall acceptance of Drake as their new military leader was going decent. A few holdouts didn't feel they could ever accept a man not from Tyradis to be their military leader. Even after Kaius had explained his lineage. That had been expected, though, and Drake couldn't blame them. That would be a tough adjustment for him. The funeral for Atlas was almost planet-wide as everyone came through the capital city to pay their respects to their fallen hero; Drake found it hard to attend. There was no body to bury, and everyone just wanted to meet the military Commander. Drake did his best to just smile and get through it. But everyone had adored Atlas; some blamed Drake. Others gave their condolences. The restructuring of leadership within the military did not take too long; Drake knew precisely who he wanted to promote, and Kaius didn't have a single objection. Aziel refused to take any sort of promotion. He said he preferred to keep his hands dirty in the field, and Drake respected that.

Admiral Talis had been promoted to Grand Admiral. She was delighted with this promotion. Thatcher was promoted to Admiral, and Jason was promoted to Commander. He was now Thatcher's second-in-command; it was funny how things worked out like that. All of the officers beneath him called him Commander Ross, and he absolutely hated it. Drake would still deploy on missions with them. The newly remade X-Caliber would be Thatcher's ship, while Drake got to command a brand-new vessel. The Imperium had been working on it for a while. The Cherubim was a massive command vessel. Drake had named it in honor of Atlas's command ship. He still hoped he'd get to run missions on his old baby from time to time.

Drake walked by his window, looking out and seeing the beautiful mountain ranges in the background. Drake had requested somewhere secluded for him and his son's home. Thatcher decided to have her home close as well. They had been given a large plot of land in the nearby mountain ranges. Being in his position and of the Vantari lineage gave them a lot of good things. The home was still conveniently within a five-minute speed plane ride back to the capital, where the palace was located. Drake would fly back to the Imperium military base daily for work, and Thatcher would accompany him. Liora had been given the position of Axton's primary nanny and caretaker. Drake had settled on that name to honor his distant grandfather and in hopes that some of the man's bravery and courage would be instilled into his son. She was thrilled to take the position. And Drake ensured she would never have to work again after Axton was grown.

Kaius really liked the name as well. He said the name Axton Drake held real power. Drake walked outside to his back porch overlooking a beautiful lake. The cotton candy sunset cast over the mountain range in front of them. There was still snow on the peaks. It reminded Drake of Earth in a lot of ways. Back before humanity had destroyed it. He thought back to Vorterra and the ravaged landscape of the planet; he wondered if it had once been as beautiful as Earth once had been. Trees of all sorts surrounded the land and made them truly feel like they were in nature. Drake walked out on the dock that sat out into the water.

Thatcher held Axton, feeding him a bottle as Cody ran around the entire place, loving every moment of his freedom. Thatcher would throw his ball in the water, and the dog would run to retrieve it. Drake sat in the rocking chair that was next to Thatcher. He had his coffee in his hand, and he was wearing his old Yankees cap. Drake looked out over this beautiful landscape. He wondered if it would ever truly feel like home. But this place, where they were now, a million light years away on a planet that was not their own. In a war, they had never asked to be a part of, fighting for a cause that still felt foreign. Most called it luck or chance that Drake was still alive; he should have died that day. But then again, that's just who he was and had been his entire life, a man who defied the odds.

Drake sat back into his rocking chair and looked down at his forearm, the skin still red around the fresh black ink, the ancient letters arranged in a beautiful display. Drake had found the exact artist Atlas had used all those years ago. The words etched into his arm, once meaningless a lifetime ago, now burned like a blazing fire in his heart…

…ONLY THE BOLD DARE DEFY THE VOID.